She Likes It Irish

by

Sophia Ryan

She Likes It Irish

Contact Information: info@thewildrosepress.com

Cover Art by *Angela Anderson*

The Wild Rose Press, Inc.
PO Box 708
Adams Basin, NY 14410-0708

Visit us at www.thewilderroses.com

Publishing History
First Scarlet Rose Edition, February 2013
Print ISBN 978-1-61217-813-4
Digital ISBN 978-1-61217-814-1

Published in the United States of America

"Do you want me?"

"I'll tell you plain, Kristin…it's you I want. And it's you I'll have. If that makes me a bad guy, then so be it."

His mouth found hers, giving sweet hot kisses that ignited her blood. He held her head closer, opened his mouth wider over hers, and tilted his head to better fit their mouths together. His tongue found hers, and together they conducted a symphony of carnal delight.

She slipped her hand inside his T-shirt and ran her fingers across his hard stomach, up to his smooth chest where she traced the flat button of his nipple until it peaked. Feeling his heart pounding against her hand, she explored his chest thoroughly, letting her fingers dance across his ribs and the defined muscles of his stomach, before moving down to the band of his jeans that barricaded the part of him she wanted most.

The very part stiffening beneath her bottom.

She couldn't help but give a little wiggle, just to entice him. His sharp intake of breath pleased her, telling her that despite the control he seemed to have over his urges, he wasn't immune to her.

Breaking the kiss, he shifted her around in his lap so that her back faced their neighbor, giving them more privacy. She watched as his fingers went to work undoing the closed buttons of her shirt. His fingers moved slowly, taking care and building the heat and tension in her body.

"Since that first night I saw your breasts, I've wanted to see them again. Wanted to taste them," he said when all the buttons were loose and her shirt hung open almost to her navel. "I'm going to do that tonight."

Dedication

To my family for your love, support,
and encouragement, and to Kelly O
for your brilliant suggestions.

Chapter One

Randy fumbled with a key that seemed three sizes too big for the lock.

"Hurry!" Kristin's hungry whisper in his ear and a squeeze of the bulge in his jeans proved the magic combination to unlocking the door, and the two burst through into his dark dorm room.

Lips fought to stay connected as coats were yanked off. Boots kicked off. Shirts ripped away. Zippers scraped open. Jeans and underwear tangled hopelessly at ankles then wrestled off as one. Amid the clutching and grabbing, one of them remembered to kick the door closed before the soon-to-be lovers fell naked across the unmade, extra-long twin bed.

Kristin grabbed Randy's erection, stroking it. It wasn't as big as she'd hoped, but she moaned at the thought of it filling her slick, hungry tunnel, plunging in and out, stroking every nerve, like his probing fingers were trying to do.

The tension in her body ratcheted up, and her body ached for the hard, sweet KO that would give her what she needed so badly that she'd hook up with just about anybody. Even her somewhat socially awkward classmate.

Now, she screamed silently. *Oh, God, now!*

"Condom?" they asked in unison.

"What?" Again in unison.

"Fuck!" Three for three.

"You're kidding. What guy doesn't maintain a stock of condoms?" Kristin sat up and pushed out of the sexual fog that had made her somewhat desperate but, thankfully, not stupid.

Randy shrugged. "I, uh, ran out last weekend. C'mon, we could still have fun." He grinned and lifted his eyebrows. "We could do a sixty-nine."

She paused to consider the idea then quickly shook her head to dismiss it. She needed long, hard dick filling her, not a flicking tongue teasing her. In the moment of silence before her dream crashed and burned, the dull thump of a deep beat called to her through the wall from the room next door.

"What about your neighbor?" she asked, nodding her head toward the sound.

Randy's eyes rounded, and he looked a little scared. "You want him to join us?"

She released an exasperated sigh, complete with an eye roll. "No. Would he have condoms?"

"Uh, yeah, I'm positive he would, but it's not a good idea to ask him."

Kristin bounded out of bed at "yeah," grabbed one of the shirts piled on the floor, and pulled it on. From the cluttered desk, she grabbed a mug stuffed with pens and dumped them onto the floor with the rest of the mess.

"Kristin, wait," Randy began, but she ignored him and rushed out of the room, rapping on the neighbor's door.

The pounding beat blasted out of the room at Kristin when the door opened, a god standing at the door with a ridiculously large dumbbell in his hand.

The song commanded her to *look at that body*, and she did. Tall, ripped, glistening, and tight from his workout. Thick, blond, sun-kissed hair, a bit curly and endearingly unkempt, framed a made-in-heaven face. The man was as sexy as they come, from head to toe, made even more so by the fact that he wore nothing but boxers—green ones with red lips perched atop the words "Kiss The Legend" scrawled across the Blarney Stone.

A rush of lusty heat engulfed her body as his dark-as-dusk eyes gave her the same long, slow once-over before making their way back up to her face. Then his gaze tangled with hers, and she couldn't move. Breathed in but found no air in her lungs. Heart pounded so hard she was sure it would fly out of her chest. Goosebumps marched over her skin as his full lips curled into a wide, sexy smile. The floor moved under her feet, and she stuck out a hand and grabbed the doorjamb to steady herself.

"Well, hello, darlin'," he said in a thick Irish lilt that trilled across her skin like a caress and made her legs wobble. If his gaze hadn't been holding on so tightly to hers, she surely would have toppled over into his arms.

She couldn't stop the smile taking over her face. "It's Kristin." Her voice came out breathy and husky, and she felt her face warm at her intense and unexpected reaction to this stranger. But she kept her eyes on his as if her survival depended on it.

"What can I do for you...Kristin?"

The soft sound of her name on his lips made her go all gooey inside, struggling to remember why she had even come to his door in the first place. He moved a step closer, raised his arm, and leaned it on the doorjamb near her hand. The movement shifted his body closer to hers, and she could feel him, as if he was pressed against her. It suddenly became very clear why she was here.

Her eyes dipped down to the kiss on his boxers. Sex. Condoms. Her eyes rose to his again. He stared at her as if he was a heartbeat away from pulling her into his room and locking the door behind them.

She swallowed. When had her throat gotten so dry? Why was it so hot in here? Breathe, dammit!

"We're mixing something up next door," she finally said, nodding her head toward Randy's, "and wondered if we could borrow a cup of condoms." It had seemed like a good idea at the time, coming here to ask for condoms. Hearing the words come out of her mouth now, she knew it was a bad idea. Especially when a better idea had since formed, one that involved this Irishman pulling her into his room and using the condoms on her.

He blinked. "You want to borrow what?"

"A cup of condoms."

"Randy needs condoms?" He threw back his head and laughed. Before she could respond, Irish put the weight down and stepped out into the hall. He took her hand in his. "Darlin', let's you and I go have a little talk with your boyfriend."

"He's not my…" she started and then realized she should shut up.

Irish smiled and led her back to Randy's room, the empty cup dangling on one finger of her other hand.

Randy sat on his bed, dressed, his head slumped in his hands.

"Sorry, *boyo*. You want to tell the lass or should

I?" Irish said, the grin on his face suggesting he wasn't sorry at all.

"Tell the lass what?" Kristin asked, pretty sure she wasn't going to like the answer.

"You have to leave," Randy said, his voice thick.

She snorted with a laugh, but when no one else laughed, she lost her smile and stared at Randy. "You're kidding."

"No kidding," Irish responded when Randy couldn't seem to. "So, get your—"

She snatched her hand from his large, warm grip and stared into his sinful, devilish eyes. Her temporary interest in Randy was obviously a mistake, but she didn't like someone else making that decision for her. Especially the Irish hottie standing beside her, smiling like he was enjoying spoiling her plans, and enjoying her embarrassment. "Who are you? The sex police?"

He had the nerve to laugh.

"He's the RA. Sean," Randy explained, finally finding his voice. "He enforces dorm rules."

"What rules?"

"No women on the floor after midnight—it's now twelve forty-one—and I kick out the women I see," Sean answered.

The ones he SEES. His meaning dawned on her and she shook her head. "Ah. So, if I hadn't chosen *your* door to bang on—"

He nodded. "You'd still be holding an empty cup, but we wouldn't be having this conversation."

"This is ridiculous." She tossed the empty cup at Randy, who caught it and cradled it like something precious. She crossed her arms over her chest and glared at Sean. "We're grad students. Adults. We don't need anyone regulating our sex life." She turned her glare to Randy. He dropped his eyes to the floor—or to the cup again, she couldn't be sure. She shook her head in disgust.

"Get your clothes on, darlin'," Sean said, a chuckle in his voice that she found both endearing and annoying. "I'll escort you home."

"Thanks, but you've already been *too* helpful tonight." She hoped her sarcasm wasn't lost on him.

"Kristin…" Randy began.

She held up her hand to stop him. "Don't even."

Embarrassed to the tips of her toenails by this whole fiasco, Kristin rushed around the dimly lit room, tossing aside clothes, towels, books, and shoes to find her hastily discarded clothing, mumbling about little boys and their big egos, while the two guys watched quietly.

"How do you find anything in this dump? It's a health hazard. Why don't you enforce a rule about that, Mr. RA?" Spying her panties hanging on the lamp by the dresser, she quickly and discretely pulled them on, pretty sure she had flashed her pale cheeks to one or both of the guys, who were watching her intently when she turned around.

Sean held out a pair of skinny jeans that clearly didn't belong to Randy. "Yours?"

She grabbed them from his hand and, as she pulled them on, a flash of neon purple winked at her from a pile of clothes. She dug in and pulled out her shirt.

Turning her back to her audience, she stripped off Randy's shirt and tossed it onto the pile, wrinkling her nose at the unidentifiable smell clinging to it. As she was turning her own shirt right-side-out, she realized, too late, that she was standing in front of the full-length mirror hanging on the closet door.

Not only did she have a full view of Sean, but he had a full view of her.

His eyes held tight to her body, like a lion watches the gazelle he's stalking. The heat of his stare skated across her skin, and she felt the fine hairs on her body stand up. His eyes met hers in the mirror and he grinned, making her nipples pucker and her pussy tingle as if he'd touched them with that smiling mouth.

Her heart rose high in her throat and she tried to swallow, but her mouth was too dry. *Oh, shit!* She remembered that feeling swirling through her heated flesh like liquid heat. It wasn't simple attraction. It was lust. Desire. Pure. Red-hot. Hungry.

What was wrong with her? How could she crave this perfect, hot, gorgeous, sexy-as-hell man she knew nothing about other than his name?

This was not good.

After almost two years of staying away from men, two in one night had seen her bare breasts and her naked ass. One of them she never wanted to see again. The other she wanted to donate her body to.

Pulling her shirt on forced her eyes away from his, but did nothing to staunch the loud humming in her body that said, "Gotta have me some of that."

Careful to keep her eyes from the mirror, she found her jacket near the door and put it on, zipping it to her chin. One boot stood against the desk, along with her backpack.

"I can't find my bra," she said as she stuffed one foot into the boot. "It's pink, it's expensive, and it makes my breasts look spectacular, so I want it back."

When she straightened, Sean stood at her side, the matching boot in his hand. She tried to avoid his eyes, but they compelled her to look. So she did. They looked into her, holding her, devouring her. He wanted her, too!

A sigh purred up from her throat, but she swallowed it before it could leave her mouth. Taking the boot from his hand, she dropped her eyes to focus on pulling it on, then rushed to the door. She picked up her backpack and slung it over her shoulder as she looked back at Randy.

"You do your half of the project, I'll do mine, and *this,*" she wagged her finger between the two of them, "never happened."

"Kristin…" Sean and Randy both began as she flung open the door.

"Give me a sec to get dressed," Sean said.

"Sorry," Randy whined.

She ignored them both and rushed out of the room, leaving the door open. She was down the stairs, out the front door, and several yards away from that dorm of regret when she heard footsteps clomping behind her on the crusty, frozen ground. Had Randy decided to do the right thing and walk her home? A glance over her shoulder told her it wasn't Randy, but Sean jogging toward her. He had pulled on a thick hooded sweatshirt and hiking boots, which he'd left untied, but only those thin boxers covered his lower half.

Frigid air assaulted her lungs and nose when she breathed in, and she was cold even wearing jeans, boots, and a jacket. Guilt rose in her like foggy breath, knowing that Sean's bare legs were probably freezing in the 32-degree February night.

"I'm fine on my own, really," she said. "Go back in before you freeze."

"Which dorm are you in?" He pulled the hood over his head and tucked his hands in the pockets at the stomach, ignoring her insistence that she was fine.

Fine, let him freeze. "Zia."

"On the other side of campus?"

His shivering legs and chattering teeth brought a little smile to her face. "That's the one. Still think I need an escort?"

"I kicked you out, so it's my job to protect you. If your cute little arse got assaulted walking across campus at one in the morning, I couldn't live with myself."

She stared into desire-filled eyes, remembering his sinfully hot body, and, God help her, what was inside those damn-ugly boxers. "Who's going to protect me from you?"

He laughed.

She didn't. "You do realize frostbite hits large exposed areas first?"

"Aye. I also realize those areas are less likely to freeze if I keep moving, so if you don't mind…"

They trudged across the still campus, the only sounds their footsteps on the icy brown grass, their breathing, and the occasional chattering of Sean's perfect white teeth.

"Most of the guys on the floor have come to my door for condoms. But tonight's the first time a beautiful, half-naked woman has asked for a whole cup."

"Hmm, well, don't be impressed or anything. It was just plain old desperation that sent me to your door," she said, thankful for the darkness that hid her smile. He had called her beautiful.

"Desperation? For condoms or because you regretted your choice of partners?"

"Wow," she said with a scoffing chuckle. "Someone has a high opinion of himself."

"You didn't answer my question."

"Look," she said, and stopped, turning to face him. "It's been a really long time since I…"

She couldn't concentrate with his dark eyes shining, smiling, staring deeply into hers as if he were absorbing her every word and very interested in learning how long she had been celibate.

Swirling sensations of awareness for this perfect stranger were stirring up long-buried wants and needs. The heat of his body rushed out to meet hers, and, oh God, she could smell him, a delicious aroma of soap and sweat and man that made her want to lick him all over. She wanted to ask him to plant his flag in her and claim her for his own. Right here. Right now.

His very presence, his nearness, sucked the air from her lungs. And he grinned at her like he could read every single thought slip-sliding through her passion-filled brain. She strong-armed her inner slut back and tore her eyes from his, but that didn't make the sensations burst like soap bubbles as she'd hoped.

"Never mind." She started walking again, then stopped when she noticed he wasn't beside her. She looked back. In the light of the half moon, she thought she saw his eyes glued to her butt. She spun around to face him.

"Are you looking at my ass?"

The grin he gave her said, "Aye, I was." But his mouth said, "Why don't you have a boyfriend taking care of your needs?"

"That's none of your business." She turned her back to him and continued walking, smiling when he jogged to catch up.

"Girls like you usually have loads of boyfriends to pick from."

She stopped again, facing him with a spark of anger. "Girls like me? What's that supposed to mean?"

"Ones with gorgeous green eyes that could stop a man's heart and sweet lips that could bring him back to life with a single kiss."

Though she knew a line of bull when she heard it, that damn sexy accent sent chills skating up and down her body and left her blushing and struggling for a response that didn't include giggling or babbling.

"I'm not *incapable* of getting a boyfriend, if that's what you're suggesting."

"I didn't say that."

"I'd have one if I wanted one."

His eyes were staring so deeply into hers that she was sure he could read the real reason she didn't have a boyfriend. She lost her mind completely when he reached out and brushed a thick strand of hair from her face with his fingertips. Her skin heated under his touch and her bones began to slowly melt.

"Do you?" Sean breathed the words more than spoke them.

Shit! She'd forgotten the question. "Do I what?"

"Want someone?"

"What I want is…" *Oh, my God, you!* "…to focus on finishing my degree."

"Can't you juggle the books and a lover at the same time?"

"I could. I choose not to." She kept walking and

took a deep breath to steady herself. He was right beside her.

After a short pause, he interrupted the quiet night again with another question. "Would you like to know whether I have a girlfriend?"

Oh, God, yes! "I have a feeling you're going to tell me whether I want to know or not."

"I'm unattached...like you."

"What!" she said, increasing the volume of her sarcasm. "You mean a charming guy such as yourself hasn't found someone special even with a whole campus full of women to choose from? Hot-blooded American women, by the way, who fantasize about dropping their drawers for a guy with an Irish brogue."

"Tell me, Kristin, is this your fantasy as well?" She felt his hand brush hers, and then one finger hooked hers, sending tingles up her arm and straight to her heart. "If so, I'd be happy to make it come true."

Her face burned hot in the cold night as her mind scanned her list of top ten fantasies and found being with an Irish hunk sitting at *numero uno*. It was crazy how he knew just what to say to stop her heart. It was as if he could see inside her, see all her bottled-up secrets that longed to come out and be shared with that special someone she'd been looking for her entire life. *Damn him!*

She struggled for control over her emotions and moved her hand away from his. "Now I understand the problem. With that ego, I bet you're looking for someone with the face of a movie star, the body of a model, the skills of a porn star, and the IQ of a gnat."

He stopped and grabbed her hand so she would stop, too. His gaze locked on hers as he slid his hand around her waist and settled it at her lower back. Applying almost imperceptible pressure, he maneuvered her closer until mere inches separated her body from his.

"No," he said, his voice somewhere between a whisper and a caress. "I'm looking for a woman who is so filled with passion that she'll beat down a stranger's door for a cup of condoms just to have me."

Cold air wrapped around them in the stillness, uniting them. Breaths of steam exited their mouths in sync, mated in the air, and dissipated as one.

Shivering to dislodge the troupe of chill bumps that had settled down on her like snowflakes, she swallowed and steadied herself to speak.

"Don't mistake my actions," she answered, her voice low and soft, like she was confessing her sins to him. "I just needed someone tonight."

"I don't mistake your passion." His voice matched hers in tone and volume, once again showing how in sync they were. "I saw it on your face when I opened my door." He ran his thumb along her jaw line then touched the corner of her mouth. "And it wasn't for Randy."

He was right, of course. The second he'd opened his door, she had known without a single doubt that Randy had been a mistake. The desire she had felt for Sean at that moment was still alive and well. She could feel it, and he could see it. His eyes roamed hungrily over her face. She felt the warmth of his touch and his breath on her skin. Smelled his hard body, his desire. She felt the tug of him deep inside her. He wanted her, she wanted him. All the pieces were in place.

It would be a simple thing to shift closer, ease

deeper into his embrace. Lift her mouth to his and let his kisses drive away all thoughts from her troubled mind. Let his hands remind her that she was a woman, with a woman's need for a man. And not just any man…a man like him. No, not *like* him…*him*. Let his sexy, hard body satisfy that need. And he could do it. Of that she was fully convinced. The man radiated strength and sexual prowess. He would know how to fuck a woman, how to please her, to distraction.

Even as she shivered at the idea of what he could do to her, she knew it would be a mistake. He was her type—a love-her-and-leave-her kind of guy who would thrash her heart as easily as he had won it—unfortunately. The type she was trying to stay away from. She forced herself to step back from his embrace.

"Why would you think that?" she said and turned away from him to keep walking.

"Because Randy's not your type," Sean said, right by her side.

Shit! Was he a mind reader, too? "After knowing me for all of, what, five minutes, you're an authority on my type?"

"I know the guys on my floor. Randy's definitely wrong for you."

"I hope the university is paying you mega bucks for your amazing talents of deduction."

"No mega bucks. But I do get to escort beautiful women to their dorm."

She felt her heart swell as his meaning sank in. That was twice he'd called her beautiful. "Doesn't sound like much of a reward, if you ask me," she said.

"All of life's miracles are rewarding, darlin'. Some are just more…pleasurable." At the last word, he let his eyes roam over her body, then took a deep breath and released it slowly.

His emphasis on the word, and the knowledge that he appreciated her body, settled hot and heavy between her legs. Realizing she was holding her breath, she exhaled.

"Is that some old Irish saying?"

"New Irish saying. I made it up myself. Just now. Are you impressed?"

"I'm impressed you can still move after being out in this cold without pants."

"If you're worried about me, you could invite me in." He nodded his head toward the building looming before them. "A little body-to-body contact could save my life."

Sudden and deep regret filled her when she saw they were already at the entrance to her dorm. "Well, I would, but men aren't allowed in the dorms after midnight. And it's now," she glanced at her wrist where her watch would be if she'd worn it, "later than that. But thanks for the escort."

She turned away from him and grabbed the door. It wouldn't budge. Locked.

"Shit." She cupped her hands on the window and peered into the building to check for any movement. The front desk and reception area, which closed at one, were dark and deserted.

"Lost your key in that mess at Randy's?" he asked.

"No. It's in my room, sitting on my desk." She tapped her head on the window, feeling like an idiot.

"Can you call someone to let you in?"

"My phone's sitting next to my key, so I don't have anyone's number."

"Now that's a real shame. Well, good night." He held up his hand and turned to leave.

Regret scurried across her skin. "You're just going to leave me here? Alone? In the dark?"

He turned back to her, and the warm gleam in his eyes chased away the chill sheeting her skin.

"I'll stay... If you warm me up." He stepped closer as if to pull her against him, but she moved back and crashed into the glass door.

"It's your fault we're out here, Irish. If you'd just stayed out of my business, we'd both be warm right now."

"You invited me into your business when you knocked on my door, asking for condoms. Who's your RA?" he said, pulling his phone from his pocket.

She shrugged. "I don't know. Natalia something."

"Nattie Jones?"

"Yeah, maybe."

He punched in several numbers. "You'd have been warm but miserable because you slept with the wrong guy. Hey, Nattie. Sean O'Neill. Good. You? Oh, sorry to wake you, but I'm downstairs with one of your residents who needs in. Fantastic. Thanks, love." He hung up. "She'll be right down."

"My, aren't you the charmer. I could hear her giggling from here."

"Now, darlin', don't be jealous and hating on poor Nattie."

"Jealous?" she scoffed. "Why would I be jealous?"

"I saw you checking out my boxers."

Heat bloomed in her cheeks as Kristin fought to keep her mind and her eyes off his boxers—well, what was in his boxers. She couldn't help herself. Her gaze went right to where the red lips seemed to pout atop the Blarney Stone. The material rose. She shifted her eyes quickly to his face. To the sexy little grin on his face. To his laughing eyes. *Busted!*

The buzzer sounded and the door clicked, signaling that it was unlocked and she could turn away from those smug, knowing eyes.

"Good night, Blarney Stone," she said and reached for the handle, but he was already behind her, opening the door for her.

"Sleep well, darlin'." The whisper in his voice tickled her ear, and she turned to face him. He was so close she could smell the minty sweetness of his breath. So close she could see that his eyes were indigo not black. So close that if she lifted her face but a few inches she could taste his lips.

Sean was absolutely right: Randy was the wrong guy for her in every way. Sean, on the other hand, was looking more and more like a wish she had made on a four-leaf clover. Despite the fact that his body shivered from the cold, he was holding the door for her until she got inside. He didn't know her, but had escorted her all the way home in the cold February weather and stayed until she was safely inside her building. Randy hadn't even offered and she knew him—had been heartbeats away from sleeping with him.

The tenderness she felt for Sean at that moment lifted her hand to his shoulder. She let her hand slide down his arm slowly from shoulder to wrist, her fingers caressing every muscle along the way and helping her remember what they looked like without the jacket covering them. "Thank you."

He caught her hand when it ended its trek and slid

his fingers softly between hers, casually linking them. "For walking you home or for ruining your night?"

"Both," she said. "And sorry if anything..." she glanced down, "...froze."

"If it did, it was worth it."

She smiled. "Well...see you around."

"Count on it." He winked at her.

She turned to go in, and he let her hand slip away.

"Oh, about your breasts..." he started.

She nearly ran into the door spinning back toward him. "What?"

"Never mind. You better get inside. G'night." He smiled, released the door, and moved away slowly, still facing her.

"No, tell me," she said.

Sean was just out of reach. She could grab his arm, stop him, get him to finish his comment, but she'd have to let go of the door. A girl doesn't let a comment about her breasts go she reasoned as the door locked in place behind her.

"Sean," she said, grabbing his arm.

"Yes?" he teased, the ever-present smile in place.

"Tell me!"

He reached his hand into his sweatshirt pocket, pulled out something pink, and held it up by a strap. Chuckling, she lifted her bra from his finger, but he closed his finger over the strap before she could free it.

"Just so you know—it's not this pink thing that makes your breasts look spectacular."

Her breath left her lungs, and she longed to yank him hard against her and kiss the breath from his lungs.

"Are you coming in or not?" someone shouted from the door.

The voice broke their connection and they turned toward it. Nattie stood in the open doorway, hands on her round hips, blonde hair wound up in a massive clip.

Sean released Kristin's bra and she stuffed it inside her jacket.

"I'm giving up my beauty sleep holding the door open for you," Nattie said. "Not to mention freezing my ass off."

"Nattie, love," Sean said. "If you get any more beauty sleep, you'll have to keep the men away with a tazer."

She giggled. "Sean, you do my ego good. Now kiss her goodnight so I can get back to my warm bed."

Sean looked at Kristin and grinned. "You heard her, darlin'," he said and stepped closer. "She thinks I should..." his hands settled low and hot on her hips and he eased himself against her, "...kiss you."

The touch of his fingertips, his palms, burned through her jeans and singed her skin all the way to her toes. Hot and achy tendrils tugged at her core as he moved even closer, the Blarney Stone brushing against her, his breath warming her lips. He was going to kiss her, and she was going to let him. There were a lot of reasons to stop him. But as her brain fogged over with desire, she couldn't think of one.

Unfortunately, she didn't have to stop him. He stopped on his own. And she realized with a cold and hurtful shock that she was deeply disappointed. Time stood still as he stared into her eyes, and she waited for him to say why.

"When I kiss you for the first time, I want you to taste only me in your mouth." He backed away slowly then, maintaining eye contact. A few paces away, he turned and ran back across campus. Pretty fast for someone wearing half-laced boots and thin boxers, she noted before she went in, floating on a warm, fluffy cloud.

****

Sean jogged the rest of the way back to his room, thoughts of Kristin warming him despite the cold.

What the hell had just happened? That sexual tension running back and forth between them? That electricity sizzling when they touched? His hands still tingled from their brief contact with her hips. Had she felt it too? *Fuck, yeah.* She wanted him. He was certain of it. The thought spread through him like a licking, consuming fire.

There wasn't a thing about her he hadn't noticed. A cute little nose that turned up slightly at the tip. Green eyes that set his body on fire. A perky round ass that would fill his hands perfectly. Full breasts that would give his mouth and hands hours of pleasure. A smile that sent a bolt of desire straight to his heart. A sexy laugh that made his pulse surge and his cock leap to attention. He was already imagining her long, silky chocolate hair tangling around him during sex. He could hear the sound of her sweet voice screaming his name when he made her come.

He'd been with a few women since he'd arrived a month ago, always at their initiation, and he willingly lay with them. But he hadn't wanted them enough to have done the asking or to have invited them back for an encore. He wanted this woman, and once wouldn't be enough. He was going to have to touch her again. And kiss her. All over her body. Often. And she'd let him. He knew it. And he couldn't wait.

Chapter Two

Kristin prepared herself for the awkwardness of seeing Randy in class by convincing herself that nothing happened.

So they had kissed.

So they had seen each other naked.

So he'd sucked her breasts and fingered her pussy.

So she'd held his little dick in her hands.

They hadn't actually fucked.

Besides, he had to know that their encounter had been nothing more than a weak moment, brought on by the stress of the assignment and, for her, a long period of abstinence. There was no need for anxious explanations or hasty apologies, she was sure of it.

That surety, however, didn't keep her face from flushing hot when Randy looked up from his seat when she walked into class. All through class, she felt his eyes on her. After class, she bolted out as quickly as she could, but he caught up with her outside.

"Kristin, wait up." He grabbed her arm to stop her. "Didn't you hear me calling you?"

"Hey, Randy." Her voice was neither friendly nor rude. She didn't want to be a bitch, but neither did she want him to think they had something.

"I thought we should talk about, you know, the other night."

She held up her hand to stop him. "No, we shouldn't."

21

"Yeah, but—" He stepped forward and his chest touched her hand.

"No." Jerking her hand away, she took a step back and folded her arms across her chest in a protective gesture. Her stomach pitched at the thought of having to hurt his feelings. But she'd do it if he persisted in his attempt to continue what she'd so foolishly started. She would, dammit.

"Let me finish, will you?"

She clamped her mouth closed. Fine. She'd hear him out. Then break his heart.

"Uh, look..." He swallowed. "I regret what happened the other night."

A breath of relief rushed from her lips, and her heart lifted out of her stomach. "God, I'm so glad you said that. I totally regret it, too. Good thing Sean stopped us, huh?"

His eyebrows drew together in an irritated frown. "No, what I mean is that I regret not being prepared. That we didn't get to, you know, finish what we started."

Kristin's heart dropped back into the pit at every word. *Shit!* She was going to have to hurt him. And it was all her fault for getting mixed up with him in the first place. She didn't care about him. Had been willing to use him to satisfy her urges. Stupid urges!

"And that thing you did," Randy continued, "asking Sean for a cup of condoms—that was the best thing any girl has ever done for me. We would have used them all." He stepped closer and tried to take her hand.

She stepped back, away from his touch. "Look, Randy. You're a nice guy, but what *almost* happened the other night is not going to happen again. Ever."

"I know," he said with a chuckle, not getting her point. "Cuz I bought some condoms."

Shit! "No, that's not what—"

"Yeah, a whole box. With ribs for your pleasure." He waggled his eyebrows.

Frustration spiked her temperature, her temper, and her tongue. "It was a mistake! A big, fucking mistake!" Seeing the hurt look on his face, she inhaled, counted to five, and then exhaled. "Sorry. Shit," she gritted and stared down at the space between them. When her temper was once again neutral, she looked up into his eyes. "You and I will never happen." She shook her head for emphasis. "And we're not talking about this again. Ever. Now, excuse me. I have to get to my next class."

She turned and rushed across campus, feeling his eyes on her the whole way. Only once did she glance back over her shoulder, just to convince herself that he wasn't following. The look on his face as he watched her go—his face red, his eyes narrowed, his mouth a clamped line—would stay with her a long time.

****

When she got home that afternoon, her roommate, Zoe, handed her a note scribbled with *Sean* and a phone number.

"Who is Sean?" she asked, one eyebrow raised.

Kristin glanced at the note then tossed it on her bed along with her backpack. Her heart pounded like she'd just run a marathon, but she willed her face not to show any emotion. The last thing she needed was for Zoe to start digging into her business. She adored her roommate, but she tended to get over-involved. And she'd hated every guy Kristin had ever been interested in.

"Nobody." Kristin zigged.

"Mr. Nobody sounded hot. And that accent. Yum-yum-bubble-gum!"

Kristin pulled off her boots and curled up on her bed and tried not to smile.

"Well?" Zoe asked when she didn't respond.

"Well, what?" Kristin zagged.

"Who is he?" Zoe sat beside her. "And why didn't he call your cell phone?"

"He's just some guy I met the other night, and he doesn't have my number."

"You must have made quite an impression for him to take the time to look you up."

Your breasts are spectacular. Kristin felt her face warm as she remembered his comment. She gave a noncommittal shrug.

"Kristin…"

"What?"

"You're blushing." Zoe smiled.

"No, I'm not," she denied, but she felt heat crawling across her cheeks and down her chest, where it settled between her legs. She started to get off the bed, but Zoe stopped her.

"Don't make me beg. Tell me about him already."

"I don't know him, so there's nothing to tell."

"At least tell me what he looks like."

Kristin sighed and accessed the clear images of Sean in her mind. "Tall. Broad shoulders. Muscular arms. Six-pack abs—"

"Wait, you saw him without his shirt? In this weather? Where did you meet him? Between his sheets?" Zoe laughed.

"No!" Kristin got up again, but Zoe stopped her, again.

"Tell me more."

"All right! Damn, you're bossy! Messy blond hair—"

"Like Matthew McConaughey?"

"No, more like Paul Walker in that archaeology movie. You know the one."

"Mmmm, yeah." She closed her eyes. "Okay. Got it." Opened them. "Go on."

"Blue eyes." *So dark they're almost black.* "Great smile." *So amazing it stops my heart.* "Great legs." *And arms and abs and face and...*"No piercings or tattoos I could see." *And boxer shorts that revealed his strong Irish pride.*

Zoe slid her hands between her legs and arched her back like a cat. "He sounds Gosling-alicious. I'm horny just thinking about him. Are you guys going to hook up?"

God, I hope so, was her first thought, but she waved off Zoe's comment. "No."

"You know I love you, but really, you're way overdue for some cock."

"Zoe!"

"Honey, it's been two years. And you know what they say about Irish men."

"No, what do *they* say about Irish men?"

"They don't wear anything under their kilts, so their package always swings low to grow long and strong."

At the thought of Sean's long and strong package, shivers flashed across Kristin's body and met at her crotch to spiral against her like a tongue.

"I thought it was the Scots who wore kilts?" Kristin asked, trying to get her mind off Zoe's statement.

"That's *so* not the point," Zoe said.

"How about you whip out your laptop and do a search on that while I grab a shower," Kristin said and started to rise from the bed.

"Oh no you don't." Zoe lay across her lap, blocking her. "You're not getting out of here until you tell me what you're hiding."

Kristin knew she'd only end up telling Zoe everything eventually, so she plopped back onto the bed.

"There's this guy in my forensics class. Randy. He's kind of a geek, but sweet. The other night we were alone in the library, working on a report we'd been assigned. I'm not into him, but I suddenly needed someone. Of course, it didn't take any time at all to get him to take me back to his room."

"Of course. And then?"

"We almost had sex."

"Almost? What, couldn't he get it up?"

"No, it was up. But it had nothing to wear…if you know what I mean."

"No way," she scoffed. "I've never known a guy who didn't have at least one condom with him at all times."

"Yeah, me too, but anyway…In desperation, I went next door to borrow some from his neighbor, who turned out to be his RA—that Sean guy—who then kicked me out of the dorm because women aren't allowed on the floor after midnight. By the way, the rule is they kick out the women *they see*, so just don't get *seen* while you're with Mason in his room."

"Actually, the rule is no women after one o'clock, and then they only kick out the ones they see…and they usually don't even follow that rule," Zoe said, waving away the warning. "But go on."

"After one? Are you sure?" *Did he kick me out early so I wouldn't have time to have sex with Randy?*

"Positive. Why? Is that important?"

She shook her head. "I must have misunderstood. Anyway, he—Sean—walked me home."

"And?"

"And that's it. End of story."

"No, *not* end of story. You're into this guy."

She shook her head. "No, I'm into school. Relationships get in the way."

"You can't spend your remaining year of school in celibacy. It's not healthy."

"I have plenty of sex."

"Survival sex with your nympho roommate and your trusty vibrator doesn't count."

"I never heard either of you complain."

Zoe's pale blue eyes grew bright. She leaned over and pressed her lips against Kristin's. "And you never will," she said, before pushing her back onto the bed.

"I really need a shower." Kristin's protests were half-hearted.

"Later." She smiled. "For now, close your eyes and pretend I'm Sean." She shifted her hands to the hem of Kristin's sweater and lifted it past her stomach and over her breasts. Kristin felt a spark finger her pussy when Zoe's mouth found a puckered nipple and sucked it, starting the juices flowing and flesh throbbing before moving on to the other nipple.

Zoe sucked and licked and bit her way down across

her stomach, lower to her mound. Kristin's mind throbbed with the image of Sean. Sean's hands stripping her of her clothes. Sean's hands spreading her legs wide. Sean's tongue diving into her wet pussy, lapping and licking. Sean's cock plunging deeply inside her. And it was Sean's name she called out at her moment of release.

When she opened her eyes, it was Zoe's blonde head on her stomach, not Sean's. She had to find a way to turn her sex fantasy with Sean into reality.

When Kristin got back from her shower, Zoe was gone. Her note said: *Gone to Mason's. Call Sean. Invite him over for some lovin'! Z.* On top sat a condom.

Kristin grabbed the note with Sean's number on it and stared at it, seeing his face, eyes, smile, body. Hearing his sexy voice say her name.

She crawled onto her bed, taking the note and her cell phone with her. She was ready to punch in his number when the landline rang. She answered.

"Hello?"

"Hey, darlin'."

She'd recognize that lilt anywhere. "Who is this?"

"Your friendly condom supplier."

"The way I remember it, you didn't supply me with anything except a hard time and an escort home. And, on top of that, you lied to me."

"What did I lie about?"

"Women are allowed on your floor until one in the morning. I still had at least twenty minutes left when you kicked me out."

His soft chuckle shimmied up her spine. "My mistake, darlin'. Guess I owe you."

"Guess you do."

"When would you like your apology and cup of condoms delivered?"

"Whoa. Not so fast." She stretched out on her bed. "You didn't just rob me of condoms that night."

"Ah. Well, in that case, I'm going to need more time to satisfy this debt."

"More time? Hmm. I don't know…"

"I'll make it worth the wait."

Yes, yes, yes! "What do you have in mind?"

"I'll work out the details and let you know tomorrow."

"It better be good."

The silky sound of his soft laugh wrapped around her heart.

"It'll take your breath away, Kristin. I promise."

It already was.

****

An emerald green satin bag sat in her mailbox at the front desk the following afternoon. Inside was a mug emblazoned with a four-leaf clover, holding one extra-large lubricated condom and a note laying out Sean's payment plan, starting the following morning.

Saturday @ 8 a.m.	Breakfast
Sunday @ 3 p.m.	Walk
Monday @ 8 p.m.	Movie
Tuesday @ 12:15 p.m.	Lunch
Wednesday @ 8 a.m.	Coffee/escort to class
Thursday @ 7 p.m.	Dinner
Friday @ 7 p.m.	Massage
Saturday	Condom payoff

****

"You're going where?" Zoe lifted her head an inch

off her pillow to squint at the time on her cell then over at Kristin, who was dressed and brushing her hair.

"Breakfast with Sean."

She groaned. "Why don't you just do him and get it over with."

"His plan to draw things out means we get a chance to get to know each other. I think it's clever—and pretty sweet." Kristin pulled the brush through her dark strands a final time, and then flipped her hair. "Besides, breakfast is my favorite meal of the day."

"He better not make all his payments this early in the morning." Zoe plopped her head into her pillow and pulled the covers over her head when Kristin laughed. "You're both weird and perfect for each other."

Kristin took a final glance in the mirror. Her eyes were shining and there was an excitement to her actions that had absolutely everything to do with the fact that she couldn't wait to see Sean again. Zoe was right—she needed some big cock—and if she had her way, she'd remedy that problem today.

Chapter Three

Sean waited at the front desk for her, and Lord if he didn't look even better in the light of day. He was decked out in faded jeans, his hiking boots from the other night—tied this time—unbuttoned shirt over a T-shirt, a rough and faded jean jacket. He was magnificent, muscular, and powerful. He grinned at her, that same sexy smile he gave her the last time she saw him. The one that said he could deliver everything a smile like that promised.

She greeted him with a teasing gaze that took in his entire body. "I almost didn't recognize you with pants. No Blarney Stone boxers today?"

He laughed. "If you're nice, I'll show them to you later."

"Tease."

To her surprise, he took her coat from her hands and held it out for her. She slid her arms in and turned back to him. He lifted her scarf out from under the coat and held onto it where it hung by her breasts. The backs of his fingers brushed against her nipples, which hardened instantly and thrust against her shirt and jacket, bringing a flushing heat her face that made her want to drop her gaze from his knowing eyes.

"Last chance to change your mind," he said, his words brushing her lips.

"About?"

31

"About whether you want me to pay back everything I owe right now. In one payment. Because once the schedule is in progress, we won't be deviating from it."

The idea of having him deliver everything right now was super appealing, but the idea of spending time with him and drawing out the pleasure—and the anticipation—offered the greater appeal. "I haven't changed my mind."

His eyes danced with a light that showed he was pleased with her answer. "Okay then. Hungry?"

"Starved."

"Then let's roll."

****

"How did a sweet Irish boy like you end up in this depraved little square of the world?" Kristin asked as she devoured her *carne adovada* burrito.

"I came here for the spicy food and the pretty girls." He winked at her and took another bite of his green chile burrito.

"'Tis a load of blarney you be whispering in me ears," Kristin said in her best Irish accent.

He laughed. "I'm helping put on the university's archaeological field school this summer, and I arranged permission from my university to take my final master's coursework here so I can prepare for the school."

"How long will you be staying?"

"I go home the first week of August."

Five months? It wasn't nearly long enough.

"That will give you plenty of time to satisfy me…I mean, satisfy your debt to me." She smiled then put her mouth to the straw, let her tongue jab the hole, her teeth bite the straw, then her mouth suck it.

She watched him and could see his mind giving her suggestive little move his rapt attention. He swallowed hard, his throat bobbing as if the mere thought of satisfying her, and the things her mouth could do to satisfy him, overwhelmed his ability to breathe.

"I have a feeling I'll never have enough time to fully satisfy you." He smiled. "Your debt, I mean."

"True, but you're willing to try, right?"

"Oh, aye. I'll be giving it a go, all right."

"Funny running into you two here…together." Randy appeared at their table as they were laughing at their private joke and plopped down beside Kristin. He reached into her plate, grabbed a potato cube, and popped it into his mouth.

The laughter died in her throat. She rolled her eyes and pushed her plate away, wanting to smack Randy for shattering the moment with Sean.

"I didn't think you knew each other well enough to have breakfast together," Randy continued when neither of them said anything.

She lifted her gaze to Sean and returned his grin. The longer the silence hung on, the clearer it became that there was *something* between them, something that neither was willing to discuss with Randy.

"Okay, awkward," Randy said, a flush crawling up his face. "Anyway…We should get together today to *finish our report*." He lightly jabbed Kristin's arm with his elbow to emphasize his final words.

She shot him a stern look. "As I said the other day, I think it's best that you do your part, and I do mine—separately." She kept her tone clear and firm so he couldn't misinterpret her words or her wishes.

"Sure, whatever. You going to the Pike party

tonight? We could go together." He laid his arm behind her across the back of her chair.

She leaned forward, away from his touch. "I don't go to frat parties." Feeling uncomfortable at his closeness, she found Sean's eyes again. He winked at her, making her smile. Making her feel safe.

"You can't do this, Kristin." Randy's words, delivered in a low tone, caught her attention. His mouth was a tight line, his eyes narrowed on hers, and his cheeks bore red patches. One hand had balled into a fist on the table, while the other bit into her shoulder.

"Knock it off," Kristin said, and twisted her shoulders to break his hold, but he didn't release her.

"You can't come on to a guy then just ignore him like he's nothing." His fingers dug in harder the louder his voice grew.

Sean stood and held out his hand to her. "Are you ready to go?"

"Yes." She grabbed his hand and stood, breaking Randy's grip. Sean maneuvered her behind him and away from Randy, then leaned in to grab her jacket and his backpack.

"She told you she's not interested, so I'll ask you to leave her alone from now on." Everything about Sean screamed stern, from his low, hard voice to his tightly restrained menace. "And if you lay a hand on her again, you and I'll be having a little man-to-man. Nod your head so I know you heard me clear."

Randy nodded once.

"Good." He turned and, taking Kristin's hand possessively in his, the two left the café.

****

"That was weird," Kristin said as she and Sean

strolled back across campus, her hand still in his. "I know Randy was disappointed about the other night, but...wow."

"That guy wasn't just disappointed; he was angry." An unmistakable chord of irritation sharpened his usually lilting brogue.

"Yeah, and I don't get it. Until we became partners for this project, we never spoke to each other. Not in class, not outside class. Yet, he's acting like—"

"Like a jilted lover."

"Yeah."

As they walked, she noticed they had matched pace and gait. It amazed her that they had connected so soon. She smiled up at him. "Thanks."

"For?"

"For being there when he freaked out. I'm glad you were with me."

He met her smile with one of his own. "Are you, now?"

She nodded.

"How glad?" he asked, his voice so full of heat that she felt wisps of smoke swirl in her stomach.

She stopped, parted his jacket with her fingers, and rested her palms on his hard stomach. Sparks traveled through her hands as she slid them slowly up his chest.

"Very glad," she whispered, and saw the moment her whisper crawled into his skin.

His eyes got heavy. His body tensed slightly, as if all nerve endings were on alert.

"Show me." The words exited his mouth on a whisper, but her body heard and understood the request.

Her hand left his chest and rose to his face. Slowly, teasingly, she outlined his lower lip with her thumb before raising both arms and sliding her fingers into his hair. She eased his head down to her as she raised hers to him. Their gaze held. Their lips poised in place, ready to come together.

His warmth, the smell of his skin, the touch of his hands warming her lower back set a fire burning inside her that she knew only he could extinguish. Fireworks lit inside her, and they hadn't even so much as kissed. He ran his tongue across his lips to wet them, and a pulse zapped through her, pushing her to eliminate the final sliver of space separating their bodies. She was starved for the taste of him, his mouth, his tongue.

She touched her lips to his and breathed him in. At first the kiss was about nothing more than getting to know the feel of him, enjoying how they fit so perfectly, how he tasted so sweet. Then, craving more, her mouth opened slightly and moved over his. She sucked his bottom lip, then his top. She ran her tongue along the smooth skin just inside his mouth. His tongue greeted hers warmly.

Lights flashed behind her eyelids, and fiery tingles pulsed at her mouth, the tip of her tongue, at her palms where they caressed him, all through her body where it touched his. She kissed him long and slow and deep, and he matched her, move for move, touch for touch. When they finally came up for air, his eyes gleamed and his breathing was as scattered as hers.

"That's the best thank you I've ever received."

She wanted to kiss him again, but he had already left her embrace, taken her hand in his again, and continued walking.

"Where are we going now?" she asked, hoping to hear the answer, "my room" or "your room."

"Your dorm."

Oh, God, yes! Her heart shouted the words and swelled with desire. It had been easier to get him naked than she thought it would be after his speech about not deviating from the schedule. Then she thought she better make sure of his intention.

"You mean, to my room?"

He chuckled. "Darlin', I told you we wouldna be deviating from the schedule. Besides, do you really think I'm the kind of guy who would try to make love to you on our first date?"

She stared into his sinfully hot eyes. "Yes, actually."

He laughed out loud and wrapped his arm around her neck, hugging her to his side and kissing the crown of her head. He dropped his arm to her shoulders, holding her tight, and she held onto his hand where it hung in front of her breast.

It made her smile that he hadn't denied it. "So…You're not interested in charming your way up to my room or into my panties, and you're dropping me off early. Sounds like you have another date."

"I do."

Disappointment and jealousy raged through her body. She let her hand fall from his and stared straight ahead. "Oh."

He laughed and hugged her closer. "Not so much a date as an appointment. I tutor to help pay my way here. My next appointment is in…" he glanced at his watch "…about twenty minutes."

"Oh." She breathed and took his hand in hers again.

"With a *male* engineering student," he added.

She smiled and met his teasing gaze. "You don't have to explain. It's not like you and I are...you know."

He smiled down at her. "You looked like you wanted to knock my head off."

She looked away, embarrassed that he had seen through her so easily.

He stopped and faced her. "It's your eyes," he said, even though she hadn't asked, and brushed a finger down the side of her face, pulling her gaze back to his. "They say everything your mouth doesn't want to."

She stared at him, opening a pathway to her deepest emotions, willing him to see what was written there. To see her desire for him. "And what are my eyes saying now?"

He paused as if reading, trying to translate the symbols he saw in the depths. "They're saying I'll miss all my tutoring appointments today if I don't get you home fast. Oh, and just to clarify, I never said I wasn't interested in getting into your panties."

She laughed, but there was nothing funny about how the sweet spot between her legs heated up as her mind rolled around in the idea of him getting into her panties. They again set off toward her dorm, but instead of heading for the front door, he pulled her into a patch of sunlight crawling up the adobe-style building. He removed his arm from around her and stuck his hands in the front pockets of his jeans while she settled back against the warm wall.

"We still on for our walk tomorrow?" he asked.

As an answer, she grabbed onto his jacket and yanked him against her, pulled his face down to hers, and kissed him.

He pulled his hands from his pockets and settled

them on either side of her to steady himself, but he did little more than allow himself to be kissed. But soon, as if her kiss had touched off something inside him he couldn't resist, his hands left the wall. They moved inside her jacket and went around her waist, pulling her into his body. But he wasn't done touching her. His hands slipped beneath the hem of her shirt and caressed the feverish skin of her back, and his tongue, which had previously been only a teasing heat, suddenly became a licking flame in her mouth.

She felt hot all over. Grabbing his hips, she held him tight against her. A moan crawled up from her core when he slid his thigh between her legs, and she arched herself hard against him.

Her erotic sounds and moves seemed to cool his ardor because he eased back from the kiss and braced his hands against the sandpaper-rough wall. His face hovered inches from hers, his eyes holding tight.

"So…You're one of those kinds of people, are ya." The growl of his low voice skittered lightly across her skin like fingernails.

"What kinds of people?" she asked, frowning.

"The ones that don't play by the rules," he whispered in her ear, then nibbled her lobe with his lips, sending a battalion of shivers racing across her body.

She released a slow smile. "Is that a problem?"

"No. Only a challenge."

His eyes dropped to her mouth, and she knew he wanted to kiss her again—and she was waiting for it, ready for it—but then he didn't. He stepped out of the pocket of desire enveloping them and eased his hands back into his pockets. The movement further stretched the tight and tented crotch of his jeans.

His chest rose and fell in sync with hers, as if the two of them couldn't get enough air when they were this close to the other. Her body screaming in agony at losing his heat, his touch, she stared at him, her eyes asking why.

Their gazes held for long, hungry seconds when neither could say a word. He took a breath and released it slowly.

"See you tomorrow at three."

If Sean had looked back as he sprinted across campus, he would have seen her touching her scorched mouth with her fingers and known that she keenly regretted not asking for the lump-sum payment.

****

"How was breakfast?" Zoe asked when Kristin came in from her date.

"Fabulous."

Zoe sat up in bed, the sheet clinging loosely around her naked body. "I thought you didn't like that place? You said the green chile tasted like sour pickles."

Though what Zoe said about the café was true, today it didn't matter. She would have eaten anywhere, even at a roach coach, as long as it was with Sean. "It was the company that was fabulous."

Kristin peeled off her coat and her boots and curled up on her bed with her backpack to get some homework done so she'd have more time with Sean tomorrow should they decide to expand their walk to include a tour of his bed.

She felt Zoe watching her and looked up at her. "What?"

"You didn't get any, did you?" she asked.

"We don't even know each other, yet."

"Yeah, I didn't think so…I don't smell his cum on you. I'd notice a new smell like that."

Kristin shook her head. She never knew what Zoe was going to say, but more often than not, it shocked the polish off her toenails.

"No, I didn't bring any strange cum home with me."

Zoe pushed back the covers, jumped onto Kristin's bed, and laid her head in her lap. "But I can smell the sweet peach juice he stirred up in you."

"Don't get any ideas. I have tons of homework."

"Ideas like this?" Her fingers moved up the inside of Kristin's leg in little swirling motions.

Kristin was horny as hell, but she wanted Sean to satisfy her, not Zoe. Not that she didn't enjoy what her roommate did for her—she just craved Sean.

"Stop," she said with a smile, swatting away her teasing hand.

She buried her face in Kristin's lap, exhaling her breath on her crotch. "I can do what Sean wouldn't." Zoe mouthed her mound through the jeans. Need spiraled like a tornado in Kristin's body, but she knew she didn't want to be satisfied this way. Not this time. Not after what she'd felt with Sean. He was still running through her veins like a drug.

Kristin caressed her friend's head gently. "Thanks, but not now."

After a moment, she eased back. "Okay. Fine." She got off the bed and dropped down onto hers. "But keep in mind I may not be in the mood later."

Kristin laughed and shook her head. The nymphomaniac was always in the mood.

Zoe laughed, too. "You owe me one."

Kristin didn't respond. A sudden, sharp feeling had stabbed her heart, telling her she and her friend-with-benefits would not be intimate as long as Sean was in the picture.

Chapter Four

The pinging sound of the rain slashing against the windows sent shivers across Kristin's back. She pulled her blanket tighter around her body for warmth. Through the wet rivulets, she saw Sean rushing toward her building, head down, eyes squinting to see through the rain, the ever-present grin on his face. Her heart sped up and her smile beamed when she saw the unopened umbrella he carried in his hand.

They weren't calling their walk due to rain.

Losing sight of him when he entered the building, she left the window, tossed the blanket onto her bed, and slipped on a hooded raincoat. She dug in the back of her closet for her rain boots and pulled them on.

"Are you going somewhere?" Zoe looked up from her textbook.

"My walk with Sean." The words danced out of Kristin's mouth in a happy stream.

"But it's raining. And freezing." She tucked the blanket around her and shivered.

"Sean'll keep me warm." Kristin smiled at the thought, her heart buzzing like a swarm of bees in a field of wildflowers.

The throbbing strains of the ringtone she used for Sean's calls caught her ears. Her phone was on the table by Zoe's bed. As she reached for it, Zoe snatched it and put it in her lap to prevent Kristin from answering it.

"Tell him you can't go, that you need to stay with me and do homework."

"No. I want to go with him." She tried to grab the phone, but Zoe folded herself over it. "Give me my phone."

"No."

"Give it to me!"

"No!"

Kristin lunged at her, pulling at her to uncover the phone. Zoe held firm, but Kristin managed to get a hand on it and drag it from her grip just as the music stopped.

"Dammit!" Kristin shot her friend the evil eye. "What the hell's the matter with you?" She grabbed her room key and stormed out of the room, slamming the door soundly behind her.

She raced down the stairs, hoping Sean was still in the building and hadn't left thinking she'd stood him up. Rounding the corner to the first floor, she burst through the door leading into the reception area. Several gazes spun toward her but Sean's was the only one she cared about.

He was by the TV, phone at his ear. Water misted his hair, the tips of his eyelashes, and his face. Joy danced in her heart as if rows of spring daffodils had bloomed there in the past second. He glanced up, his eyes capturing hers.

His smile felt like sunshine on her face. She wanted to run into his arms but wasn't sure whether he'd welcome it after the way he left her yesterday.

"Hi," he said, tucking his phone into his pocket.

The grin alone was enough to make her moan with pleasure, but she collected herself enough to speak. "Hi."

He held out his hand to her and she took it. "I missed you."

"You did?" She smiled. "How much?"

He pulled her closer until she was right in front of him. "This much." His hands cupped her face, his fingers in her hair, and he kissed her, his rain-slicked lips greedily drinking her in as if trying to quench an unquenchable thirst.

Her arms were around him, holding onto him with all her might, as his mouth devoured her. This was the response she'd dreamed of! How was it possible that after only a couple of days, she already felt like "next to him" was where she belonged?

Sounds of TV laughter, people chatting, phones ringing, music playing vibrated against her boots and radiated up through her body. She unlinked her body from Sean's and allowed a breath of air to slip between them. She was damp where he was damp, and it felt like heaven.

"I've wanted to do that since I left you yesterday morning." Sean's words, said low and quiet through a smile, were like a rare gift just for her. "And judging by the way you kissed me, I'd say you missed me, too."

"Maybe a little." Her words carried a breathless tone that she couldn't contain.

"A little?" he repeated her words with a grin. "Maybe I'll leave now and come back when you miss me more." He turned away.

Laughing, she grabbed his arm and pulled him back to her.

"Okay. I missed you more than a little. And I'm glad you didn't bail on our walk because of the storm."

He slid his arm around her, the grin full on his face

again, and led them to the door. "Darlin', where I come from this is nothing but a gentle mist."

She peered outside at the steadily falling rain. "A gentle mist? Here it's called raining cats and dogs."

He held up the umbrella. "This won't do much against cats and dogs."

"I'll take my chances."

"What a trooper."

They clutched each other, as if life depended on being able to touch each other, and pushed outside.

He popped opened the umbrella and raised it above his own head, leaving her exposed to the elements. Laughter danced in his eyes as he looked at her. "Didn't you bring one? You're going to get soaked."

She shoved him playfully, a grin on her face. "And you're not going to get any more of my kisses, that's for sure."

He caught her and tucked her safely against him and under the protective dome. "I'd give up everything I have for one more of your kisses."

Pure joy surged inside her like an erupting volcano and she dipped her head into his chest and giggled to release some of it before she exploded.

He put his hand on his heart and stumbled dramatically backward as if her giggles had wounded him. His eyes closed in mock pain. "I pour my heart out and you laugh at me?"

Kristin yanked him flush against her, still laughing. Her eyes on his, she invited him to push his gaze deep inside her to see the truth and the rolling desire in her heart.

"I laugh like a little kid who's ripping the paper off a present she's waited a whole year for."

It took him a moment to respond, as if he couldn't find the right words. "I must be rubbing off on you. That's the most Irish load of blarney I've heard you say. But I liked it."

She laughed again, and through the layers of his clothing, she felt him melt against her, telling her the corny words had touched him.

Arms around each other, they walked the campus, rain pinging on the umbrella above their heads. Being tucked up next to Sean, the sound of the rain, the smell of the air, the chill blanketing them, washed goose bumps across her body in waves. It felt like they were in their own little bubble and that made everything they did, everything they felt, everything they said, heightened, almost magical.

He showed her his favorite spots on campus—the usually sunny spot at the duck pond where he soaked up the sun, the little chapel where he went to hear himself think, the place by the archaeology building where the tree branches formed a serene tunnel, and the bench near class he sometimes sat on just to avoid being inside for too long.

He told her about his life in Ireland and asked her about hers here. He touched her face, her hair, her fingers. He kissed her with his mouth, his eyes. He set her on fire with need.

On the way back to her dorm at the end of their walk, they went into the coffee shop inside the library. She ordered a latte with whipped cream, he a black coffee with four sugars.

She tried to pay for hers, but he refused, fishing his wallet out of his back pocket and handing a ten to the cashier. She got a peek at his driver's license before he closed his wallet. After getting their drinks, they settled at a corner table and pulled off their coats.

"Did you have to get a state driver's license when you came here?" she asked.

"I did."

"Can I see it?"

"If you show me yours," he said with a grin.

They each took out their wallets and pulled out the licenses. He handed his over and her eyes zeroed in on the picture. There was a touch of a smile on his luscious mouth as if he were amused by something. His hair was a bit shorter but just as untamed. The eyes looked as if they were a blink away from laughter. He had turned twenty-four in November, making him four months older than she.

"No one takes a good license photo, Sean, but somehow you managed it. I think I hate you."

He laughed. "Okay. Hand over yours."

She kept hers against her chest. "I was getting a cold when this was taken, and I didn't want to go back for a retake. Promise me you won't laugh."

"I promise."

"Promise what?"

"Promise I won't laugh." He made a show of wiping the smile from his face with his hand.

"Okay." She handed it over, making a face as she watched him.

A smile twitched at the corners of his mouth. His eyes raised from the picture to her face then back to the photo, then back to her face again. "Were you smoking something?" His smile was full-blown on his face.

"You promised!" she said with a laugh and playfully hit the arm holding the license.

"I promised not to laugh. I didn't promise not to smile." He continued to study her license. "You have the same birthday as my best friend back home. Ian. You'd like him."

"Why would I like Ian?"

"You two are a lot alike."

"So he's gorgeous and brilliant, too?" She tossed him a teasing grin.

He laughed. "All the women in his life think so." His eyes dropped back to her license. "Your middle name starts with H. What is it?"

"It's a secret I'll take to my grave, that's what it is." She reached out for her license, but he pulled it back with a grin.

"How bad can it be?"

"Really bad." She reached again, and again he pulled it away.

"Now I have to know," he said.

She took a sip of her latte and shook her head. "No way."

"If I guess it, will you tell me if I'm right?" He handed over her license and she put it away.

"You'll never guess it."

"Hannah."

"No."

"Haley."

"No."

"Hortense?"

"Hortense?" she chuckled. "Just for that, you lose your guessing privileges, and I get to ask you five questions about the things in your wallet." She plopped her hand on his wallet and with a grin slid it across the table to her.

"You're not going to stop me?" she said, teasing him with her smile and eyes.

"Seeing as it's already in your hands, I can't very well tackle you to the floor and take it back, now can I?"

"Ha! I've seen your muscles. You definitely could. But you won't."

She held the thin wallet in her hands, felt the worn-leather smoothness of it against her skin. "I've always been fascinated with men's wallets…what's in them, I mean." She brought it to her nose and smelled the seasoned aroma of it mixed with Sean's own scent. "You guys keep them so secret and off-limits. This is a rare treat for me, O'Neill. I feel a little wicked just holding it."

"Remember this moment when I ask to explore your bag," he said, drawing a chuckle from her lips.

"No promises." She felt his eyes on her, studying her face as she opened each flap of the trifold, laying open his secrets. She slipped his license back into its slot next to a credit card, his university IDs—one from here, one from Dublin—what looked like a medical card, and a few business cards—one related to immigration, one to the Irish embassy, several to personnel at both schools, and one to a local law firm.

The other side held a few neatly folded receipts, including the one for their coffee. Several bills were lined up by denomination in the long slot. No condoms. No personal mementos like torn ticket stubs. No pictures or girls' phone numbers…but then he had his phone for the last two.

"I figured you'd have at least half a dozen condoms tucked away in here somewhere," she teased.

He shook his head, light dancing in his eyes. "Heat and pressure degrade condoms, making them less effective."

"Oh…so if you're out and about when the mood strikes, and Ms-Right-Now doesn't have protection, you're SOL?"

He leaned back a bit in his chair and stuck his hand into his front pocket, pulling the tip of a gold condom package out to show her.

She raised an eyebrow. "Only one?"

He glanced around to make sure they weren't being watched, then pulled out a three-piece string of condoms for her to see. Before he stuffed them back into his pocket, she noticed the packages said extra-large, lubricated, and they looked just like the one in the four-leaf clover mug he'd given her. So, it had been from his stash.

How big was he that he needed an extra-large condom? She swallowed and squeezed her thighs together, trying to diminish the zaps of electricity suddenly popping between them and imagining the answer to her own question.

"Did you load up just for our walk?" she asked, giving him a sexy look.

He smiled, his eyes closing half way in a sleepy-sexy look that made her want to jump onto his lap and make him rip open a gold package.

His expression changed like a storm had stopped right over his head just as a hand touched her shoulder.

She turned her head. Randy stood at her side, his eager face smiling down at her. The guy was book smart, but he wasn't the sharpest crayon in the box when it came to social convention.

"Hi, Kristin," Randy said. "I thought that was you. Oh. Hey, Sean."

"Randy," Kristin said then turned back to Sean, who was giving Randy the death stare.

"Can I talk to you outside?" Randy asked, trying to draw her attention away from Sean.

"No, Sean and I are—"

"It'll just take a second. I have a question about our project."

She put her hand on Sean's, linking her fingers with his. "Do you mind? I'll make it quick."

He made a gesture of acceptance, but continued to glare at Randy.

She stood and walked out of the coffee shop, Randy behind her. Once outside, she turned toward him, ready to remind him that she had already turned in her part of the project and that they had nothing further to discuss, but he spoke first.

"I didn't want to talk about our project. I wanted to ask you to go to the movies with me tomorrow night."

She blinked in surprise at his request and shook her head. "I told you I'm not interested in you." Though she delivered the rejection softly to spare his feelings, she didn't want to give him any room to hope that she'd change her mind. "You only make me hurt your feelings when you keep asking."

He shifted on his feet, his face reddening. "Who *are* you interested in? Sean?"

Her heart jumped as if it knew the answer. "That's none of your business."

"There's stuff you should know about him before you—"

"I'm not interested in hearing anything you have to

say." She turned toward the door, but he caught her arm.

"He has sex with a lot of different girls. They show up at his door, they have sex with him, and then they leave. Alone. He doesn't even walk them home. He's a user, and I don't want him to use you like that."

Her heart hitched at Randy's words, but she breathed through it until it righted. "He tutors. Maybe they're doing homework."

"Oh, he's tutoring them, all right, but it isn't for any class. That wall between us is paper thin. I hear everything…and it's not like the girls are quiet, either. They all scream out 'Fuck me, Sean' or 'Oh, God, Sean,' sometimes both. He's a manwhore."

The news sat heavy in Kristin's stomach. She and Sean weren't *together*. They weren't really even dating. They were…what? Foreplaying? But knowing that he was having sex with a lot of girls made her wonder whether all his attention was about adding one more conquest to his list. But if that were the case, why had he dodged every attempt she'd made to get into his boxers? She hadn't exactly been subtle about what she wanted. And unless she was completely off base, their whole payback plan was meant to end in sex. Was it just a control issue? Or was he, like her, interested in more?

"He'll hurt you, Kristin. But I won't. I…I love you." Lightning quick, Randy leaned forward and kissed her hard on the mouth.

She pushed him away, and fury swung out her hand to connect with his face. "Dammit, don't you ever do that again!"

He grabbed her hands and his black eyes stared

into hers with an intensity that shook her. "I'll do whatever I have to to save you from him."

"I don't need saving." She was yanking her hands away when he suddenly released them and took off running. A second later, Sean burst through the door and was at her side, their things gripped tightly in his hands.

"Did that little *shitehawk* do what I think he did?" Concern filled his voice and eyes. He helped her on with her coat then held out her wallet.

"I'm not exactly sure what a *shitehawk* is, but if you think Randy kissed me and confessed his love for me, you'd be right."

"I'm going to have to kick his arse," Sean growled, his body stiff as he stared after Randy, who hadn't stopped running.

"Don't worry about it. The slap I gave him will make him think twice about touching me again. Besides, he's harmless."

Sean didn't look like he believed her statement any more than she did, but he let it drop. He looked at her, putting his arm around her. "Are you all right? Did he hurt you?"

She put her arms around him. "I'm fine."

"Well, I'm not. That'll make twice his kisses have stopped me from kissing you."

"Don't be such a baby." She leaned up and kissed him on the mouth, her hands on his face, holding his mouth to hers.

And when Sean forgot about Randy's kiss and wrapped her up tight in his arms, her head spun, and Randy's words washed away.

****

"Our movie date is tomorrow night," Sean said as they stood outside her dorm.

It wasn't a question or a demand, but a simple statement of fact. And it was the second time he'd referred to his payments as dates.

"Yep. Eight o'clock?"

"I'll pick you up at seven-thirty so we can get a good seat." He kissed her.

The deep kiss she gave him would, she hoped, tell him how much she wanted him. *I'll never grow tired of kissing him*, she thought as she pulled back to capture his eyes.

"You wanna come up?" Her breathing was ragged as the words passed her throat. Couldn't he hear the obvious invitation in her voice? See it in her eyes? Feel it in the way she touched him? When he didn't respond, she pressed against him to help him decide. "Try out those condoms in your pocket? I'd love to see why you need an extra large." *And I'm really interested in finding out whether you can make me scream your name.*

He inhaled a quick, quiet breath at her soft plea, and his eyes revealed a mix of desire and hesitation. Clearly he wanted her. Why was he waiting?

"No, darlin'."

The answer stabbed her heart, but she pushed through the pain and smiled. "Another tutoring session?"

"No."

She paused, giving him time to explain why he was refusing her, but he didn't offer one. The cold pain pushed back and released a burst of jealousy in her, along with a feeling that he was playing with her...and not in a good way.

"Then, why not?"

A slow grin stretched across his face. "It's not on the schedule."

She smiled, relief rushing out of her lungs at his response. "So, you're one of *those* kinds of people."

He lifted his eyebrow in surprise at hearing his own words thrown back at him. "What kinds of people?"

"Those who think schedules are carved in stone and can't be deviated from."

He laughed, caressed her cheek and then her mouth with his thumb. "I won't rush my debt to you, Kristin, no matter how much you ridicule or tempt me."

He didn't want to rush. He wanted it to last. If the words themselves weren't enough to convince her of that point, his touches were. His hands slipped inside her jacket, around her back, under her shirt, and on her skin where they seemed to belong. He pulled her close to him, his eyes on hers, and slid his luscious mouth over hers in a branding touch that would live on long after he'd left.

Her knees weak, her lungs out of air, her body aching for all the things his kiss promised, she protested when he slowly pulled back and looked into her eyes. But he didn't give in to her need to continue the kiss.

"See you tomorrow at seven-thirty...Henrietta," he whispered against her mouth.

She tried to chuckle but she didn't have the air for it. "Yes to the time, no to the name."

He backed away from her, keeping his gaze locked to hers, then pushed out the door. She watched him through the glass until she could no longer see him and then rushed up to her room to find the pleasure he wouldn't give her.

Zoe wasn't in the room, which was good, since Kristin needed a quick release to ease what Sean had started. She stripped, got under the comforter, and pulled her vibrator from its resting place in her little Friends Never Die pillow.

Centering her mind on Sean's face, the feeling of his mouth on her, his large, warm hands on her skin, made it easy to imagine him beside her, touching her, ready to take her. Her heartbeat pounded through her tense body as she slid the vibrating plastic cock between her legs.

At the first touch to her throbbing pussy, she cried out Sean's name. In her mind, it was Sean's tongue vibrating against her, inside her. Her temperature spiked and sweat beaded her forehead. Burning up, she kicked off the covers. She spread her legs wide, wanting to feel every nerve clenching and releasing inside her. She closed her eyes at the pleasure surging through her pussy, rode the spiral up, up, higher than she could go and still breathe. She cried out, the powerful release wringing the pent-up tension from her body. Her core pulsed from the intensity of her orgasm.

After a minute, her heart slowed its crazy rhythm. Her eyes began to focus again. She came back into herself—relaxed, but not fully satisfied because it hadn't been Sean who had given her what she needed.

She heard a key in the lock, and she quickly covered up and put her little friend away.

Zoe came in, took one look at Kristin lying on the bed in the middle of the day, and knew what she'd done. "You and Sean didn't fuck today either, huh?"

Kristin avoided her eyes. "What makes you think that? Maybe he just left here."

Zoe laughed. "No, he didn't." She slid her jeans off her hips and kicked them toward the laundry basket in the corner of the room. "Don't you want to fuck him?" Her shirt and bra followed.

"Of course I do!" Kristin's words were sharper than she'd intended them to be. Frustration sharpened her tongue.

"Maybe he doesn't want to fuck you," she shot back without missing a beat.

Hearing the words said aloud that she had been thinking sent a jolt of pain through her, but there was a real possibility it was the truth.

"I thought of that. He kisses me like he wants to. But when I ask him to come up here or suggest we go to his room, he always has a reason not to. I mean, he told me from the beginning we wouldn't be deviating from the plan, but I want him so bad I feel like I'm going to explode."

"Yeah, and he probably knows it." Zoe pulled on her big, soft sleep shirt and curled up on Kristin's bed.

"You think he's doing it on purpose?" Kristin asked as she scooted over to make room for her.

She laughed. "Yeah, I do. But that's okay. When you guys finally come together, they'll be able to hear the explosion from Cruces to Raton." She grabbed Kristin's vibrator from where it was half hidden under the pillow, held it up, smiled. "I'd offer to take care of you, but it looks like your Little Friend here has already taken care of things."

Heat washed over Kristin's face and she smiled. "Shut up! Bitch!"

Chapter Five

Kristin wiped her drenched forehead with the back of her wrist but the action did little more than smear the salty beads of sweat, since her entire body was slick with moisture. Her heart pounded in her ears as she pulled cold morning air into her burning lungs to feed her oxygen-starved body. Her legs were the only part of her not burning because they were ice cold, and she cursed the decision to wear shorts instead of sweats or leggings.

She glanced at her watch. An hour down, half an hour to go, and she'd be done. Her time was way off today—probably because her mind wasn't on her daily run. It was on Sean. His touches. His kisses. How he made her melt with a look.

Deciding to lift weights for the remaining half hour of her workout, she cut across campus toward the gym, smiling as she thought about their walk yesterday. How his hands had slid up her shirt and touched her skin. How the fingerprints he left on her still tingled in warm little swirls on her back. How their wet kisses lasted for eons and unlocked the doors to her desire. She couldn't wait for their movie date tonight, couldn't wait to see what part of her body he'd touch or kiss.

She'd never wanted a man the way she wanted Sean, but it wasn't just about sex anymore. She liked being with him. It felt right, easy...perfect. Destined.

Yikes! Her heart pitched. No. She wouldn't go that far.

She skirted a small group of students filing into the little sixty-something-year-old adobe campus chapel, the one Sean said he sometimes went to hear himself think.

Her family wasn't religious in the traditional sense of the word. Her mother followed pagan rituals that worshipped the seasons, and her father worshipped the almighty dollar. She hadn't yet discovered what she was going to worship, but was pretty sure it wouldn't be done in a church with a mere mortal deciding she was wrong for wanting to share herself with Sean without benefit of marriage.

That said, she felt that she and God were good. They talked regularly. Their latest talk—just last night—had been about Sean. About how much she wanted something with him that lasted beyond his debt.

"Kristin!"

She stopped and looked around. Speak of the vision that haunted her dreams day and night! Walking toward her in black jeans, black shoes, and a black leather jacket over an oatmeal-colored sweater was the man she had asked God to give her.

Before turning to walk toward Sean, she glanced heavenward. *Ask and ye shall receive, yeah, thanks. But couldn't I have been clean and dressed nicer before he was delivered?*

"Hi." Sweat ran into her eyes, and she swiped her arm across her brow, the sleeve of her sweatshirt absorbing some of the moisture from her flushed face. Her breath was ragged, as much from seeing him as from her run.

"How are you, darlin'?" he asked.

"Good. A little sweaty," she said with a laugh, "but good. You?"

"I'm good, too. Nice shorts."

His eyes on her legs warmed them a bit. "Thanks. I like your outfit, too. Where are you headed this early all dressed up?"

The grin on his blushing face gave him an endearing look that caressed her heart. "I'm headed to church." He nodded toward the chapel.

She loved the sound of the word coming from his mouth—it sounded like "charch." But she wasn't as crazy about his being religious enough to actually step into the chapel for a service. One of God's tricks—sending her a pious man? Her mother always said that the universe sends you what you need. Maybe Sean would tap an undiscovered part of herself.

"Oh." She dropped her eyes to the sidewalk, nodded, swallowing her laughter. "Right." She raised her eyes to his. "Going in to confess your sins?"

His smile grew and he nodded slowly, keeping his eyes on hers. "I am."

"Any of them about me?" she asked.

"All of them."

Those three little words squeezed her heart and tossed it into the air. She moved closer to him, ran her hands up the front of his knobby sweater, and settled her palms atop the thudding beat in his chest.

"Am I the evil temptation you're praying God will deliver you from?"

His blue eyes grew dark and heavy, and he stepped closer to her so that their bodies touched, chest to thigh. He smelled clean and fresh and innocent, and she felt like the forbidden fruit.

"You are my temptation, Kristin. But God won't keep me from you. He and I made a deal about that the night I first laid eyes on you."

Before she could protest how sweaty she was, he cupped his hand at the side of her face, leaned in, and gave her a very non-pious kiss on the mouth that made her blood run hot.

Organ music rang out from the small chapel, which seemed to be the signal to end the kiss, because he did. He touched his forehead with hers. "See you tonight, darlin'," he whispered against her mouth.

"I'll be clean by then," she whispered back and brushed her open mouth across his lips, just barely touching them.

"So will I." He kissed her once more, twirling his tongue with hers, then backed away. Giving her a cherubic smile, he heeded the hymn that called him to come to the table.

Her muscles seemed to have atrophied at his confession, locking her in place as she watched the man of her dreams slip into the chapel. For a split second, she felt a tug pulling her to join him. To share something pure with him. Only when the doors closed was she able to shake off the feeling and move toward her dorm. The gym would have to wait. She needed a long, cold shower to get her body, if not her soul, clean.

****

Kristin shut off the blow dryer and listened intently. Sean's ringtone blared from her phone. Wearing nothing but a smile on her face, she raced to grab the device from the charger on her nightstand. The time was 7:02. He was early.

"Hey, darlin'. You clean?"

She chuckled. "I'm clean, but I need another twenty-eight minutes to get ready."

"I'll take you as you are right this second…gorgeous or merely beautiful."

"Right this second, my hair is wet and I'm naked."

"Naked's good…Heloise."

She laughed. "No! See you in twenty."

"Hurry! I can't wait to see you."

She couldn't wait to see him, either, and that was the only reason she made it downstairs fifteen minutes earlier than their agreed upon time.

****

The smell of popcorn and candy, perfume and cologne, sex and desire greeted Sean and Kristen as they strolled hand in hand into the tiny but packed makeshift theater in the Student Union Building a little before eight. They had kept stopping along the way there to kiss and touch or they would have arrived sooner. Sean pointed to a few empty seats in the last row by the corner. Kristin nodded, and he led them that way.

Zoe, her boyfriend Mason in tow, intercepted them, grabbing Kristin's hand.

While Kristin tried to withdraw her hand from her grip, she noticed Sean and Mason did the fist pumping male greeting ritual as if they knew each other.

"Come sit with me up front," Zoe insisted. "We have a whole row of seats saved, and we're going to throw popcorn at the screen."

"Thanks, but we've already got a couple of seats picked out." Kristin nodded to the dark corner.

Zoe stared at the seats with disgust. "You can't even see the screen from there."

"We're fine, but maybe we'll catch up with you guys later." She hugged her and stepped away to give Mason a brief hug. "Bye, Mason."

"But—" Zoe started.

"See ya, Kris. Sean." Mason interrupted Zoe's protest by taking her hand and leading her away before she could throw a fit.

"Mason'll have his hands full tonight," Kristin whispered to Sean. "She is *not* happy."

"Hey, if you want to go up front—"

"No, I don't. I mean, unless you want to?"

"I don't want to share you tonight."

She smiled. "Good answer. Let's get to our seats."

They slid into the back row and headed toward their seats, but only one chair remained. Someone had nabbed the other while they'd been fending off Zoe.

Kristin stared at the chair, then at him. "We could take turns sitting."

He shook his head. "You take the chair. I'll sit on the floor."

"You won't be able to see the screen."

He looked toward the front. Sighed. "There's always those seats up front with your friends."

She put her hands on his chest and moved in close to whisper against his neck. "I could sit on your lap. If it wouldn't be too uncomfortable for you."

"I like the way your mind works...Hermione."

Laughing, she shook her head.

He sat in the chair, she eased onto his lap, and he wrapped his arms around her. Cradled in his arms with her back resting against him, she could hear his heart beating, could smell the just-from-the-shower-clean of his skin, could feel the heat of his body wrapping around her like it always did when they were together. With a smile and a contented sigh, she held onto his hands, which were clasped around her waist.

"How do you know Mason?" he asked out of the blue, his breath brushing her ear.

"We went to high school together, and he's Zoe's boyfriend. How do you know him?"

"He's on my floor...right next door, actually."

She grinned. "No kidding?"

"No, why?"

"That night you walked me home from Randy's and I couldn't call my roommate because she was with her boyfriend somewhere in your dorm?"

"Yeah."

"She was with Mason."

He grinned. "Those two have kept me awake many nights, her instructing him how to do it better, him calling out his thanks to God."

She chuckled. "Sounds about right." Her mind flew back to Randy's comments about the screamers who had visited Sean's room, and she couldn't resist. "And what about you?"

"What about me?"

"Do you keep your neighbors awake at night?"

The room went dark and the movie started, but their eyes remained locked.

"Not since I met you."

Her heart skipped a beat and, in the space of that missed beat, she fell a little more for Sean O'Neill. She touched his face, kissed his mouth, softly, tenderly, letting him know he was the only one she wanted to make noise with, too.

They settled in to watch the loud, action-adventure.

From their corner seat in the back row, only the upper half of the screen was visible and a pole bisected the screen, which made it difficult to keep up with what was going on and who the characters were.

"Is that the bad guy?" Sean whispered against her hair about a third of the way through the movie.

She turned her face toward him to whisper back and found his lips inches from hers.

"No, that's the hero."

Nearly a half an hour later, he whispered again. "How can he be the hero? He just shot that woman."

"She's a bad woman."

She saw his gaze fall to her lips as she responded.

"Oh, yeah? What did she do?"

She licked her lips. "Cheated on him."

"With the bad guy?"

"Yes."

In the middle of a love scene, he again whispered. "Anybody watching this movie would think American girls like bad guys."

She chuckled at his half question. "Some do."

"Do you?"

"I like guys who go after what they want."

"Even if what they want is you?"

"Only if I want them back."

He took her hand and brought it to his mouth, kissing her palm, swirling his tongue at her wrist.

"Do you want me?"

At his question her heart rose in her chest like a helium balloon, and shivers spread like fire across her body. His eyes were hot, needy as they held hers, and she felt dizzy with the desire she saw and felt.

"Are you a bad guy?" She'd meant the words to be

funny and light, but they came out scratchy and almost inaudible as they passed through the need stuck in her dry throat.

"I'll tell you plain, Kristin…it's you I want. And it's you I'll have. If that makes me a bad guy, then so be it."

His mouth found hers, giving sweet hot kisses that ignited her blood. He held her head closer, opened his mouth wider over hers, and tilted his head to better fit their mouths together. His tongue found hers, and together they conducted a symphony of carnal delight.

She slipped her hand inside his T-shirt and ran her fingers across his hard stomach, up to his smooth chest where she traced the flat button of his nipple until it peaked. Feeling his heart pounding against her hand, she explored his chest thoroughly, letting her fingers dance across his ribs and the defined muscles of his stomach, before moving down to the band of his jeans that barricaded the part of him she wanted most.

The very part stiffening beneath her bottom.

She couldn't help but give a little wiggle, just to entice him. His sharp intake of breath pleased her, telling her that despite the control he seemed to have over his urges, he wasn't immune to her.

Breaking the kiss, he shifted her around in his lap so that her back faced their neighbor, giving them more privacy. She watched as his fingers went to work undoing the closed buttons of her shirt. His fingers moved slowly, taking care and building the heat and tension in her body.

"Since that first night I saw your breasts, I've wanted to see them again. Wanted to taste them," he said when all the buttons were loose and her shirt hung open almost to her navel. "I'm going to do that tonight."

She was nearly breathless from his words and his actions, so she nodded her acceptance of his plan. He slid a finger under the flap of material and moved it aside, then moved the material on the other side, too. He made no move to touch the two rounded breasts heaving out of her lacy bra like she hoped he would, but lowered his head and brushed his lips along her jaw line, against her neck, and across her chest.

"I want you, Kristin," he whispered into her feverish skin.

"I want you, too," left her lips just as his mouth reached her breasts, and she gasped and grabbed his head in anticipation. His mouth swept across each half-moon in a languid crawl, his tongue tracing the path his parted lips traveled. He rolled his tongue around her hard nipples through her bra, sucking and nipping each one in turn.

Fingers in his hair, she held his head to her breast in case he was tempted to stop. Then he did stop, and she heard herself whimper a protest.

Biting the front clasp of her bra with his teeth, he twisted it until it popped open, releasing her breasts. He buried his face between them and turned his head back and forth to nudge aside the cups with his nose and chin. Her breasts exposed, nipples reaching up to his mouth, he stared at them, a hungry grin on his shadowed face. Then his eyes met hers. They were soft and drowsy as if he were drunk on the taste of her. "Ready, darlin'?" he whispered.

At her nod, he kissed her mouth then kissed down her face, her neck, her chest. He licked the nipple of one breast, and she about came out of his lap. He put his mouth on it, sucking it lightly into his mouth, nipping the point with his teeth, circling it with his tongue. His hand cupped the other breast, bringing it closer to his mouth so he could treat it with the same attention. When both tips were hard and wet, he breathed on them, the cool breath tightening the points further. He sucked each of them hard, sending pleasure roaring deep inside her body.

Kristin bit down on her lip to keep a chorus of moans from escaping her mouth. She was torn between enjoying everything he had in mind and ripping his jeans down and sucking his cock—the crowd be damned. But his mouth shifting from breast to breast had caught her up in a frenzy of feeling that she didn't want to let go of.

Wetness dampened the crotch of her jeans and she squirmed in his lap, pressing her thighs together, trying to relieve a tingling pussy that cried out for attention. She was panting, unable to catch a full breath. Her eyes and ears were unfocused, but her mind was sharp on the tornado of pleasure roaring inside her.

His mouth left her breasts and found her mouth seconds before the lights came up. With a muffled curse, he broke off the kiss and hugged her to his chest, helping to hide her breasts until she could adjust her clothing.

In a blinding, dizzying fog of desire, with fingers that didn't seem to belong to her, she snapped her bra then buttoned her shirt. Her legs felt boneless and unable to stand. By the feel of the bulge tightening his jeans, he would need a few minutes as well. They remained seated while everyone around them filed out.

Embarrassed to let him see the raw and naked desire so close to the surface, she avoided his eyes, but she could feel his gaze on her hot face. His finger brushed along her jaw. Her face burned but she raised her eyes to his.

"That wasn't on the schedule," she teased. "I would have remembered."

"It's part of the movie experience," he said, his breath finally returning to normal.

"Hmm. Like snacks?"

He laughed. "Exactly."

"Here in the U.S., we just grab a bag of popcorn and a soft drink."

"I like the Irish way better." The way his gaze shifted to her breasts then back to her face made her crave his touch.

She dropped her eyes. "Me, too."

He pulled her back against him and pressed his cheek to her head, inhaling deep as if he were breathing in the scent of her.

"Are you sniffing me?" she asked, touched by the tender act.

"Makes me hungry, you smell so good."

Sharp need replaced soft tenderness as she imagined him satisfying that hunger.

After the movie crowd cleared, they stood and walked out, arms around each other. It staggered her how much closer she felt to him. As if one simple act of intimacy had opened their hearts to each other, giving each other a bigger slice of real estate to claim as their own.

Although what she wanted more than anything was to run back to her dorm so she could convince him to deviate from the schedule, he took his time, talking to her, taking time to stop and kiss and hug in the cool night air. It was as if he knew her plan and wasn't going to let it happen.

****

The woman was driving him mad with need. And she knew it. Was pulling out all the stops to get him to deviate from their schedule and make love to her. Having her lovely arse sitting on his cock during the movie had turned him inside out. He hadn't planned to suck her breasts in the middle of the fucking movie but they were right there, her nipples hard and practically begging him to take them. When he'd started unbuttoning her shirt and she didn't stop him, he couldn't stop himself. He would have them or die. The taste of her nipples in his mouth almost sent him over the edge. He had been ready to take her right there when the lights came up. Now, he was this close to saying to hell with the schedule.

He drew in a deep breath, trying to get control restored to his system so he wouldn't act out of pure emotion, pure lust. He'd never felt this discombobulated before. Not with a woman. What spell had this American woman cast on him? In such a short time, he already saw her as his. His heart did somersaults when he realized he didn't want it to end. He stopped and pulled her in for another kiss. He couldn't seem to get enough of her mouth. With her, he felt right. It felt easy. Fun. And really good.

"Next time, we'll get there early so we can get a seat where we can see the screen," he said.

"Oh, I don't know," she said, "I thought we had the best seat in the place."

It pleased him that she meant their back-row love making. "You liked it, huh?"

She nodded.

"What was your favorite part?"

"Chris Hemsworth."

She chuckled at the look of surprise and disgust that he was sure had materialized on his face at her answer.

"Hemsworth? He's what does it for ya, huh?"

She grinned at him. "As a matter of fact—"

"No, don't even say it. You'll pay for that nasty remark."

"Oh, will I, now?" she said, mimicking his accent. "And just who will be collecting from me? You, Sean Patrick O'Neill?"

"Glad to see you got the name right, love."

He took a step toward her, and she retreated. He took another, and the fire in her eyes sent him chasing her across the crusty grass, her laughing the whole way. She zigged, he zagged. He rushed, she swerved. Rounding a light pole, she grabbed hold of it and swung back around and into him where he easily caught her. Giggling at their fun, she taunted him. Kissed him. Teased him.

"Now that you got me, what are you going to do with me?"

Lightning fast, he bent and lifted her up and across his shoulder, his hand on her ass, and headed for the duck pond. The icy-cold and slimy duck pond.

She shrieked in mock terror. "Sean! What are you doing?"

"You've been a bad girl, and bad girls must be punished." He delivered a playful slap to her backside, hoping the action sent a wave of vibrating pleasure to her crotch. Thinking about it sent one through his dick.

Laughing, she kicked her legs and pounded his back with her hands. "No! Sean! Don't you dare!" For her struggles, he gave her another enticing slap and stopped at the edge of the water.

"Have you learned your lesson or do I toss you in?"

"I think you need to take me home and give me a proper spanking."

Laughing, he set her down in front of him, slowly, so their bodies rubbed against each other on the slide down. "You're bad, Kristin DeMarco," he whispered, "and my only temptation these days."

She wrapped her arms around his hips and pulled him against her, rubbing slowly against his dick, which was standing at attention in his boxers. She was soft against his hard and she clutched him as if she wanted to crawl inside his skin.

"I'm not bad," she said just above a whisper. "I'm just a woman who is so filled with passion for you that she'll do anything to have you."

Her words, the way she looked at him, her eyes soft and deep, her lips parted, her breathing labored, touched him and reminded him of their first conversation about the kind of woman he wanted. His breath caught in his throat and he couldn't speak.

"Got a problem with that?" she asked, a bit of an attitude coloring the words.

Shifting his hands to her ass, he cupped both cheeks and pulled her even tighter against him. He shook his head. "No." His voice was rough with need. "Not at all."

He kissed her, sliding his mouth wetly over hers, giving, taking, and making her want more. And she did want more. He could tell by the way she pressed her breasts into his chest and ground her mound against his erection. She wasn't playing hard to get with him...Christ, he hated when women did that. He knew Kristin was filled with passion for him, and it made him feel wanted, like no other woman had before.

He wanted to take her home and love her all night long. Hear her sigh his name as he made her come again and again. Spend hours exploring her body with his mouth and tongue and hands. It was *his* damn schedule. He could alter it if he wanted. And fuck if he didn't want to. Bad. His mind made up, he pulled back with a groan, then bent his knees and stooped over, presenting his back to her. "Get on."

She hopped on his back, wrapping her legs around his waist and her arms around his neck. "Where are we going?"

He stood upright, shifting to make sure he had a good grip on her legs. "To adjust the bloody schedule."

"Yippy!" she said and giggled with joy as he headed toward her dorm.

Chapter Six

As Sean and Kristin neared the dorm, a crying Zoe ran past them as if she didn't see them.

"Zoe?" Kristin called out and slid off his back.

She stopped, turned tear-filled eyes to Kristin, and ran into her arms. "Oh, Kristin!"

"What's wrong?" Kristin patted her back awkwardly. She wasn't a crier and had never been comfortable easing people through emotional outbreaks like the one playing out all over her.

Hiccupping and sniffing, Zoe swiped at her nose. "Mason br-br-broke up with m-m-me." The words seemed to unleash a fresh torrent of tears.

Kristin stepped out of the clinging arms. "Mason broke up with you?" she asked, just to make sure she'd heard the warbled words right. Zoe nodded.

"That doesn't sound right. He's crazy about you."

"Not anymore," she moaned, and flung herself against Kristin. "Take me home!"

Kristin looked longingly at Sean over her friend's shoulder. He shrugged then winked at her as if to say there'd be another time.

"Sure. Let me say goodnight to Sean."

Zoe let loose with another sob as Kristin moved away.

Kristin went easily into Sean's embrace. "Sorry," she whispered. "Rain check?"

He swept a strand of hair away from her face and brushed his thumb across her mouth. "We'll have another chance. I promise." She captured his hand, holding it against her cheek, against her mouth. His other hand slid onto her neck and pulled her into him. His kiss was filled with passion and promises that would have to be left for another time.

"Lunch tomorrow," he whispered against her hungry lips as his gaze darted to Zoe then back. "Unless you're unavailable...Harriett."

Kristin smiled. "I wouldn't miss it," she said. "And no to Harriett."

He kissed her again before she slowly, reluctantly, left his arms and led her friend toward home.

****

"Sorry I ruined your date with Sean," Zoe said from her bed as Kristin handed her a cup of hot tea.

"You didn't. I had a great time. Now tell me what happened between you and Mason." She sat at her side, holding her hand.

"We went to his room after the movie. We usually tear each other's clothes off and jump on each other. But when I started kissing him, he pushed me away. I asked him what was wrong. And that's when he told me that he didn't want to see me anymore."

"Did he say why?"

She shook her head. "I asked him if I'd done something wrong or if there was somebody else. He said no. But he had to be lying. Why else would he break up a good thing like us?"

"Maybe he just needs some space. Give him time. He'll realize how much he misses you and how stupid he was for letting you go."

"You think?"

"Absolutely."

Zoe set her cup on the bedside table. "Can I have a hug?"

Kristin hesitated for a split second. She knew Zoe—sex was her go-to salve for everything, good or bad. Kristin had Sean's touch, his smell, his kisses on her, and she didn't want it to rub off. But Zoe was a friend. A good friend who needed her comfort.

Kristin leaned over and hugged her. Zoe wrapped her arms around her and held her tight, pulling her body against hers.

Through their clothes, she could feel Zoe's nipples pressing into her breasts, could feel her warmth hook into her, connecting them. Kristin knew what Zoe wanted and needed, but it was no longer what she wanted and needed. She wanted Sean. Only Sean. Slowly, gently, she pulled back.

"Drink your tea. It'll make you feel better," she said with a small smile, hoping to change the subject.

Zoe caught her arm. "I don't want tea. I want you. I want to feel you." As if sensing the coming refusal, her eyes teared.

Knowing she couldn't break her friend's already fragile heart, Kristin stood, pulled back the covers, and crawled into bed. She put her arm around her and let her lay her head on her shoulder.

She felt Zoe's hand slip under the hem of her shirt. Felt her fingers tease across her stomach. She put her hand over hers, stopping her. "I'm sorry, but I can't."

"Why not?"

"Sean and I are, I don't know, getting...closer. I don't want to be with anyone else while we're—"

"I'm not just *anyone*. I'm your best friend. I need you."

"And I'm here for you...to talk, to comfort you. But I'm not going to have sex with you." Kristin kept her tone soft and sympathetic, but it bugged her that Zoe kept pushing.

"So that's it?" Zoe scooted away from Kristin. "You're with *him* now, so I can go fuck myself?"

"That's not what I mean and you know it." Kristin reached out her hand, but her friend swatted it away.

"I'm always here for you," Zoe said. "I never refuse you when you need me. Now, when I need you, you brush me off."

"Try to understand about Sean. I really like him. He's—"

"I don't want to hear it." Zoe pulled the covers over her head with dramatic sobs.

Kristin sat on the bed for a minute longer, unsure whether to leave or stay. In the end, when Zoe showed no signs of leaving her blanket cave to talk rationally, Kristin rose and got ready for bed. She was growing tired of her tantrums and no longer wanted to play these childish games.

It was deep in the night before Kristin heard Zoe's soft snores begin. She swallowed against a ball of confusion in her throat. What would Sean think if he knew about her and Zoe? Many guys found girl-on-girl a turn on, or at least that's what they claimed. Would Sean be one of them? Or would he be angry? Shocked? Offended? Amused? Titillated? Curious to watch? Eager to participate? She didn't know.

And what about her relationship with Zoe? Would her desire to be with Sean exclusively destroy it?

She didn't have any answers. This was uncharted territory for her. Until last semester, she had never been with a woman, never had any real interest in being with a woman. Oh, she had been curious, but not enough to follow through with it. Then, she and Zoe roomed together. To Zoe's free spirit, sex was like air, water, food—something the body needed to function, to thrive. She had given Kristin the courage and the opportunity to explore her sexuality and learn what her body wanted and needed.

The new truth in her life was that, with Sean in the picture, she no longer wanted sex with anyone but him. While she cared about her friend, she felt something growing strong in her heart for Sean. And she wouldn't do anything to risk losing that or him.

Maybe she didn't need answers right now. She and Sean hadn't even slept together yet. Maybe sex would be a part of his payment plan and nothing else. Maybe one time would be enough to scratch her itch. Maybe they wouldn't be sexually compatible. Maybe he wouldn't be any good in bed.

She smothered a laugh.

Yeah, right. He'd be a lit stick of dynamite in bed. She knew it by the way he kissed her, slow and hot, like he was eating her up, drinking from her soul. By the way his slow hands seemed to know where to touch her body for maximum pleasure, even if that place was as innocent as the curve of her shoulder, her wrist, her neck, her fingers. By the way his gaze bore into her, as if he was reading her desires with the intent of making them come true. The man knew how to pleasure a woman. And she had a feeling that, once she'd tasted the pleasures he offered, no one else would satisfy.

She pictured them tonight, his mouth loving her breasts, his hands cupping her butt, his hard dick pressing into her. Her hands slid between her legs on a low moan, and she knew that tomorrow, and another chance to convince him to deviate from their blasted schedule, couldn't come soon enough.

Don't wait—call him, her heart said. *Tell him you're thinking about him, can't wait to see him tomorrow.*

No, her mind countered. *You're already moving way too fast with him. Playing hard to get will keep him interested.*

"The hell with that." She grabbed her phone and her pillow and went to the lounge on her floor. It was dark and quiet and somewhat private. No one would hear her, bother her, watch her as she made a fool of herself.

****

Sean lay in bed, wide awake, seeing Kristin's face in the light and shadow of the ceiling. His mind focused on remembering every moment of their night...imagining what their night could have been. If not for her roommate, he'd be holding Kristin in his arms right now, would know the feel of her body connected to his. Zoe was trouble. He knew the type. The strange thing was that he usually felt those territorial signals from a man who thought he was losing his woman, not from the woman's girlfriend.

He would have Kristin. No matter who got in his way. He closed his eyes, felt her mouth on his. Felt her warm, curvy body fitted against his. Ah, shit, he wanted her. All the fucking time. His hand moved under the covers and grabbed his swollen cock at the base. He stroked it to the sensitive tip, Kristin flooding his mind.

His phone buzzed and he almost ignored it. But a sixth sense told him it was her. With his one unoccupied hand, he grabbed it.

"Missing me are ya?" He said the words through a smile.

"You got me all stirred up tonight with a promise to ditch the schedule, then you left me to dangle."

He chuckled softly, the melody of her low, sweet voice wrapping around his heart. "What can I do to help you feel better, darlin'?"

"Tell me…tell me what we would have done tonight had our plans not been interrupted."

Her voice was a bit hesitant, as if she wasn't sure calling him like this was a good idea. "And spoil the surprise?" He kept his voice soft but eager to let her know it was right.

"How about a taste," she said, "just to build excitement?"

"I can talk to you 'til I'm blue in the face, but I can't touch you or taste you."

"I've got the touching covered. You just talk."

Her words spiraled up his cock like a tongue, and he squeezed the swollen rod filling his hand. Maybe she wasn't such a novice after all. She was making him sweat. "I could use a little talkin' myself."

"Is it hot in your room?" she asked, her voice low and sultry.

"It wasn't before you called."

She chuckled. "Take off your boxers."

"Oh, so you're driving this ride?"

"We'll take turns. Are they off?"

"They were off before you rang."

He heard her murmur a low mmmmm. "All that naked skin against the sheets. It's making me hot just thinking about it."

"What are you wearing?" he asked, wanting to participate in their game.

"T-shirt and panties."

"Take them off."

He heard her moving, shifting, heard the rustle of clothing. "Panties are off. The shirt stays on. I'm in the lounge, and I don't want to be caught naked playing with myself."

"Take off the shirt, Kristin."

"Sean."

"Kristin. The risk of being caught makes it hotter."

"Easy for you to say. You're not the one taking the risk."

He could hear in her pause that she would relent.

"Shit. Let me put the phone down," she said, and he heard the material shush in his ear. "Okay. I'm as naked as you, except I don't have a sheet."

He kicked the sheet off and laid spread eagle on his bed, his cock rising in the air like a monolith. "The sheet's gone. We're the same."

"Good. I'm touching my breasts, like you did tonight. What are you touching?"

He loved that she jumped right into it, eager to be with him this way. "Mmm. Your breasts are delicious. Too bad you can't taste them, like I did."

"It felt so good. I liked when you sucked them, then bit them. I wanted to do the same thing to you, but in a spot quite a bit lower."

"What did you want to suck? Tell me."

"I wanted to suck your dick."

Fuck! His hips rose, stuffing his cock deeper, harder into his fist. He stroked it, imaging her lips on his head, his shaft, taking him full in her mouth. A groan slipped from his mouth before he could stop it.

"It was so hard," she continued, her voice strained. "I could feel it growing as I sat on your lap."

He was enjoying the image of his hard cock on her ass as much as she seemed to be.

"I felt your arse wiggling on me. Had the lights not come up when they did, I would have embarrassed myself, walking home in wet boxers."

She laughed. "My panties were pretty wet, too."

"Are you wet now?"

"Oh, yeah."

"Close your eyes. Pretend I'm there. Are they closed?"

"Yes."

"I'm climbing on the bed—"

"Couch."

He laughed. "Couch. Crawling up toward you, between your legs. Do you see me?"

"No. My eyes are closed."

Chuckling, he tried again. "Your eyes are open in the fantasy."

"Gotcha."

"Where was I?" he asked.

"Crawling between my legs."

"I'm there, between your legs, now. My hands running up your thighs. Your skin is so soft and smooth, I want to touch it all. With my hands, my tongue, my lips. I lower my head to your inner thighs, kiss you. You shiver it feels so good."

"Yes. Yes, I feel it."

"I kiss up your leg until I come to the spot where you're wet and hot for me. I'm there, Kristin. Can you feel my breath on you?"

"Yes. I feel it. Hot. I want your mouth on my pussy. God, Sean, I'm shaking I want you so bad."

"I open my mouth and slick my tongue between your wet lips and lick all along the opening, tasting you, sucking your juice into my mouth."

He could hear her panting. "It feels so good. More."

"My tongue breaks through your silky lips and digs deeper to find the little spot that'll drive you to your pleasure."

"Right there. Right on my clit."

"I go deeper, sliding my tongue into your wet pussy. In. And out. Fucking you." He was panting, too. He could see her laying back, her legs wide for him, opening herself to his mouth, his tongue. She would taste like heaven to him. His cock was so tight that he had to come soon or risk the skin splitting right off. The jerking motions of his hand got faster when he thought about tasting her juice, tongue-fucking her pussy.

"Then I can't wait any more, so I pull you on top of me and glide your cock inside my pussy." Her words rushed out in one long breathy sentence.

The thought of being inside her warm, tight pussy, of thrusting his cock inside her, had him thrusting his cock into his hand, fighting for release. "I'm inside you, loving you. Can you feel it?"

"Yes. Yes. Faster."

His fist pumped his flesh hard and fast, and he felt his cum rising. His heart was pounding as fast as his hand was pumping, and he couldn't catch a breath. His tightly closed eyes were focused on that singular image of her on that couch, him between her legs, pumping into her wet pussy, kissing her wet mouth, feeling her bucking beneath him, calling out his name.

"Love me. Ahhh! Sean! Sean!"

Hearing her groan his name as she found her pleasure pushed him the rest of the way. His body tensed and then released, cum shot from his dick in a great explosion that took all his energy. For a moment, neither of them said a word, just lay there trying to catch their breath.

"You okay, darlin'?" His voice couldn't seem to go above a whisper. There was nothing left in him.

She released a small laugh. "Much better now. God, you're good." She whispered, too, her voice soft and loving.

He wished she was by his side, whispering in his ear. "You're pretty good yourself."

"I'm better in person," she said.

"So am I."

"I can't wait to find out. Don't make me wait too long."

"Couple more days, darlin'. We can wait that long. Think how good it'll be."

"Mind blowing would be my guess."

"It will be. I promise."

"I trust you."

Warmth spread through his core out to his limbs at her words. She trusted him. She wanted him. As much as he wanted her. They would find great pleasure together, he was sure of it. As they said goodnight and hung up, he wasn't sure he could wait another couple days either to have her. He rolled over, a smile on his face, and fell asleep. Kristin on his mind. And Kristin in his heart.

****

Her professor/master's thesis coordinator kept her fifteen minutes after class to discuss her progress, so she rushed all the way to the Student Union Building, hoping to catch Sean before he gave up on her meeting him for lunch.

She checked all the sitting areas, all the food kiosks, even the private rooms students could check out. No Sean. Disappointment swirled inside her as she realized he must have thought she wasn't showing up and left. Maybe after last night he didn't want to see her? Had the phone sex been a mistake? Too soon? Shit!

She bought something to drink and sat down at one of the tables in a section that saw the most traffic in case he came back around. Maybe he was just running late, like she was? She grabbed her phone to call him and saw a text from him from over a half hour ago.

"K—got held up in a meeting. Have to reschedule lunch. Sorry."

Shit. That sounded like a brush off.

A second text from him came through as she was trying not to swallow her tongue.

"Won't be able to sleep tonight without kissing you today. Can I see you tonight?"

She smiled. That did *not* sound like a brush off. She was preparing a response when a large pair of hands gripped her shoulders and a familiar voice tickled her ear. "You mad at me?"

Her heart fluttered in her chest and a wave of heat coursed through her as she inhaled Sean. If he mentioned

86

last night, she'd die of embarrassment. Smiling, she leaned her head back to stare into his eyes.

"Furious. I'm going to have to charge you a penalty for missing a payment."

He grinned as if he was relieved she wasn't angry. "Name it."

"A kiss. And make it a good one. I missed lunch and I'm starving."

He leaned forward, his lips hovering over hers.

She closed her eyes and held her breath in anticipation of his kiss.

He kissed her fully on the mouth, the tip of his tongue gliding across her teeth, swirling inside her mouth, making her head spin and her nipples pucker. When she feared she would pass out from the sheer pleasure of the moment, his lips left hers. It was the kiss they would have shared last night had they been together.

Her eyes cracked open in time to see him raise his head and smile. "Did that satisfy your hunger?"

He slid into the chair beside her and took her hands in his. The heat in his eyes made her cheeks hot. Was he thinking about last night, too?

She shook her head. "It only made me want more." She put her hand to his face and brushed his mouth with her thumb. "Do we have time now to adjust the schedule?"

He brought her hand to his mouth, kissing her palm. "Sorry, darlin', no. I teach class in about ten minutes but, if you can wait until tonight, I'll make it up to you."

Her heart fluttered in her chest at the thought of how he'd make it up to her. "Call me. If I'm available, I'll invite you over. If not, you'll just have to—"

"Wait for you to call at one in the morning?"

Heat burned her face at his teasing comment. She laughed, lowered her eyes, and nodded. "Something like that."

He leaned forward, ran a finger along her jaw, and brushed her mouth with his thumb. "Look at me, darlin'."

She met his eyes. Their dark blue depths were filled with light today.

"I love that you did that. I love that you want me as much as I want you. I love—" His hands cupping her face, her eyes staring deep into hers, he looked like he was going to say something more to her, but the words never came.

He pulled her up against him and kissed her. A long, wet, deep kiss that left a passion fog hanging thick like a curtain of red velvet in her head. She groaned in his mouth and ground her hips against his, wanting more. Instead of giving her more, he eased back.

"Tonight."

She smiled. "Tonight, what? We'll actually deviate from the schedule, or you'll torture me again with promises to deviate?"

With a damn, sexy grin, he dropped his arms from around her and stepped back, grabbed his backpack.

"You'll have to let me up to your room to find out." He turned and walked away.

She had gathered her things and headed off to her next class when another text buzzed in.

"See you at nine, Hazel?"

She grinned and texted him back. "Yes, no."

****

At just past eight, Sean's personal ringtone blared and Kristin grabbed her phone.

"Are you always early?"

"For the important things I am. I'm dying to see you."

"For?"

"Hugging."

"And?"

"Kissing."

"And?"

"And...I'll tell you the rest when I get up to your room."

"You'll have to do better than *tell* me if I'm going to let you up."

"How about I show you?"

"I'm on my way down."

She quickly brushed her teeth, swished with mouthwash, and ran some balm over her lips. At the last minute, she removed her bra and panties, then rushed downstairs to escort him up to her room.

As soon as the door was closed behind them, Sean tore off his coat and slung it aside, grabbed Kristin around the waist, pulled her to him, and kissed her long and hard on the mouth like they hadn't seen each other in weeks.

Her body was ready for him—hot, wet, and ready to be fucked. Fortunately, Zoe should be gone at least another hour, giving them time to do everything she'd been dreaming about since the first time she'd seen his face. They would not stop at kissing and touching tonight if she had her way.

Keeping their lips locked and her arms around him, she walked backward until she felt the edge of the bed against the back of her legs. She yanked his T-shirt over his head and pulled him down with her onto the bed, shivering with joy at the weight of his hard body on hers in contrast to the fit of his soft, firm mouth on hers.

He spread her thighs with his knee and tucked his leg against her core. She grabbed his ass and held him tight against her, grinding against his leg. The crotch of her yoga pants was already wet with desire for him, and she craved the feel of his fingers inside her, his tongue on her, his dick filling her, like they'd talked about last night.

He broke the kiss long enough to grab the hem of her shirt, and she bowed up to allow him to pull it off. He paused, staring at her breasts and smiling.

"Thoughtful of you, lass, to remove your bra for me."

She smiled back. "Yes, it was. Now show me how much you appreciate it."

He took her nipple in his mouth and sucked hard enough to tug at her womb and rip a groan from her mouth. His tongue and teeth took turns teasing and tasting the hard bud.

The moans and groans she released sounded a lot like, "Oh, Sean," and, "the other one, too. Please," because he gave the same delicious attention to the other breast.

Her head reeling and her body on fire, she wanted his hands and mouth everywhere, wanted him to finally satisfy her hunger. As if she'd spoken aloud, he slipped his hand into the tight space between their bodies and found his way past the low band of her yoga pants. She gasped as his fingers moved lower and lower, finally tickling the trimmed edge of her landing strip.

Noticing the absence of underwear, he paused, arched one eyebrow, and grinned at her, a question in his laughing eyes. "No clean panties?"

"I have a drawer full of clean panties. I chose not to wear any tonight."

"I think I love you."

"Less telling, more showing."

His eyes locked with hers, he palmed her mound, and traced her aching folds with one long finger. Her needy, wet flesh easily parted at his touch and his finger plunged deeply. His hips moved against her, like it was his cock inside her and not his finger. She could see his pulse jump at his throat, but it was like he was holding his breath.

"Oh, Sean, yes. It is better in person." Her eyes fluttered closed and her legs opened wider. She wrapped one leg around his back, making it easier for him to glide in and out of her pussy, building her desire. His thumb, slick and wet, rode her clit until it throbbed and she thrust up against his hand, begging for release.

She reached between their straining bodies and pulled at the strings on his sweats, untying them. "I have to touch you." She stuck her hands into the waistband. No boxers stood between his hard dick and her eager hand. "No clean boxers?"

"I chose not to wear them." His laugh sounded more like a groan as she wrapped her hand around his cock and stroked it.

Her fingers weren't going even half way around his rod. And he was long. Math was never her best subject, so she could be off, but he felt nearly ten inches long and growing as she stroked him.

"God, you're huge!"

"Is that a problem?"

For some reason, he sounded worried, but she purred in pure delight. "I think I love you."

His eyes were closed and he was smiling. "Less telling, Kristin, more showing."

"Roll over."

He removed his hand from her pants and rolled to the side as she slid out from under him and knelt by the bed. He shifted and faced her.

She lifted his cock from his pants and took it firmly in her hand. She stroked its length, massaging the swollen head, getting to know the silky feel and clean smell of him. A drop of cock honey beaded at his slit, telling her he was turned on. He put his hand on her head gently. He obviously needed to hold on to something, because she was about to blow him away.

"This is what I wanted to do at the movie and last night," she said and dipped her head, eager to taste him.

The door flew open.

"Kristin, you'll never guess who I—"

Kristin spun toward Zoe's voice, then back around to Sean, who moved his hand from her head.

"Oh my God," Zoe said. "What are you...? Is that...? Oh, damn!"

Chapter Seven

"Shit!" Kristin murmured and put a pillow over Sean's crotch so he could cover up. She took a last look to make sure he was decent before she grabbed her shirt and yanked it on. She then sat on the bed next to him.

"Thought-you-were-with-your-study-group." Her words rushed out in one breath.

"We finished early. Hey, Sean." Zoe's voice carried that sexy come-fuck-me tone Kristin had heard her use on more guys than she could count, and it pissed her off.

Sean put his arm around Kristin's shoulders, kissing the crown of her head. "Hey," he muttered.

"We're in the middle of something..." Kristin didn't finish the curt sentence, thinking Zoe would understand her meaning.

"I can see that."

"Then how about you go to Jessica's or Addy's for a half hour or so."

She dropped her backpack on the floor by her bed, kicked off her boots, and pulled off her coat. "Why?"

Frustration answered for Kristin. "Why do you think?"

Zoe glared at her. "From what it looked like, you want to suck him and fuck him."

Sean muttered something in Irish and shook his head at the crass frankness.

Kristin bit her lip to hold her tongue, not wanting this to escalate into something even more embarrassing and uncomfortable. "Come on. Give us some time alone."

"Nope. I'm going to bed. But please—you guys go on with what you were doing. I don't mind." Facing Sean and Kristin, she pulled her sweater over her head and dropped it to the floor. She, too, was braless, and her nipples were hard tipped peaks, standing at attention on her pert breasts. She undid the snap on her jeans, lowered the zipper, then shimmied them over her hips and down her legs. Her pink see-through thong revealed a small diamond patch of neon pink curls.

"If you ask me nicely, I'll even join you."

She had hooked a finger on either side of the thong and pulled it down when Sean cursed in Irish again. He stood, found his shirt, and pulled it on, then grabbed his coat and headed for the door.

Kristin didn't understand his words, but his tone was clear—he was disgusted. With her? Zoe? Or just the turn of events?

Kristin shot Zoe a look so sharp it could maim as she pulled on her yoga pants and slipped into her flips before following Sean out the door, slamming it behind her.

Sean and Kristin headed down the stairs in silence. She kept waiting for him to say something, anything, and prayed that he would. But they reached the front door of her building and he still hadn't spoken, so she did.

"I'm guessing you're not into threesomes?" She smiled to let him know she was joking. But he wasn't amused.

"There's something seriously wrong with that girl," he said and yanked on his coat.

"She's having a hard time since Mason broke up with her. She sees us, and I think she's jealous."

"What she did up there, that's beyond jealous."

"It's just the way she is, but look, I don't want to talk about her." She slid her arms around his waist. "Let's go to your room and finish what we started," she whispered. "I want you in my mouth."

He held her close and cupped his hand over her cheek. The smell of her pussy juice on his fingers made her want to beg him to take her.

"I want you, Kristin. But not in my room."

The words hurt her to the quick. "Why not?"

"Darlin', it's a guys-only floor. They'll be listening to our every sound, flogging themselves thinking about what you're doing with me in my bed. I'd end up punching a couple of them after they looked at you."

She eased back out of his arms, the frustration zipping through her body and making her words sharp. "You didn't seem to have any trouble bringing those other girls to your room."

The second it was out of her mouth, she wished she could bring it back. But the shocked look on Sean's face told her it was impossible. She dropped her eyes, ashamed of herself. After a moment, she felt his hand on her face, lifting it so he could see her eyes and so she could see the truth in his.

"Those girls didn't mean anything to me," he said, his voice soft but firm. "You do."

She threw herself against him and hugged him. "We can't go to my room. We can't go to your room. Do we just give up?"

He wrapped his arms around her for a deep and soulful kiss filled with a promise that he would find a way.

"I'll never give up on being with you...Heather."

She choked on a chuckle. "No! Don't you dare speak another woman's name after giving me a kiss like that."

He kissed her again, defusing her frustration into particles too tiny to sour her mood.

"See you tomorrow morning at eight with your..." he closed his eyes, remembering "...latte, no sugar, with whipped cream."

She smiled, pleased that he remembered her favorite coffee drink from their walk. "Dream about me tonight," she whispered against his mouth. "What I was going to do to you."

"That'll be all I think about, darlin'." He kissed her, left her embrace, pushed open the door, and disappeared into the darkness.

****

Zoe was in bed, innocently typing on her laptop, when Kristin came in.

"What the hell's wrong with you?" Kristin seethed through gritted teeth. On the climb up to her floor, her anger had risen to bubbling-over proportions.

"You could have gone to *his* room for your little fuck-fest. You didn't need to kick me out of the room." Her eyes never left the computer as she delivered the bitter words.

Kristin stormed over to her and slammed the laptop closed. "I've left *my* room for you plenty of times when you brought some guy here. The one time I ask the same of you, and you act like a bitch."

"Oh, I'm a bitch just because I don't do what you say? Thanks…*friend*."

Kristin released a frustration-filled growl and dropped down onto Zoe's bed. "I thought you'd be happy I've found someone I like after everything I went through with Nick. But ever since I met Sean, you act like you hate that he's in my life."

Zoe was silent, her finger tracing the paisley pattern on her comforter, her eyes following it. Then she looked up into Kristin's eyes. "He's going to hurt you."

The statement came like a blow to Kristin, reminding her that only a couple of days ago she'd heard the same thing from Randy. She leaned back and stared at Zoe. "I don't get that from him at all."

Zoe chortled. "Sorry, honey, but when it comes to guys, you don't have a great record."

"That's not true."

"Oh? There's Nick, who ditched you. Before him was that basketball player—what was his name? Reese?—who cheated on you with another basketball player. Female, but still. Before that was—"

Kristin held up her hand. "Enough already." She stood and climbed into her own bed, pulling the comforter up to her chin. It smelled like him, like her, like their combined scent. "Sean's different."

"The only difference between Sean and those other guys is that his package is bigger." Zoe opened her laptop again. "Much, much bigger."

"You saw?"

"Duh! Only wish I'd whipped out my phone and snapped a pic before you smothered it with a pillow." She sighed. "But it's in here," she added, tapping her temple, "and it's going to fuel my fantasies for weeks."

"Leave him out of your depraved fantasies."

"I will if you will."

"No promises. But really, Sean's a good guy, and even if you can't find it in your heart to be nice to him, at least be happy for me and support what I want. Can you do that?"

"No promises—not as long as what you want is him." Zoe's eyes were sharp flints of ice, telling Kristin that she was serious about not giving her an ounce of help with Sean.

Her phone dinging through a text from Sean curbed what she really wanted to say to her, but throughout her hour-long conversation with Sean, Zoe's words stayed with her.

Sean hadn't done or said anything that would make her question his sincerity or his honesty. With guys from her past, even Nick, she'd always felt a little off, like she was walking on a sloped sidewalk that could pitch her at any time. And to be honest, the possibility of being pitched had been part of the appeal. Being with Sean was like floating through a summer-blue sky—no clouds, no rain, just a light breeze to carry them forward.

Could she be wrong? Again?

****

Seeing Sean's handsome, open, smiling face the next morning just before eight, her latte in hand, Kristin knew Zoe and Randy were wrong.

"I stayed awake all night thinking about your roommate," he said as he walked her to class.

"Oh, goodie. Just what every girl wants to hear from her guy."

He chuckled. "What I mean is, I thought about why she's acting the way she is."

"Did you come up with any conclusions? More importantly, any solutions?"

"No solutions. It's crazy, but she's acting like a jealous lover."

A chill shot through Kristin at his words. Was now the time to tell him about her and Zoe? Before they got any closer? She opened her mouth to say something, but one look at him and she knew she couldn't. Besides, she hadn't been with her since she and Sean got together, so why tell him? He hadn't been real open about his ex-lovers.

"Was she this bad with your other boyfriends?" he continued.

"She's never liked any of the guys I dated, but she's never been this…territorial."

"So, it's me she doesn't like."

She shrugged. "She thinks you're going to hurt me."

He stopped and faced her, his gaze serious. "And you, Kristin? What do *you* think?"

"I think she's wrong."

"I want you to *know* it…" he put his hand on her heart "…in here. Know that I won't hurt you."

She covered his hand with hers and brought it to her lips, kissing his palm. "I know it."

He dropped his arm around her shoulders and hugged her, dropping a kiss on her head.

They got to the building where her class was but, instead of letting her go, he sat on the adobe *banco* and pulled her onto his lap.

"Where are you taking me for dinner tomorrow

night?" she asked, her arms loosely looped around his neck.

"No place with sushi, that's for sure," he teased, knowing it was one of her favorite foods.

"No place with food that comes on a bun, either," she countered, knowing of his passion for green chile cheeseburgers.

"Nah. Tomorrow we're going someplace nice where you can wear a dress cut down to here." His finger drew a line from her neck to her belly button, then his hand stayed to splay across her lower stomach.

"I'll see what I can do," she said on a ragged breath.

His other hand cupped the side of her neck and pulled her in for a goodbye kiss.

As she watched him go, she noticed how many looks he got from women—and a few guys. He was beautiful and oozed sexuality, from the way he walked to the way he looked, and clearly she wasn't the only one who saw it. Her mind flew back to Randy's comment about the girls who visited his room, and she wondered whether Sean was telling the truth—that no girls had been in his room since the night they met.

All her doubts blew away like piles of ash when Sean looked back over his shoulder at her as if he needed just one more look. The smile on his face when he saw her still there, watching him go, warmed her head to heel.

Shaking his head, he stopped and rushed back to her. She moved toward him, too, and they met in a tangle of arms and mouths, their bodies merging like two flames, his hands splaying out across her ass, pulling her tight against him.

When they came up for breath, his eyes were heavy and glazed like he was high on some pleasure-inducing substance. His heartbeat was as thunderous against hers. "I can't get enough of you."

"You could have more if you'd agree to adjust the schedule."

"If I wasn't teaching this class..." He held her gaze, telling her everything he'd do to her if there was time.

"Go," she said. "They'll only wait ten minutes before they decide you're not showing up." She smiled. "Besides, we have tonight."

With a groan, he kissed her again then backed away, still holding her hand. Right before his fingertips slid off hers, he said, "Tonight." He turned and ran toward his class.

She drew in a few strong breaths to calm the racing desire washing over her, knowing she wouldn't have the brain power to focus on anything the professor had to say until the wave had receded. Zoe was right...she needed to do him and get it over with. Maybe then her hormones would settle down and let her get back to her normal, rational self.

As she pulled open the door to the building, a woman behind her stopped her. "Hey, Kristin."

Kristin faced the unfamiliar woman warily. "Do I know you?"

"You haven't fucked Sean yet, have you?" Her mouth was smiling and her eyes were shining, but nothing about her looked friendly.

"That's none of your business." Kristin frosted her words into shards of ice to leave no doubt that she wasn't going to continue this conversation. The woman grabbed her arm as she tried to move through the door and stuck her face close to Kristin's.

"The way he was with you, just now? He acted like that with me, too. But once we fucked, he never spoke to me again, not even to tell me why he was ending it."

Kristin yanked her arm from the woman's grip. "Maybe it was your breath."

The woman narrowed her eyes at Kristin and moved back a step. "Don't fool yourself into believing he cares about you. He wants you, that's clear enough from the way he was all over you. But after he's had you, he'll toss your ass aside, just like he's done all the women he's been with since he got here. Take my advice and end things with him before he takes your heart." The woman left as quickly as she arrived.

Kristin's face burned. Did Sean already have her heart? Had she let her desire for him morph into a deeper feeling that would only get her hurt? She stood outside for a few seconds, quieting her restless mind and stomach with a few deep breaths before going inside to make her way to class.

As she turned the corner toward her class, she saw the woman talking with Randy, heard him say, "thanks." He handed her money, and she left the building. When Randy turned to head down the hall, Kristin was there, waiting for him with her arms crossed over her chest.

His face went pale as his mouth and eyes rounded in surprise. He closed his mouth and swallowed. "Kristin!" His voice cracked and he swallowed again.

"I know you paid that woman to trash Sean." She advanced on him, and he backed up until he hit the wall. "Why?"

"Okay, yeah, I asked her to tell you about what

happened when she was with Sean, but she wasn't making any of those things up. He really did drop her and the other women...just like she said. For no reason."

"Hell, Randy, even I can see she's not right for him."

"And what happens when he suddenly decides you're not right for him?"

The concern in his eyes and in his voice pushed her to take time to check in with her heart. Feeling Sean's hand there, hearing his promise to not hurt her, tasting his kisses on her mouth told her everything she needed to know. Her heart was safe with Sean O'Neill.

"I'm willing to take that chance."

Randy looked like he'd been stabbed in the heart. "You're in love with him, aren't you?"

She released a deep sigh. "I don't enjoy hurting you, so this little ambush of yours will stay between us. However, if I even suspect that you're pulling something like this again, you'll be explaining to Sean why you're interfering in our lives. He won't be as easygoing as I am."

He lifted his hand to her arm as she turned to go. "I care about you, and don't want him to hurt you."

She smiled, her face warm from thinking about Sean. "He won't hurt me."

"I'll do everything in my power to make sure he doesn't."

The concern in Randy's eyes was touching, but the barely veiled threat in his words was troubling. Should she warn Sean or leave it alone? What real harm could Randy do anyway?

Chapter Eight

Sean was so damn beautiful he took her breath away.

He was standing in the TV/lounge area when she came downstairs. One look at him in his charcoal slacks, white button-up dress shirt with a black-print tie, black shoes, and the leather jacket he'd worn to church locked her knees and stopped her heart.

He must have felt her eyes undressing him because he turned to her. The appreciation in his eyes and the smile on his face told her she didn't look half bad in her low-cut, black dress and sky-high black heels. She had added silver bling to accent her wrists and ears. He walked to her and took her hands in his.

His eyes opened wide and so did his mouth before he grinned. "Wow."

"Wow, right back at you."

"My only non-jean clothes." He held out his arms and turned slowly to give her a full view. "Take a good look because this may be the last time you'll see me in it."

"You're totally hot, no matter what you wear."

"We're a perfect match then. Ready?"

"Yes."

He helped her on with her coat and they walked out the door.

"Hope you don't mind riding on the back of my motorcycle," he said.

"Are you kidding? I can't wait!" She actually giggled.

****

The hostess sat them toward the back of the dimly lit restaurant. Kristin slid onto the padded bench while Sean took the chair to her right. The waitress took their drink order and left menus for them to peruse.

"You weren't lying," Sean said, scanning the menu. "No sushi or cheeseburgers in sight."

She laughed. "I thought it would be nice to spend a few hours outside our comfort zones tonight."

He took her hand in his, brought it to his lips, and kissed her palm. "Next to you *is* my comfort zone."

The glow from the candle danced in his eyes, and she basked in the desire she saw there. It sounded like—felt like—he meant every word. But as Zoe so thoughtfully reminded her the other night, she had been burned before from getting too close to the heat in the eyes of a handsome man.

She smiled. "Be careful, handsome. I might actually start to believe all the sweet things you say to me."

"I expect you to believe every word," he said and dropped a kiss on her lips.

His mouth was minty, wet, and delicious, and she wanted more than the appetizing peck he teased her hunger with. It had ignited her desire for him, and she was ready to jump ahead to the main course. Before he could move away, she dug her fingers into his thick hair and pulled him back to her, giving him a long, languid kiss that was more appropriate for the bedroom than a fine restaurant.

"Excuse me."

They glided apart at the waitress' gentle

interruption. To Kristin, it felt like they were moving in slow motion, as if their bodies were strongly opposed to the separation and resisting.

Their waitress set a glass of water before each other them, a lemon drop for Kristin, and a dark beer for Sean.

"Have you decided what you'd like for dinner?" the woman asked.

Sean looked at Kristin, who was smiling behind her glass. He smiled and smothered a laugh. "We'll need another moment."

If the waitress was exasperated, she hid it well. She simply smiled at him and agreed to come back in a few minutes.

"When you get us kicked out of here, we're going for a green chile cheeseburger," Sean whispered, making Kristin laugh out loud. He chuckled. "Look at your menu."

"On one condition."

"What's that?"

"Come sit next to me. You're too far away."

He scooted back his chair, got up, and slid next to her into the booth. "This is much better," he said and laid his arm along the top of the bench, his hand brushing her shoulders.

She turned toward him. "I hope they don't seat another couple close to us. I might want to play footsy with you under the table."

"If I'd known you wanted that much privacy, I'd have rented out the room they have in the back."

"Next time."

"Uh-oh," he said grabbing his menu. "She's headed this way again."

Kristin put her hand on his menu. "Do you trust me?"

"Completely."

"Is there any food you hate or are allergic to?"

"I like everything…except sushi and haggis."

The waitress eyed Sean like he was the dessert of the day. "Are you ready to order?"

"Yes," Kristin said, capturing her attention. She opened her menu. "We'll be sharing the petite beef filet, medium, the baby greens salad with red wine-honey vinaigrette, asparagus spears, and the walnut and cheese-stuffed grilled figs."

A smile lifted the corners of the waitress' mouth as she repeated the order and committed it to memory. "Excellent choices. I'll have it right out."

"Odd combination," Sean said, a look of confusion on his face.

She smiled but said nothing.

He took her hand in his. "Why do I get the feeling you have plans for me you're not telling me about?"

"Aren't you the suspicious one?" She sipped her drink. "Do you get that from your mom or from your dad?"

He laughed, but didn't answer right away, as if he were gathering memories and weighing which ones could be shared and which ones had to be kept hidden. "My brothers and sister and I joke that if we tell our mum the sun's out, she'll make us bring in a bucket of the stuff to prove it. So, I guess I got that from her. I'm always looking for proof, too. My da was just the opposite. He believed everything and everyone."

"Is your dad…gone?"

He nodded. "Two years ago this spring."

She squeezed the hand holding hers. "I'm sorry. How?"

The corner of his mouth rose as if he were listening to a small private joke. "Dancing. If bands were playing trad at the pub near home, Da was there. He'd drink too much, laugh too much, and dance like he was twenty instead of fifty."

"He was young. His heart?"

He nodded. "He died doing what he loved—living life full out."

"We could all take a lesson in that—live life to the fullest while you can."

"Yeah. I guess. But in his odyssey to cram everything into his own life, he sometimes forgot the other people in his life had needs, too."

"A bit of an absentee father and husband?" she asked.

"Nice way of putting it. Mum was there for us. But having to shoulder everything made her a bit fanatical."

When he paused to sip his beer, she jumped in. "My mom was the dreamer, the painter and poet, who refused to acknowledge life's unpleasant moments…refused to acknowledge anything, really, but her own whims. My father, the corporate lawyer, thought being a good parent meant hiring people—nannies, cooks, housekeepers, etc.—to take care of things."

"No siblings?"

"Nope. My parents are such polar opposites, I often wonder how they found their way to each other long enough to conceive even one child."

"Were you lonely?"

Kristin paused, peering backward into her

childhood. "I used to wish for a house full of brothers and sisters so I'd have someone to laugh with, fight with, keep secrets with. But..." She shrugged. "It wasn't to be." She had been lonely at times. But being a single child was all she knew, so it was almost as if she didn't realize what she was missing.

"So are you a dreamer like your mum or a driver like your da?"

His question pulled her out of her memories and set her back down into the middle of the present with him. She linked her fingers with his and smiled to show him she was back.

"I try hard not to be like either of them."

"Maybe you're the best of both...reflective, impulsive, positive, and open like your mum. Strong, capable, intelligent, and practical like your da."

"That sounds a whole lot better than ditzy and detached."

"But then there's the qualities that are uniquely you."

"Oh, yeah? Like what?"

"Passionate, giving, independent, fun, a sharp and creative mind."

His words touched her. She smiled. "You could make a lot of money reading palms and telling fortunes in Nob Hill."

He laughed as if he could see the humor and gratitude lighting her words. "If I could see the future, I'd already know your middle name. I've become obsessed with names beginning with H."

"Then we have something in common." She took a sip of her sweet-tart drink then let her gaze tangle with his.

"How so?"

"I've become obsessed with finding out more about you."

He ran his thumb across her bottom lip, brushing away the liquid clinging there. "What do you want to know?"

"Let's start with...why archaeology?"

His eyes brightened as if she had hit on his favorite topic. "I like having proof for things going on in my world. Excavations—holding an artifact or a bone in my hands—give me proof of what went on before, which can tell us about ourselves today."

A smile twitched on her lips. "But archaeology studies human societies of the past. When it comes to people, especially people of the distant past, you can never be certain of their motives and desires for doing things. Applying modern-day reasoning to a culture that didn't have the same frame of reference doesn't really provide you with proof...it only provides more questions."

"True enough. The proof for me is that we came from somewhere, from a group of people that had similar desires as we do—food, water, shelter, and love. It tells me I'll be here in the future through my children, my children's children, and so on. That connection is proof enough that what we do here matters."

"I love the way you look at it," she said. And she meant it. The fact that he wanted children, wanted to leave a part of himself behind, touched her...made her long to be the one he made children with, forgetting her vow to never have any.

"You sound less than convinced." He took a sip of his beer.

"No, it's not that." She shrugged. "I guess I never thought of it in those terms. I'm in archaeology, too, but with a focus on forensics, where one can satisfy the need for proof easily. The skeleton shows evidence of disease or it doesn't. It was a male or a female. He died young from a blow to the skull or old from the ravages of age. She was of this race, not that. And so on."

He was quiet for a moment, studying her face, with a small smile on his face, and she started to wonder whether she had offended him.

She laughed. "I'm sorry. I'm sounding like one of those geeks feuding with a fellow scientist over whose area of expertise is better."

"Can we agree that our chosen paths complement the other?"

"Yes." She squeezed his hand.

"Will you do research or field work?" he asked.

"Research. I'm a lab rat. But maybe a little in the field just to get my hands dirty. See where it all comes from. You?"

"Field, definitely. I like being outside, working with my hands, getting them dirty, as you say."

"You're good at it." At his confused look, she added, "Working with your hands. But go on."

He kissed the hand he was holding. "You know, if you're looking for an analyst position after graduation, there's an excellent university in Dublin with a world renowned lab devoted to archaeology. There's also the commercial archaeology company I work for now. They're always looking for good lab rats who want to get their hands dirty."

"That company—is that where you'll be after leaving here?"

"Yes. I'll go directly to a dig site with the team I've been working with since I started college."

She found her breath then her voice. "Is there a woman waiting for you there? Someone I'm going to have to open a can of kickass on to get her out of your life? If I were to go to Dublin, that is."

Even though he chuckled, his gaze dropped from hers to the table and his body tensed against the seatback. "No," he said, and shook his head.

"There was someone, though, wasn't there?" A flare of jealousy ran up her spine at the plume of silence that swirled up between them. His tone, his reaction, his hesitation before answering told her that the relationship had been important to him. And hurtful.

"There was. It ended a few months before I came here."

"Why?"

He brought his beer to his lips and drank deeply. "That's a conversation for another time."

"Do you miss her?"

He caught her eyes, then leaned forward and reached out his hand to caress her face. "Not anymore. Someone else fills my mind these days."

She breathed in. "*Moi?*" She kept her tone light and a smile on her face so he'd know she was teasing, but she meant the plea.

He nodded. "*Tu.*"

She kissed his smiling lips, releasing the tight hold she'd had on her breath, the beating of her heart.

She was tired of leaving this man, of going home alone and wanting. To hell with his schedule. To hell with his not-in-my-room policy. Tonight, she'd get into his bed.

The waitress arrived with the feast Kristin had carefully selected to arouse Sean's appetite for sex, but she could barely taste it.

****

"I wasn't sure about grilled figs, but they were good," he said as they walked hand-in-hand toward her dorm from the parking lot. "I'll let you order for me next time."

Excitement bubbled through her that he was thinking beyond their payback schedule. "There's going to be a next time?"

He stopped and linked his fingers behind her back. "You want there to be?"

It was a risk to tell him the truth. But she wanted to. Had to. She slid her arms around his neck, leaned into him. "Yes."

His hands slid down her back and settled on her ass. He pulled her against him and kissed her slowly, softly, so fully that her bones felt like they were melting.

"Whatever makes you happy…" he said.

His hands on her ass, squeezing, pressing her into him, made her very happy. "Do you really mean that?"

He nodded. "I mean it."

"Then, take me to bed, Sean. Now. Tonight. Not two days from now when it's on the schedule. If it really is on the schedule…Honestly, I can't even really tell."

He stared at her in the dark, speechless. Had her bold request troubled him? Or was he just unwilling to go that far to make her happy?

She slid her hand down the front of his pants to cup his dick. "I don't care who might be listening to us or what they might be thinking or doing. I want to go to your room. I want to make so much noise that we keep the neighbors awake. I want you to fuck my brains out."

His cock hardened against her hand and she saw his pulse thumping at his throat, but still he said nothing. He remained motionless, letting her handle his rod, letting her go off at the mouth, and letting his eyes swallow her.

"And I'm a smart girl, with a lot of brains, so it's probably going to take all night long."

Suddenly, she realized he'd been silent for a long time, and that his gaze hadn't budged from her face. *Shit!* Her audacious words suddenly felt like a huge mistake that she wished she could take back.

Her hand moved off his arousal. "But if you don't want to, I—"

"Kristin…."

"Is it the whole 'schedule' thing?"

"Kristin…"

Her face hot, she held up her hand to stop him. "You know what, it's okay," she said, putting her hands to her stomach, trying to calm the embarrassment rolling there. "Forget I said anything." She backed away from him. "Thanks for tonight. I had fun, but I'm going to go, now."

Before she got three feet away, he grabbed her hand and pulled her back into his body. He cupped her face with his hands, gently, like she was a rare and delicate flower, and stared intently into her eyes as if that would ensure she was focused on every word he said or didn't say.

"I want you." He kissed her again, deeper, more passionately than any kiss she'd ever had. His heat closed around her, creating a raging embrace that made her squirm with desire. She felt his desire course through her body, too, and had to ask.

"Then why don't you want to be with me?"

A little smile lifted the corner of his lips. "Darlin' I've wanted to fuck your brains out since the night you came to my door looking for condoms."

She laughed. "It's taken you this long to make your move? I never knew the Irish to be such a timid bunch."

"Timid?" he repeated, and she shivered when his hand rounded over her breast. "It took all my control not to pull you into my room and make love to you all that night, the next day, and the day after that. A gentleman I was being that night."

His palm slipped into her dress and kneaded her flesh, while his fingers tweaked her nipples, making her knees go weak and her eyes flutter closed.

"I wanted you to pull me into your room. But you didn't even try."

"You weren't ready for me then."

He leaned in and kissed her neck, sucked on it, drawing a low moan from her mouth.

"Look at me, love," he whispered, and she opened her eyes.

"Are you ready for me now?" His voice was low and deep and dangerous, and she suddenly felt as if she'd opened the tiger's cage. A shiver raced up her spine. Her eyes wanted to look away from his face, but he wouldn't let her. His eyes chained her to him and demanded she answer.

She swallowed and even managed a little smile. "I asked you to fuck my brains out, O'Neill. I don't think I could be any more ready."

His laughter rang clear and rich, warming and lighting the cold, dark night.

"Let's go make some noise, darlin'." He wrapped his arm firmly around her shoulders, she wrapped her arms around his waist, and as one they headed toward his dorm.

Chapter Nine

As soon as the door was closed behind him, Kristin attacked, throwing her arms around Sean's neck and kissing him with a fierceness that showed her need. He gently detached himself from her.

"We have all night, darlin'," he said. "I want to make this something you'll remember forever."

His bold promise sent shivers raging up and down her body.

He walked over to his laptop and clicked through until he found the playlist he wanted and let it play. He moved across the room to the window, where he opened the blinds, letting silver moonlight spill onto the tile floor. Returning to Kristin, he took her hand and stepped into the spotlight. His hands at her back, hers at his chest, they swayed to the soft, soulful music, kissing softly, whispering words of desire.

As good as the tender and soft loving touches felt, Kristin was desperate for something bolder. So far, he hadn't come near the places screaming loudest for his attention. She wanted to rip his clothes off and take him on the floor, but he held her passion in check, insisting they go slow.

"I know you're hungry for it all now," he said, as if he could read her mind and her body, "but I want to prepare you...prepare your body...to accept me inside you. I'll get you there. I promise."

"I trust you."

He kissed her then extracted himself from her embrace. Slowly, he kissed her face then moved on to her neck and her shoulders. His lips were like a match to her already fiery body. He made her burn with want. There wasn't enough air in her lungs, and it made her dizzy.

He slid his hands lightly up her arms, sending chills through her. Moving behind her, he lifted her hair and let it fall over one shoulder, exposing her back. He kissed and nipped the sensitive skin at her nape then lower to where the zipper of her dress began mid-back.

He slowly lowered the zipper, following its descent with soft kisses along the length of her spine and on a wave of her soft sighs. The zipper stopped at the top edge of her panties, but his kisses didn't. They reversed and slowly climbed back up as he grasped each side of the open dress with his hands and slowly pushed it away over her shoulders.

Her skin tingled at the feel of the material parting and sliding away. She made no move to hold the dress in place over her bare breasts, but let it fall softly to her hips and then to the floor. She shivered, not from cold, but from the sparks dancing across her skin where Sean's mouth and hands caressed. Every nerve in her body was standing at attention, screaming his name and begging for his expert touch. If he happened on the right nerve now, touched it or kissed it just right, she would explode. She was sure of it. She'd been standing on the edge of a climax since the first time he'd touched her.

Sean moved around to her front, trailing his fingers across her skin as he did, and her breath shuddered in her chest. When he faced her again, he kissed her heavy eyelids, her open mouth, her heaving breasts, then dipped his head lower.

The simple touch of his hot mouth on her swollen nipple made her cry out, and she said his name like a prayer, softly and passionately. His clever tongue swirled around the wet tip then sucked it deep into his mouth.

His tongue trailed down to the plump underside of her breast, tasted it, sucked it. The light touch tickled and she squirmed, releasing a giggle. He increased the pressure in that area and she could handle it again.

He moved across to her other breast and licked all around her nipple, but did not touch it. It was tight and hard and begging for him to suck it. She moaned again and, to her ears, it sounded more like a plea.

As if sensing she could take no more sweet torture, he captured the point and sucked hard, drawing part of her essence out in the process. She lifted her hands to his head and held his mouth to her breast. Little mewing sounds slid from her throat. The power of her climax would destroy them both.

He slid his mouth between her breasts, moved it lower across her stomach, and down her sensitive sides. Her muscles clenched in joy when his tongue paused to dip into the well of her belly button.

"You taste so good," he said, his voice low and thick.

Lower, Sean, lower, her mind screamed. *Kiss my pussy. Lick it. Suck it. Bite it. Please.* The building tidal wave of need swirled, churned, and rose, higher and higher the lower he went, heating her up from the inside. She wanted to come. She needed to come. His mouth was headed in the right direction, but not nearly fast enough.

Sean knelt before her and massaged her breasts as his mouth moved lower. He was at the band of her panties. Then he was there. At her pussy. She trembled. She couldn't catch her breath...wasn't sure there was another breath on the other side of the one she had barely tasted in her mouth. Heated desire rose from her like fragrant steam, and he was like a starving man wanting to taste it all.

Her eyes opened and she looked down at him just as his mouth captured her mound like he was taking a bite out of a juicy peach. His teeth bit her though the thin material of her panties, grazing her engorged clit. His tongue snaked inside her panties and pressed against that nib of nerves.

As if he could feel her last shred of control going, he grabbed her hips and raised her knee to his shoulder and pulled her closer. With a finger, he pulled aside the material. His mouth and tongue on her throbbing center filled her body with a swirling mass of light, heat, and color. The wave hit, crashing through her so hard it buckled her knees and had her leaning on him to keep from falling.

He caught her, held her, and pressed his hard tongue against her trembling clit until her orgasm subsided.

The whole body release was overwhelming emotionally, and she was helpless to stop the tears spilling from her eyes.

Sean rose from his knees and held her.

"I don't know why I'm crying. I'm not a crier. It's just..."

He kissed away the tears from her eyes, from her cheeks, and when he moved to her lips, she clung to his mouth with hers, giving him her thanks. She had never felt so close to another person as she did at that moment. She had never given herself so completely to another person before.

****

He had pleased her. And that pleased him. "You needed that, darlin'," he whispered against her mouth, ready to give her more. And he would make sure she had hers before he had his.

His kisses became more purposeful, more erotic. He rolled his tongue in her mouth, mating with her tongue and sucking it. He pressed his lips to hers, all the while touching only her hands, where their fingers were linked at their sides.

She tried to unlink her hand and shift it between them so she could touch him.

He captured her hand again. "Still your turn. I'll get mine later." He loved that she wanted so badly to bring him pleasure. And he'd let her.

But he wanted to give her one more with his mouth, tongue, and fingers before they tried it with his dick. If he was too big for her…it would be over. At least he could say he had pleased her. He kissed her face, her neck, her shoulders and moved around to her back.

"You make me feel so good," she said.

"Was it worth the wait?"

Keeping his hands on her skin, he slid them down her ass, exploring with his tongue and mouth.

"So worth it."

"Good."

At the band to her panties, he hooked his fingers,

one on each side, and peeled them from her body, across her hips, over her thighs, and down her legs until they joined her dress on the floor.

She was a feast for the eyes, and his heart tripled in pace as he gorged on her. Her naked body glowed in the moonlight, a silky sheen of passion on her smooth, skin that smelled like flowers in the rain. Her body was fit and curvy and soft, with long shapely legs, firm arms, ripe breasts, a deep, almond-shaped navel set in defined abs. Her ass resembled a peach, round, firm, soft to the touch and ready to devour.

His hands skimmed over that ass, massaging her cheeks before moving down her legs, positioning his thumbs to slide down the inside of her thighs, his thumbs itching to slide into her juicy slit.

"Open your legs for me. I want to touch all of you." He felt her shiver.

"I want that, too." She then spread them, giving him the access he craved.

The smell of her desire drove a spear of lust through his body, where it lodged between his legs, making his cock throb against his zipper. The need to be inside her, making her come, coming inside her, rose up hard in him. He fought to reign in his hunger.

His mouth took over. With just the edges of his lips, he nibbled at the sensitive lips between her legs. She moaned and his cock stiffened even more. His blood was rushing in his ears so loud that he knew she could hear it, knew how turned on he was just tasting her flesh.

Her body trembled, and he could feel her starting to slump against him. The wave was building inside her again, he knew. Soon it would take her.

"That's it, darlin'. Come for me again. Let me hear you scream my name."

He stood, pressed his rock hard cock against her ass.

"Ahhh," she moaned and pressed back into him. "Make me come."

He gripped her hips and let his fingers fan across her stomach, trill along her ribs. He was rewarded with another shiver across her hot body. He bit along her shoulders and neck while his hands cupped her full breasts and pinched her nipples. He wanted her to feel. No arms, legs, neck, lips, no skin. Just…him.

Her arms rose and circled his neck, giving him better access to her jutting breasts. She leaned her head back and to the side, baring her neck to his teeth, and he bit her and licked her and kissed her.

The gentle massage on her breasts changed tempo and became rougher. He released one breast and smoothed that hand down between her legs, his fingers crawling through her bush for her clit. He easily parted her smooth lips and slid a finger inside her pussy.

"You're so wet."

"For you." Her eyes were closed and her lips were parted.

She lifted her leg and wrapped it back, around his leg, opening herself to his searching finger. Leaving his middle finger inside her to plunge and stroke, he used his thumb and forefinger to tweak and tug her clit.

He ground his hips against her ass, his mouth kissed her lips, his hand worshipped her breasts, his finger filled her dripping wet pussy. He claimed all of her, the body he had craved since the first night he'd seen her. He felt the sweet pleasure rising in her body, higher and higher, knew the second it took her. He held her tight to him as the explosion rocked her. Her breath stopped, her body tensed, and she came into his hand, moaning his name in a long slide of sweet, unintelligible sounds that fed his own hunger.

"Kristin, ah my Kristin."

She rode the long wave and slumped in his arms, panting as if she'd run a marathon.

He picked her up and carried her to his bed, so ready for her he was almost out of his mind. Her boneless body melted into the mattress, arms and legs splayed in a pose of total satisfaction and relaxation. He had pleased her.

"How do you feel?" He stood by the bed, smiling down at her and unbuttoning his shirt.

She managed to slide one word through her smile, "Fabulous." Her gaze fell upon the bulge tenting his pants. She stretched to awaken her loose muscles and crawled toward him, stopping on her knees in front of him.

"Two for Kristin, zero for Sean," she said, passion still high in her eyes. "Let's even the score a bit."

"I'm ready," he said.

She kissed him softly, briefly, then focused her attention on pushing his shirt from his shoulders and down his arms. She ran her hands up his chest, letting her fingers trail over his skin. His skin tingled with heat wherever her fingers and hands touched. He burned with desire for her to explore the rest of his body. She watched his face, his eyes. Did she know what she was doing to him? Could she see the pleasure she was bringing him?

She lowered her mouth to the nipple her fingers

had teased to attention, let her tongue swash over it, her lips suck it and her teeth nip it. She kissed across his chest to the matching nipple. He felt his own pounding pulse on her lips.

A groan hushed out on a breath that had been caught in his lungs. God, she affected him like no other woman ever had. She hadn't even touched his cock yet and he was already about to come.

Her mouth kissed its way down his chest to his stomach. His abs twitched when her tongue found a ticklish spot in the valley of his ribs, but he didn't flinch from her. Her eyes found his, but her hands kept traveling lower.

"I want to taste you," she said, "here," and cupped her hand over the bulge in his pants and rubbed it. "Can I?"

Colors and lights exploded inside his head at the thought of her mouth on his cock, sucking him, loving him. Never letting go of her gaze, he nodded.

Her hands unfastened his belt and pants. She shoved his pants down then reached for the bulge that was about to rip a hole in his boxers. As if she suddenly couldn't wait any longer to get her hands on him, get him in her mouth, she yanked his boxers down. His cock bounced out toward her, tapping her stomach. It was long and thick, with a head the size of a large, firm mushroom. Would the size scare her? Or tempt her?

She smiled and pulled his rod level with her mouth, licked all around the tip. His lungs weren't working right. He couldn't breathe. With a low growl, his hands went to her head and his fingers slid into her hair, holding her against his hardness. His eyes closed as his fantasies became reality.

"Mmm. I knew you'd taste good," she murmured.

He felt her tongue roll around the head of his cock. A drop of pre-cum beaded at his slit. Her tongue tasted his pleasure before she took the head into her mouth, sucked on it, taking him a little deeper each time. Her mouth slid down his organ as far as she could go, squeezed him, sucked him, while her hand massaged his balls. His cock swelled to almost bursting at every touch of her tongue and lips. His hips flexed and pumped, searching for more. He was close to coming. His fingers tangled in her thick hair and he held her head still, pulling back and stopping her from finishing him.

"Ahhh…" His voice was low, almost inaudible and his breathing ragged. "Darlin', I can't wait any longer to have you."

"Then take me." A seductive smile on her lips, she scooted backward until she could lie back on the pillow. Wasting no time, he rushed to her, suspending his body above hers and supporting his weight with his forearms on either side of her head. But instead of taking her right then, he drizzled kisses like rain over her face and her mouth, showing her how much he appreciated her passion and wanted her. As he felt her shiver, trillions of tiny sensations roared in hunger throughout his own body.

His lips seared to her neck, her nipples, and the underside of her breasts. Danced across her ribs and teased her belly, her navel. There wasn't a spot on her body that he hadn't tasted, but he caressed her flesh, slowly, carefully, as if it were the first and last time and he didn't want to risk missing a single inch.

He moved down her body and pasted kisses on the

inside of her thigh. When he got to within an inch of her pussy, he forced himself to move to the other leg, repeating the exquisite torture. He slid both hands up her legs and palmed her mound, pressing against it with the heel of his hand, kneading. He parted her damp lips with his thumbs and framed her clit. Clipping the flesh between both thumbs, he lapped it to a hard peak.

"Ahhhh, Sean," she cried out in pleasure. "I thought you couldn't wait to take me."

"Pretty sure I said taste you."

He breathed on her swollen flesh then fully consumed her pussy with his lips, making her hips raise off the bed into his mouth.

"Oh, God!"

"Want me to stop?" he asked.

"Oh, no, no, no, never!"

She opened her legs wide to him, and he ran his tongue along her valley, parting the dewy, petal-soft lips. His mouth captured her clit again, nibbling at it, pulling it into his mouth, sucking it, flicking his tongue against her, so hot and deliberate that the room spun.

"Sean…I need you inside me now." She breathed the words more than spoke them as his tongue plunged into her pussy.

At the taste, the feel of her, a full-body rush engulfed him and he almost came with his cock arching against the sheets, but he stopped himself. "Don't hold back, darlin'," he mumbled against her torrid flesh, "come in my mouth."

She held his head tight to her pussy, and pressed herself deep against his mouth and tongue. Her body shuddered under him, releasing a wild cry of pleasure from her throat.

He lifted away from her when her last spasm died, ripped open a condom, and rolled it onto his cock. Then he was on her again, between her legs. It felt so good, his belly sweaty against hers, his chest brushing the tight, sensitive peaks of her nipples.

"I want you inside me. I want to feel you."

He knew he had to be careful, but he wanted her so bad, had held back his pleasure for so long, that he wasn't sure he could. He inched slowly inside her.

"God, you're so tight. I don't want to hurt you."

"You're not. It feels...ahhhh...sooo goooood." She arched against him, seeking more.

He pushed in, driving deeper into her creamy, slick center, then pulled out slowly, over and over, to get her used to being filled so fully. As she relaxed around his raging erection, and their lubricant eased the way, he picked up the pace and was soon plunging and withdrawing in time with their racing heartbeats.

Their mouths fed on each other, their skin blended, their hearts beat as one, their bodies fused. He breathed in the smell of her, of her desire, of his, and he knew he couldn't hold his climax much longer.

"Come with me, Kristin...my Kristin."

He had primed her body well for release, her pussy clenching around his cock. She grabbed his ass and held him inside her and she shuddered around him, clutched in his arms, groaning her satisfaction.

His eyes closed at the feel of her pussy squeezing and holding his cock so tight and deep inside her body. He let the power of it, the power of her sounds, take him, let the edges of his mind go dark, let his eyes lose focus. One final thrust and his muscles went rigid with his own orgasm.

He groaned, erupting into the condom even as she was leveling from her pleasure.

He stilled inside her, over her, still connected. Peace enveloped him. Happiness. His breathing returned to normal. His mind could focus again. And her beautiful, contented face was the first thing he saw.

The moment was too precious for words. He caressed her face, kissed her eyes, her mouth, and wrapped around her body, cradling it in contentment and pleasure.

Their union was complete. She was his. He was hers.

One thing was certain. Once would not be enough.

Chapter Ten

It was easy enough to gain entry into the dorm building. Guys think they can handle any threat, so they tend to take fewer security precautions, like locking the front doors or having security ask unescorted women who they're here to see.

No one saw her slip up the stairs to the third floor. The hallway was empty when she exited the stairwell. No one was there to see her stop at Randy's door or ask her what she was doing.

She turned the knob and pushed. *The fucking idiot left his door unlocked!*

Randy was sprawled out on his bed, yanking on his cock, moaning Kristin's name, clearly unaware that he had company. A few more tugs and he shot his creamy load in spurts into the air.

Zoe knew she'd come to the right place. She applauded, her mouth in a wide grin.

Randy jumped, pushing his still-shooting dick into the sheets. "Wha-tha-fuck!" His breath was sketchy and his words not fully formed as his body shuddered.

"Oh, relax, Randy. Don't put it away on my account." She sauntered over to the bed, sat beside him, and grabbed his flaccid, wet dick.

Randy trembled, as if he couldn't decide between scooting back away from her and moving forward to encourage her attention.

"You really love her, don't you?" Zoe whispered as she slowly stroked his sticky rod and pinched the bullet-shaped head.

His eyes had rolled back in his head with pleasure, and he didn't respond.

She gripped him hard, squeezing him to the point of pain.

His hand flew to hers. "Aowha! Fuck. Not so hard, dammit!"

"Answer me, then. You love her, don't you?"

"Who?"

She squeezed again. "Don't act stupid, Randy. The person you were jerking off to, of course."

"Yes, I love her."

She loosened her grip, letting the pain fade. As she slowly stroked him, bringing back the pleasure, she heard muffled grunts and moans and cries of pleasure coming from next door. Kristin was getting her fill of Sean's big cock tonight. The thought of someone else satisfying Kristin sliced her open. She swallowed back angry tears.

"It's hard to listen to them having sex, isn't it," she said to Randy, but it was really more a statement about how she felt. When he didn't respond, she looked at his face in the dim light. He stared at the wall separating him from Kristin, his eyes shiny and his mouth held in a grim line. Strange how both of them craved Kristin with a hunger so strong that it had the power to take over their actions.

The dick in her hand had gone soft so she resumed her careful, purposeful moves. "What would you do to have her all to yourself?"

"Anything." His mouth hung open, his eyes half

closed, and his hips slowly thrusting to the rhythm of her hand on his stiffening shaft.

"Even get rid of Sean?"

His eye flew open and his hips stilled. "He'd kick my ass."

She caressed his balls, rolling them in her hand. "If I knew a way to break them up without you getting your ass kicked, would you be man enough to do it?"

He nodded.

"I didn't hear you." She was pumping him hard and fast now, felt the cum rising in his flesh, plumping it to almost average size.

"Yes." The word came out like a long hiss as he spewed his seed.

She milked him until his spasms calmed, then wiped her sticky hand on his sheets. "Put on some underwear and we'll talk."

She smiled. No one would be able to connect her to the explosion that was about to blow apart her best friend's life.

****

Sean Patrick O'Neill had never been a cuddler. But then, he'd never had a woman like Kristin DeMarco curled up beside him in his bed. The woman was hot, naked, and his.

He had a tight five months ahead of him to teach two classes, finish his thesis, and complete the field school he'd come here to help run. All which would clinch him his dream job back home. A steady lover hadn't been in the plans for his short stay in the United States. But he'd found one. One that made him ache, made him want, made him need, made him care in a way more powerful than he ever had with anyone.

Something about being with Kristin, touching her with his hands, his mouth, his dick, made his mind blur at the edges with pleasure and the only thought of being with her again. And if that didn't turn a man into a cuddler, nothing would.

"That was the best sex of the night, O'Neill." Kristin sighed into his chest, her breath warming his skin and sending the words directly into his heart.

"That's what you said the last time. And the time before that. And the time before that." He trailed his fingers along her arm, up her back and into her hair.

She chuckled softly. "Okay. I admit it. They were all in the 'best' category. All six of them. There's just one problem."

"I made you scream *my* name, *God's* name, and *fuck me now* a dozen times. What problem?"

She grabbed his dick and tugged, laughing at his quick intake of breath. "Hey, a gentleman doesn't tease his woman about her sex talk."

Her touch electrified the blood rushing through his cock, making it come alive in her hand. They had just made love for the sixth time and fuck if he wasn't ready for her again. And she had referred to herself as his woman.

"If you wanted a gentleman, darlin', you've grabbed the wrong cock."

Her lips parted on a sigh. "I've got the one I want."

He leaned in and kissed that mouth. A hundred kisses, a million, each tasted as sweet as the last.

"But, there is a problem," she continued.

He shifted his weight, tangling his legs with hers, and pulled her back into his arms. "I give up. What's our problem?"

"It's about what we did here tonight."

He breathed in but forgot to exhale. Did she regret the sex? Consider it a one-night thing—part of their payback deal—that was now over? "Tell me."

Her fingers had found his nipples fascinating and were playing with them like a kitten with a new toy.

"You've more than satisfied your debt to me," she said, "overpaid, actually."

He smiled. "And that's a problem how?"

"There's no incentive for you to stick around." She leaned over his chest and flicked her tongue across his puckered nipples.

"Ahhh. I see what you're saying." Her mouth had left his nipples and inched down to where her tongue could surf the crests and valleys of his ribs. He forced himself to keep breathing, keep talking. "Guess I don't have to take you out to breakfast or lunch or dinner anymore."

"No," she said into his navel.

"Or to the movies again."

She mumbled a no and shook her head, using the motion to brush her mouth against his bush.

"And forget the massage."

"Damn," she groaned, lifting her head. "I forgot about the massage."

He wanted to beg her not to stop, but he was a man and a man didn't beg. For anything. "Well, lass, you showed your hand way too soon, that's for sure."

He put his hands on her head, gently, as if to guide her back to her intent. But she wasn't ready to be guided. Or she had forgotten. Or had decided to torture him for awhile.

"If only you hadn't shown me such a good time

tonight," she said, "I could claim the debt wasn't paid yet."

"I've always been an overachiever."

Her eyes left his face and moved down to the overachiever that had risen from its base almost even with her mouth. She smiled and grabbed one of the condoms spread out on the bed.

For God's sake, darlin', take me in your mouth, he thought, his pulse buzzing in his balls so hard they were tightening into walnuts.

"Well, there is the matter of the condoms you owe me." She straddled him, his erection twitching against her stomach. "A full cup, you know. That was the deal."

He gripped her strong thighs with his hands. "Ah, yes, the condoms." He could barely speak. All his blood and, therefore, brain power had shifted to his cock. "Well then, I guess there's still a debt to be paid. Though, in truth, we've used more than a half a box already."

She ripped open the wrapper, removed the condom, and set it atop his stomach. Scooting back, she leaned over him, her mouth hovering over his cock. He was nearly panting now. Ready to beg if she wasn't sucking him in ten seconds. Okay, five.

Her pink tongue came out of her mouth. She stopped. "Yes, I'd say so."

Every nerve ending in his body screamed a battle cry. His lungs were about to burst from holding his breath, and he was sure that the pain surging through his body was his balls exploding.

"Yes," he managed to say, but had no idea whether the response fit the question. The word rushed out on his shallow breath and was barely out of his mouth before her mouth captured the head of his cock. His breath dashed out of his lungs in a low rumble, and his eyes closed. "Yes," he repeated, as her lips rolled down over his growing hardness.

She took her time, keeping her lips taut to stroke his cock, moving down and taking him in as deep as she could. Her tongue took over, licking up his staff and wrapping around his width. It spiraled up to the tip top and fondled his slit. A bolt of pleasure shot through to his core.

Her teeth nibbled and softly bit all over him, as if she had to taste it all and had no self-control to wait patiently. The brush of her long, chocolate hair against his stomach and thighs only added fuel to his fire, and he buried his hands into the sex-tangled mass. His hips lifted off the bed slightly, pushing his cock deeper into her giving, tight mouth, unable and unwilling to hide his roaring hunger from her.

"God knows how I want you, Kristin."

His body gasped for release, but he fought to keep from erupting until she had found her pleasure. As if in sync with his needs, Kristin grabbed the condom, slid it onto the hard head of his dick, like a beanie, and rolled it down until it rested at the base of his erection.

She rose up and, in one strong stroke, took his blade deep into her sheath. Inside her as far as was possible, he stamped his mark on her, again and again, as if to say, *"She's mine. For now. For always."*

Her eyes were fiery and glazed as she rode him hard and fast, leaning forward as if she barebacked a wild stallion on the beach of Dingle, her hair tousled, skin glowing with a silky sheen, a reckless smile on her beautiful face. He gripped her hips to steady her and to match the pounding rhythm of their single heartbeat with the rhythm of their single body.

The pace shifted, and she rocked her hips back and forth rather than up and down, letting her clit scrape against his hardness. She was close. He could smell her readiness, a sweetness that flooded his senses and turned up his own heat. Her breathing came in desperate gasps, quick and shallow through her parted lips. Then it seemed as if she wasn't breathing at all. He now knew that she held her breath when she was about to come. He felt her groin relax, open up, and she exploded on his shaft, her gripping pussy releasing the pause he had placed on his own pleasure. She pulled in gulps of air.

"Oh, Sean…Sean…Sean…"

Sex with this woman made sense. Made everything in his life make sense. Her touch made him hunger with the deepest need. He wanted her more than any other woman he'd ever had. Hearing his name on her lips, knowing he had pleased her, made his body thrust deeper into her willing, loving body. His body shook from the power of it.

"I'll want you forever, Kristin." The words were out of his mouth before he realized he'd actually spoken them.

Her eyes went soft. A contented smile lifted the corners of her mouth. "Sounds good to me."

Her words buzzed inside his body, his eyes tied to hers, he surrendered to the moment, and erupted inside her body, her name on his lips.

The sound of their breathing, their heart beat, the muted sounds of music from his laptop, the hum of the refrigerator, and other evidence of life outside their room slowly filtered back into their reality.

Kristin collapsed atop him, her head resting on his chest, her breath soft against his neck. His arms circled her and he hugged her, not ready to give up what had come to feel like part of his body. He rolled them over, so he was on top, still inside her, and pushed the head of his softening dick against the end of her pussy at just the right spot. Her legs went wider and soon she was crying out her pleasure again.

He looked into her eyes, her gaze soft and full of appreciation. He'd seen that look before in a woman's eyes. It was love. And knowing it didn't scare him. Just the opposite. The thought that this woman loved him, wanted him so deeply, enjoyed the pleasure he gave her, wanted to give it back in equal measure, made him feel warm and right. He kissed her mouth, softly, slowly, then put his hand between them, holding on to the condom.

"No, not yet," she said, her voice lush and low, but she loosened her legs, let him pull out.

After adding the condom to the growing pile in the trash, he crawled back into bed, curled his satiated body around his woman, and fell into a blissful doze.

****

Bliss flooded Kristin's body, too, but it had an opposite effect on her. She couldn't sleep. Her mind replayed the moments they had shared tonight, the words of tenderness and desire he had whispered to her, the feelings swirling inside her, and wondered what it all meant.

As he lay softly snoring, she slipped out of bed and stepped into the puddle of moonlight streaming in through the window. It was a full moon—big, fat, round, bright, and perfect for telling her secrets to.

Ever since she was a little girl, she had sneaked out of her room on the nights the moon was full, like tonight, breathed in the special scent of the magic light like her mom had taught her, then told the wise woman in the glow all her secret wishes, dreams, and sorrows.

"A full moon means fulfillment, Krissy," her mother had whispered into her tiny ear. "She is a time of celebration. Remember to give thanks for all she's given you throughout the month."

Arms around her body for warmth, Kristin faced her old confidant now and breathed her in. When all she could smell was Sean, she smiled and thanked her for him.

"I'm in love with him," she said in a soft whisper, sending chills spiraling up her legs and back and down her front like a frosty caress. The moonlight shimmied as if it understood and was happy. Seconds later, Kristin felt a warm blanket and strong arms wrap around her back and a kiss touch the top of her head.

"You're freezing, darlin'," Sean whispered against her neck.

She turned into his embrace. "Not anymore." She kissed him.

"Did my snoring wake you?"

She shook her head, too awestruck by him to speak. Silver light caressed his face, lit his hair, made his eyes shine with warmth. Her heart hitched as it always did, as if she couldn't believe he was hers.

He chuckled. "Then why are you standing in front of the window, cold and naked, instead of in my bed, warm and naked?"

Thinking about how happy I am. "I couldn't sleep. My body's still buzzing."

"Is that a good thing?"

"Definitely."

He grinned. "So, did I get it all?"

She matched his grin. "All of what?"

"You asked me to fuck your brains out."

She threw her head back and laughed. "And if I said no?"

"Then I'd have to keep trying, of course."

She *tsked* and shook her head with mock disappointment. "I'm afraid you missed a few brain cells waaaay in the back."

"Hmm." He stroked his chin with a serious look on his face. "Maybe a different position?"

"There are a couple we haven't tried, yet," she agreed in the same serious tone as he lowered her to the floor.

****

"But why do I have to tell him about the internet video of Kristin? You're underestimating how much he hates me. I'm telling you...he'll kill me." Randy wiped his sweaty hands on his boxers, showing he wasn't fully buying into Zoe's plan.

"No, he won't...if you say it exactly the way we practiced."

"Can't I just email it to him...anonymously?

"Sure. Do you have his email address?"

"Well, no, but I'm sure I could get it."

"Dammit, Randy! The two of them are getting closer every day. Right this second, they're in his bed, humping like today's their last day together." She paused, giggling at the thought that it actually was their last day together…they just didn't know it yet. "Do you really want to wait until you get his address? If they fall in love, nothing will break them up."

Randy hung his head and Zoe saw the truth slam him in the chest. "C'mon," she prodded, gently, "let me hear you say it."

He looked up at her, his face showing his fear and grief. "Uh, Sean, a friend of mine—"

"Stand up while you say it, so it'll feel the same as when you're doing it for real."

He stood. "—sent me—"

Zoe shook her head in frustration. "Start over, from the beginning. And I'll be Sean."

"All right! Damn, woman, you're bossy."

"Shhhh! Do you want them to hear us? Look, I just want to make sure you do it right. If you mess up, we're both screwed…and you'll never get Kristin."

He shifted on his feet, swallowed, released a breath, and started again. "Sean, a friend of mine sent me the link to a video of two chicks fucking."

"Good for you, mate."

He grinned at her.

"What?"

"You used his accent."

Zoe rolled her eyes. "Good for you, mate," she repeated, slowly, enunciating each word to try to get him back on track.

"Yeah, well, I think you should look at it."

"Thanks, man, but I'm not into girl-on-girl action."

"You'll be interested in this one…it's someone you know."

"Oh, yeah? Who?"

"Just take a look."

"That's where you hand him the note with the web link on it," Zoe prompted.

"Oh, yeah." He reached his hand out to her as if he were handing her the note. "Just take a look."

"Okay."

"And sorry, man. Really."

"Good, good. And then you walk away with your head down, like you're really bummed about having to tell him that his precious lover is cheating on him. And then, if I were you, I'd leave your room for awhile. He'll have questions after he sees it."

His eyes went big. "What kind of questions?"

"Who sent it to you, whether you watched it all, who else has seen it…"

Randy plopped down on the bed and dropped his head in his hands. "Ah, shit. He's going to kick my ass."

Zoe sat next to him. "Not if you play it right. Keep in mind that you're to act like you feel sorry for him because Kristin has cheated on him, because he's losing her, because she's hurt him."

"But isn't Kristin going to know right off that you're the one who posted the video? I mean, who else could it be?"

"Don't you worry about that. I'm going to tell her that someone stole my laptop—oh, I'll need to stash it here for a few days. Shamefaced, I'll admit that I recorded us. She'll be upset, but she'll forgive me. She always does. Now," she said, putting her arm around him. "You can do this, right?" When he didn't respond, she kissed his mouth, running her tongue around inside. "Right?"

"I can do just about anything if it'll get Kristin away from Sean."

"Good. At no time does my name come up. If I find out that it did, and you sold me out, I'll kick your ass myself and then drag you to Sean to finish you off. Kristin will never speak to you again much less climb into your bed."

Seeing the fear in his eyes, Zoe pushed him backward onto the bed and laid on him, grinding into him. "Don't worry. You'll do great." She kissed him, but he turned his face away.

"You're going to delete the video afterward, right?"

She rolled her eyes. "What difference does it make?"

"You have to delete it. I don't want it out there for people to see."

"Fine. I'll delete it. As soon as he dumps her. Happy?"

"Not really. I don't feel good about this."

"Well, maybe you'll feel good about this." She slid down his body, pulled his dick from his boxers, and sucked him deep into her mouth, sealing their deal with the first of four blowjobs she'd agreed to as payment for his help.

****

In the quiet, after their breathing calmed and their flush subsided, Sean wrapped the blanket around their cooling bodies. A long gurgle came from Kristin's stomach.

He laughed and ran his hands over her stomach. "You hungry?"

"Starving. What do you have in the fridge?" she asked and jumped up from the floor and went over to the small refrigerator set against the wall.

"Not much, darlin'. Sorry."

She opened the door and peered inside. "Two beers—a clear violation of dorm policy Mr. RA—a dried-up slice of pizza, half a burrito, and something that looks like it might have once been a piece of fruit."

He admired her form as she stood in the light of the fridge, letting his eyes caress her. "An apple."

"Disgusting." She opened the little freezer compartment and pulled out a pint of ice cream. "How old is this ice cream?"

"Couple days."

She pried the lid off. "Yes! It's chocolate! Do you have a fork?"

"A fork? Darlin', you eat ice cream with a spoon."

"Don't diss on the way I eat my ice cream or I won't give you any."

"In the basket on top of the fridge."

She rummaged around until she found a fork then returned to him. She dug it into the carton and ate her first bite, rolling her eyes at the creamy, rich taste. "Oh, God. I think I love you."

He loved how delighted she seemed about everything. He sat up. "Show me."

She dug up a bite and fed it to him, then dug up another bite for herself. "Am I in the presence of a fellow chocoholic?"

"It's why I work out every day," he said.

"Me, too." She fed him another bite. "Do they have good chocolate in Ireland?"

"There's this family-owned place in Mum's hometown that's been making chocolate for over seventy years. When we were kids, Da would take us there once a month and let us choose one thing."

"What would you choose?"

"It changed every month."

His eyes went to the five foot tall map on the wall. She followed his gaze.

"Wow…now that's a map. Ireland?"

He took the bite of ice cream she offered. "Yep."

"And it's to scale, too," she teased, laughing at the frown he tossed her.

"After that nasty remark, you'll not be getting any more of *my* ice cream." He grabbed the carton and forked a huge bite into his mouth.

She laughed, kissed his chocolate mouth, then crawled over to inspect the map. Moonlight streaming in caressed her smooth skin as she knelt in front of it to read the town names. "Where's that chocolate shop you were talking about?" she said over her shoulder.

Ice cream carton in one hand, the blanket in the other, he stood and joined her on the floor a foot in front of the map. He pulled her onto his lap and wrapped the blanket around them. She lay her head back on his chest. He leaned forward and pointed out a spot on the map. "Right here."

"That's your mom's home town?"

"Yes." He dropped a kiss on her shoulder. There was something about having this woman in his arms that made him feel like all was right in his world.

"Was your dad from there, too?"

He was so happy with Kristin in his arms, for the first time in a long time he didn't feel the sadness when she mentioned his dad. "No. He was from up the road…here." He finger drew a line straight north about an inch.

"Where did you grow up?"

He pointed back to his mom's town. "I lived here until I started college, then I moved to Dublin." He tapped his fingertip against the name of Ireland's largest city.

"Is that where you met the girl you left behind?"

He pulled his eyes from the map and focused them on her. "Kristin, whatever was, is past. I don't want the ghost of another woman between us, not in this room, not in each other's arms, not in our relationship."

"Sean, your past made you the man you are today. I want to know what happened that put in motion your being here with me, making all my dreams come true."

The pinch in his heart that he had been so sure was gone appeared as he fought with his memories and decided whether to share them. After a long pause he put the fork in the carton and set it aside. "Her name was Lindsey."

Chapter Eleven

Just the sound of the beautiful name spoken so tenderly from his mouth jabbed Kristin's heart, and she felt jealousy sweep into her cells and organs and flesh like high tide.

"What did she look like?"

"Long blonde hair, blue eyes, and a petite, slender body. Like a porcelain doll my sister had when she was young."

Perfect. Shit. I hate the bitch.

"How did you meet?"

"At university. We dated for a couple of months, and then moved in together."

"Looks like moving fast is a pattern for you, O'Neill."

Hearing the soft bite in her tone, he searched her face, brushing her cheek with his thumb. "Sure you want to hear this?"

She cranked down the jealousy. "No. Yes. Sorry. You were deliriously happy and in love, and...?"

"We *were*...for awhile." A look of sadness crossed his face, and he stared into the map again, his eyes taking on a glassy stare that said he was there. *With her.*

Kristin twisted until she straddled him, her legs around his waist, and she ran her hand up his chest and settled on his heart, trying to bring him back to her. "Tell me."

He blinked and shifted his attention back to her, settling his hands loosely at her back and closing the blanket. "We got along in every aspect but one. That one thing eventually tore us apart."

Kristin lifted her eyebrows in curiosity.

"Sex," he said simply.

They dropped in confusion. "Didn't she like it?"

"She did."

"What then? I know *you* weren't the problem."

"Actually...I was."

"What?" She shook her head. "You're an amazing lover, Sean...considerate, tender, amazingly gifted, and skillful. No, I can't imagine you being the problem."

"Thank you, darlin'. It pleases me you think so highly of my abilities. Our problem was less about skill and more about...size. I was too big for Lindsey. Sex with me hurt her."

She heard the pain and guilt in his voice, struggled to think of something to say to lessen it. "There are other ways to pleasure each other. I assume you..."

"Oh, yeah. I became an expert on those other ways. But it wasn't the same as me being inside her body."

Sean inside another woman. She hated the image his words conjured. She hated the jealousy the image conjured. "You said it tore the two of you apart?"

He nodded. "I came home early from work one day and she was in our bed with some guy. Fortunately, she sent him away before I could do something I would have regretted. After we'd stopped yelling and were able to talk, she told me she loved me but couldn't live the rest of her life with a man who couldn't make love to her."

"Bitch." Kristin didn't even try to hide her anger.

His mouth curved into a weak smile. "I didn't blame her. I even agreed with her. A man feels more like a man when he can bury himself deep into the body of the woman who loves him, giving her the pleasure she craves. When he can't pleasure his woman, he feels…inadequate."

Guilt is a hungry wolf that will devour you. How many times had she heard her mother say those words—usually to justify her lack of interest in parenting, but still, it was a sound belief. She smelled the guilt on Sean's skin and it made her stomach tighten and her heart tilt.

Words seemed weak, even trivial in a situation like this. He felt like he'd failed with the love of his life. Nothing she could say would change that, fix that, dissolve his pain. But she could show him how much *she* wanted him. *She* could make him know how much he pleased her. But would it be enough? She snuggled her body up against his and hugged him close.

"It's not your fault, Sean."

He tightened his arms around her and kissed her. "I know." He sighed and she felt him shrug. "It was no one's fault that we didn't fit together."

"It was just anatomy," Kristin added and he nodded, repeating the last word. She moved her hand down to his dick and caressed it. "Is that why you were so careful with me our first time? You were worried you'd hurt me?"

He nodded. "It's why I held off adjusting the schedule. I wanted to be with you as long as I could before you told me it wasn't going to work."

"It was a tight fit, but you made sure I was ready."

"Well, now, darlin', it wasn't that hard to get you

ready…you'd been panting for me since the first night you saw me in my Blarney Stone boxers."

She squeezed his dick and was pleased by the muffled "oof" that came from his mouth. "I know you're not saying I'm easy."

"No. Not at all," he said in a falsetto voice before she released him.

"Better be nice to me. I could get another boyfriend, you know. Like that." She snapped her fingers.

He smiled at her in the moonlight. "Boyfriend?"

The cold hand of panic gripped her. She hadn't meant to suggest anything of the sort. The word boyfriend suggested a relationship that she wasn't sure she wanted. Yes, she had wanted sex with Sean. Yes, she definitely felt something special for him, especially after tonight. But a boyfriend? A relationship? Was she ready to put her heart on the line again? She might have confessed to her moon goddess that she loved him, but that didn't mean she was ready to act on it.

"Do you want to be?"

"Yeah, I do."

His answer loosened the hand's cold grip, allowing warmth to flow in, allowing her to send a teasing smile his way. She kissed him and laid her head on his chest, contentment flowing through her as his heartbeat reverberated inside her chest.

"Tell me about him, Kristin."

She knew who he meant, but she asked anyway. "Who?"

"The boyfriend who hurt you so badly that you swore off guys and are afraid to love."

"I'm not afraid. I'm just…cautious."

He stared at her as if he didn't believe her.

"Why do you want to know?" she asked just to loosen the grip of his stare that was enticing her to tell him everything.

"For the same reason you wanted to know about Lindsey."

The image of Nick's face jumped before her eyes, but it took her a moment to summon the courage to pull the memories of her time with him to the surface. Surprised by the relative lack of pain the action brought, she easily summarized their relationship in her head before beginning her story.

"Nick asked me out our junior year, but I'd heard he was such a player I said no. I guess it was the chase that kept him interested, because every week he'd say, 'Go out with me this weekend, Kristin.' Every week I'd smile and say, 'No, thank you, Nick.'"

Remembering their early days brought a small smile to her face. His attention and flirting had been fun and flattering.

"One night before the end of the semester, we were studying together for our chemistry final with a study group. They all gave up and left to go to a party, but he and I stayed to finish the whole practice test. He walked me home, and we talked all night on the grass in front of my dorm. He impressed me that night, made me think I'd misjudged him. When we got back to school the following semester, and he still seemed interested, I agreed to go out with him."

"Then he tried to get you into bed, you kneed him in the nutbag, and never saw him again?"

She grinned at the jealousy she heard in his words. "Oh, you'd like that, wouldn't you?"

"Yes."

"Okay, yes. You're right. That's exactly what happened. The end." She reached for the ice cream, but he stilled her, keeping her on his lap.

"Sorry."

"Shall I continue?"

"Yes."

"We had a good time, and no, he didn't try to get me into bed. In fact, we'd been dating for over two months before he'd do more than kiss me. We were inseparable."

"Did he satisfy you?" Sean asked.

"In bed, you mean?"

"Yes."

"Well, he was no Sean O'Neill, but he did his best to put a smile on my face."

Sean didn't even smile at her compliment. "So far, it sounds like a great relationship."

She didn't even chuckle at his sarcasm. "I thought so. We began making plans for grad school and had decided on University of Washington. We weren't only planning grad school, though—we were planning our life. We were going to finish school, get jobs, get married, have kids, and grow old together. Short version: U-Dub accepted me but not him."

"And you turned down the offer."

She nodded. "I gave up my spot so he and I could be together here, which was our safety net. During our spring break trip to Maui, he told me the University of Chicago had offered him a spot, and that he'd accepted. I didn't even know he'd applied. Their deadline had long since passed, so there was no way I'd be admitted in time to go with him."

Sean released a string of Irish words that sounded really derogatory and nasty. It made her smile.

"He tried to explain his decision, saying he was doing it for our future. But I felt betrayed. I was too hurt to listen. I broke up with him and spent the remaining two months of school in a fog. I took the next semester off instead of starting grad school, deep in depression, trying to figure out how I'd been so stupid. I'd built my life around him and, when he was gone, I was gone, too."

"Kristin, you weren't stupid. He was an asshole."

His defense warmed her insides. "Either way, it changed me. I focused only on school, refusing to get involved with anyone. Until you, that is."

"Uh...until Randy, you mean."

"Oh, God, don't remind me."

"No, no...it's good. I see that now. I don't like the little *shitehawk*, but he brought us together."

"Maybe it was our destiny," she said, laying on a thick dramatic tone and chuckling. She refused to look at their joining as anything more than a happy coincidence. Then she heard her mother's voice in her head, saying there are no coincidences.

"Destiny or fate or God...whatever you want to call it, we were meant to be together."

Though her heart was pounding from joy, she laughed softly and put her hands on his face. "Sorry, babe, but to me, destiny is in the same category as leprechauns."

He wouldn't let it go.

"No, just think about it—you stayed away from all guys for, what...two years?" At her nod, he continued. "Then suddenly, inexplicably, you go after Randy, who's totally wrong for you. You end up in his room, right next door to mine, he's out of condoms, and you come to my room. Not to mention that I traveled nearly five thousand miles to get to you. You and I connected the first time we saw each other. The floor moved under my feet the first time I saw your face. And now, we're here, together, like this. That's no coincidence, darlin'."

"Are you sure it's not just hormones at work? Corresponding pheromones that make us a suitable match in the sack? I could smell the presence of your strong, desirable genes, and you could smell my readiness to take your seed?"

He cupped her face, stared into her eyes. "However it was we came together, I'm glad of it."

"I don't buy into theories about destiny and divine intervention, but I will admit that...I felt the earth move, too. The first time we met, the second, the third, every time I'm with you. I felt an immediate connection with you that I've never felt with anyone. I feel like I..."

She had to stop talking before she said the words that would be her downfall. She shook her head, as if to shake away the unsuitable thoughts. They'd known each other for such a short time. They couldn't be in love. In lust, of course, in like, definitely, but love? No! Yet, she was. Suddenly shy, she dipped her head into his chest, hiding her flaming face.

Sean lifted her face to his, found her eyes. "I know what you're feeling, even if you're not ready to say it, because it's what I'm feeling," he put her hand on his heart, "in here."

"What's in there that's telling you this?"

"I'm happy when I'm with you. Peaceful. At

home." He shook his head and laughed. "God, I sound like a chick...no offense."

Almost in tears at the depth of his feelings, she blinked her eyes and swallowed hard. "And that's all the proof you need?"

"Well, there's more, but I'm embarrassing myself." His hands tucked into her hair and his mouth slid over hers. "Yes. I have all the proof I need."

Her heart pounded as if something was in there fighting to get out. Was it love? She couldn't give it to him yet, because she still wasn't sure she had the courage. But she could give him something else. She grabbed the closest gold package, ripped it open, and rolled the condom on his erection. She lifted up, directed him into her warm wetness, and slid down until he was deep inside her. They didn't move, felt no urgency to get to the end, but only wanted the connection, the feel of the other.

"It's Honahlee," she whispered to him in the dark, his eyes shining with love into hers.

At first he said nothing, not understanding her meaning. Then he nodded, his smile tender. "Honahlee. It's beautiful." He kissed her nose. "What does it mean?"

"It's a land of supreme joy, happiness, and beauty."

"Where is this paradise?"

"In that song, you know, about the dragon."

"What?" The word tingled with mirth.

"Yeah, you know..." she cleared her throat and sang, "...Puff the magic dragon lived by the sea and frolicked in the autumn mist in a land called *Honahlee*."

He laughed. "I'm guessing your mother gave you this special name?"

"Of course. According to her, it would ensure I lived in joy all the days of my life."

"Well, Kristin Honahlee DeMarco, I plan to do my part to bring joy to all the days—and nights—of your life."

He lowered her to the floor and made love to her in the magic light of the moon—softly, slowly, tenderly— letting the moon's silver threads entwine them into an unbreakable knot.

****

"Kristin? Are you in there? Kristin!"

Kristin's eyes reluctantly cracked open when she thought she heard Zoe's voice. The dim gray light of pre-dawn stared her in the eyes, and she heard it again—pounding and her name being yelled from the other side of Sean's door. It was Zoe. She tried to sit up but Sean's arm around her, holding her against his chest, clamped her in place.

"Sean. Wake up," she said and shook him.

His eyes opened to slits and, seeing her, he smiled and pulled her closer. "You want me again?"

"No." She chuckled. "Yes, but Zoe's at the door."

"Ignore her. She'll go away," he mumbled and moved to capture her lips.

"Kristin, it's Zoe," came her voice, shouting now. "I know you're in there. Open up!" More pounding followed the insistent voice.

Sean's eyes flew open at the raucous. "That girl's a real burr up my arse!"

Kristin unhooked her leg from his waist. "She won't go away until you answer."

Sean drew in a deep breath and released it with a groan. He detangled himself from Kristin, but before she could move to get up, he rolled on top of her.

"Stay in bed and keep the sheets warm. I'll get rid of her."

The kiss and smile he gave her before exiting the bed melted her bones, stealing any ability or desire she had to move from his bed.

As he searched the floor for his boxers, she enjoyed his backside, which looked even better with the dim light of morning kissing his skin. Well-developed muscles shaped his tight ass, long legs, strong back, and wide shoulders. She knew the front looked just as tasty. They had made love all night, and she still had the desire to bite his flesh, devour him, taste him, take all of him inside her. Disappointment hit hard when blue boxers slid into place, disrupting her view.

He sauntered to the door and opened it a crack. "Go away, Zoe."

"I'm going to stay out here, yelling and pounding, until you let me in. And just so you know, there's already a crowd forming."

Sean muttered a few foreign words she was becoming familiar with right before he flung open the door.

****

Zoe tore her gaze from the nearly naked god-like form sporting a powerful morning woody and zeroed in on the numerous condom wrappers scattered on the floor among discarded clothing. That was Kristin's dress. Sean's pants. Her shoe. His shirt. Her panties.

Her gaze shifted then to the rumpled bed, where it looked as if a box of condoms had exploded. The smell of sex filled her nostrils and put a match to the wick of her own desires, especially seeing Kristin's body outlined under the sheets, and the sleepy, satisfied look on her face she got after she came.

"I was worried when you didn't come home."

Sean joined Kristin on the bed. The smile she gave him spoke volumes about her state of bliss. It was a look Zoe had never seen before on her friend's face, not when they'd had sex, not even when she'd been with Nick. She was falling for Sean. Hard.

Kristin lifted her smiling face to him, her plump lips begging for a kiss. Sean didn't disappoint. The lip-locked couple kissed as if they were alone in the room. As if she weren't standing there, watching them. As if her heart weren't crumbling to ashes at their every touch.

"Kristin!"

Kristin giggled and caught Sean's hand when it went to her breast. "Sorry. What were you saying?"

"I said, I was worried about you."

"Why? You knew I was with Sean."

"Why? Because you've been gone all night, that's why." Zoe's voice betrayed her, showing her anger as well as her jealousy.

"What time is it?" Kristin asked.

"Five-thirty in the morning!"

Kristin sat up and reached across Sean to grab her phone from the night stand. The sheet slipped down, revealing her heavy breasts, the tips pinky-red and plump as if they had been sucked hard and long and often by a ravenous mouth. Zoe's gaze left Kristin and shifted to Sean, who also stared at Kristin's lushness with desire on his face and hunger in his eyes. He knew what she tasted like, too, and a ripping bolt of jealousy gouged her heart at the thought. When she looked back to Kristin, she had adjusted the sheet to cover herself as if she had felt their stares burning into her skin and needed some protection from the assault.

"Wow. It really is true—time does fly when you're having fun." Kristin smiled at Sean. *Again.* And he kissed her. *Again.*

All their fucking ooey-gooey displays of affection made Zoe's stomach turn. She dug deep to tap her pit of pity and used it to shape her face and tune her voice.

"You were going to help me study for my chem test last night—the test that's this morning at ten. But you never showed up, you didn't call, and you didn't answer your phone. And to top it off, someone stole my laptop yesterday, with all my notes and practice tests on it, so I can't even study on my own." She collapsed her spine just a tad for effect. "Clearly, keeping your promise to me is last on your list of things to do." She turned slowly toward the door, her fingers mentally crossed. "Sorry I bothered you."

"Wait."

She stopped and turned teary eyes back to the bed. She didn't need an interpreter to decipher the look that passed between the lovers. Kristin would be leaving with her. Zoe had won. She fought to keep her satisfied smile of triumph hidden.

Kristin looked at Sean. He shook his head, whispering something in her ear. She giggled.

"Are you coming?" Zoe demanded, her tight voice a clear indication that she was irritated by the couple.

"Why don't you go on back to the room and I'll be there as soon as I can." Kristin glanced her way before turning back to accept another of Sean's kisses. "After I say goodbye to Sean."

"But—"

"I'll be there in fifteen min—"

"Forty-five," Sean said and pulled her down, covering her with his body.

"You're insatiable," Kristin whispered and half-heartedly pushed at his chest. "Thirty minutes. I promise," she said to Zoe over Sean's shoulder and giggled again at what his mouth was doing to her neck.

"I'll wait, and we'll walk back together," Zoe said and flopped on the desk chair across from the bed.

Sean muttered something guttural then pulled out of Kristin's embrace, rose from the bed, and glared at Zoe, not even trying to hide his enormous erection. And though he stayed by Kristin's side, his arm around her, he faced Zoe, his eyes burning into hers, his arms held apart from his body, his legs wide, in a stance of authority that invited no argument.

"I'll be walking Kristin home, so you can leave now."

Anger heated her face at being sent away like an unwanted intruder, but she hid it with a small martyred smile.

"Fine. See you in thirty minutes, Kristin." She walked to the door and opened it, glanced over her shoulder, stared at his dick, and smiled. "Bye, Sean."

She was traipsing down the stairs when she heard his room door slam. Triumph filled every cell of her body as she floated back to her room, laughing the whole way at her supreme manipulation skills.

She had won this battle and would win the war with what she and Randy had planned. This time tomorrow, Sean would be history, and Kristin would be hers again.

****

Half an hour later, Sean sat on the edge of the bed, his jeans on but not zipped, pulling on his socks. Kristin stood on the opposite side of the bed in her panties, stepping into her dress.

If he'd had his way, they'd still be in bed, wrapped around each other, not getting dressed so he could take her home. He had meant it when he said he wanted her forever. And he had meant for forever to begin now. It pissed the hell out of him that they were leaving because Zoe had insisted. Thrown a tantrum, was more like it. And Kristin just gave in. Like she fucking owed Zoe.

"Is she always that possessive with you?" he asked, glancing back at Kristin, his body heating up again as his gaze slid up and down her body.

She ran her hands through her bedraggled hair then began the search for the rest of her clothes. "I should have called to say I was going to be late, but for some reason," she grinned at him, "I forgot about everything but you." She found one shoe under his bed and stepped into it. "I haven't been a very good friend to her, lately."

In his mind, Zoe wasn't being a good friend. She had sabotaged every attempt he and Kristin had made to be together, even though Kristin had made it clear she wanted to be with him. Why was Kristin making excuses for her? Why did she have to keep Zoe informed about her comings and goings? Why was Kristin putting up with it?

"You put up with a lot from her," he said. "Too much." He yanked on his hiking boots, leaving the laces untied. She avoided his eyes, as if she knew her relationship with Zoe was skewed, and kept looking for her clothes like she couldn't wait to get out of here.

She found her other shoe by the door and stepped into it then walked over to him and presented her back to him.

"Zip me?" She held up her hair.

Why didn't she respond to his queries? Was she hiding something? He stood, kissed her neck, down her back. "I'd rather rip that dress off you than zip it up."

She turned toward him and put her arms around his neck, kissing him. "Tonight."

He tried another tactic. "She wants us apart, Kristin. I feel it."

"Zoe would never hurt me by trying to break us up. She knows how I feel about you."

He didn't buy it. In fact, he was sure Zoe would do her worst to get him out of the picture. His hand moved to Kristin's breast and he cupped it, pressing it deep into his palm. "How *do* you feel about me?"

"You can't tell, even after last night?"

She still wasn't ready to say it. "Call her. Tell her you're spending all day showing me how you feel about me."

"I'd love to stay with you." She kissed his neck. "Make love to you all day and all night." She kissed his jaw. "Wake up in your arms again." Kissed his mouth.

His heart softened for her. "Then stay."

"I promised Zoe I'd help her. And you teach class in a couple of hours."

Shit. She was leaving him for Zoe. What the fuck?

At his stone-faced silence, she kissed him again. He deepened the kiss, holding her face to his and tilting her head to fit their mouths better together. She was right, of course, he did have classes to teach and one to attend, but why wasn't she trying to talk him out of going? It bothered him how easily she was leaving him.

"How about we spend this weekend together?" she said, pressing against him. "I promise you—it'll more than make up for my leaving now." She kissed him and ran her hand over his zipper. "It'll be something you'll never forget."

He released a pent-up breath. "Okay. You win."

She smiled. "Zip me."

Chapter Twelve

"It's nice having you home," Zoe said. "I never see you anymore."

"What are you talking about?" Kristin kept her eyes glued to her laptop, fingers flying over the keys. "I see you every day."

"No, I mean we never get to just hang out together. You spend all your free time with *him*."

She stopped typing and looked at Zoe. Just thinking about Sean brought a smile to her face. "I love him."

Her roommate's face turned white and her mouth dropped open. She dropped her gaze to the chemistry textbook in her lap. "So you're in love. That doesn't mean you dump your friends."

Kristin heard the melancholy in her friend's voice and realized, for the first time, how much she looked like an abandoned puppy. Guilt pricked her conscience. "I'm not dumping you."

Zoe hung her head. "Feels that way." She wiped a tear from her cheek.

Kristin knew how dramatic and manipulative her friend could be when she was trying to get her way. But she also knew she really seemed upset. Setting aside her laptop, she joined Zoe on her bed, ran her hand down her hair, and laid her hand on her arm.

"I'm sorry you feel like I'm dumping you. I'm

really not. How about we set aside a day, just for us, and do something fun together."

Zoe grabbed Kristin's hand and smiled. "I'd like that." She shifted onto her knees and leaned forward. "And I know just what we can do. You're going to love me for this! My mom said she can get me tickets and backstage passes for your favorite band!"

"Oh, my God! You mean…!" She grabbed Zoe's hands.

Zoe nodded, squealed again, and grabbed her phone. "We're going to have so much fun this weekend!"

Kristin's smile faded. "Wait—they're here this weekend?"

"Yes!"

She put her hand on Zoe's phone to stop her from dialing her mom's number. "I'm sorry. I can't do it this weekend."

Guilt sliced Kristin across the heart as she watched the sheen of happiness fade from her friend's face and her body deflate like a balloon.

"And I bet I can guess why." Angry sarcasm dripped from her words.

Kristin nodded. "Sean and I already made plans, but next weekend—"

"Yeah, sure. Whatever." Zoe pushed her books and homework and notebooks and pens off her bed onto the floor, lay down, and pulled the covers over her head.

"Don't be like that." Kristin rubbed her hand across her friend's back. These childish tantrums were wearing on her.

Silence from the lump on the bed.

"I'll make it up to you."

"How?" came the muffled response.

"Next Friday, we'll find a party, or go to a club and get totally shwasted."

"You hate parties and clubs, and you don't drink."

"Yeah, but I want to do something you like to show you how much you mean to me as a friend. C'mon. Say yes."

Zoe rolled over, lowered the covers from her head. "What if there's something I'd like us to do instead of parties. Something we can do right now."

"Name it," Kristin said.

She took Kristin's hand and pressed it against her breast. "I want to have sex with you."

Kristin jerked her hand away and stepped away from the bed. "I'm with Sean. I don't have sex with anyone but him." She climbed into her own bed and grabbed her laptop.

"It's been so long since I've tasted your pussy. I'm dying for it. I need it, Kristin. I need you."

"I won't cheat on Sean." Sean would never forgive her for cheating; he had said as much last night. Lindsey's betrayal had really done a number on him.

Zoe left her bed and climbed onto Kristin's.

"It's only cheating if you have sex with another guy." Her hand slid up Kristin's leg. "This is just you and me—doing what we've always done for each other." Her fingers had reached her knee and circled the sensitive flesh on the back that she knew drove Kristin crazy. "Helping each other out. There's no cheating involved."

Kristin caught Zoe's wrist as her hand slid up her thigh and moved inward.

"It is cheating." She moved Zoe's hand aside. "I

know how it feels to be cheated on and I won't do that to the man I love." Setting her laptop aside, she stood. "I'm going to take a shower and get ready for class. When I get back, we can talk about which day we can get together to do something other than sex."

****

She came back from the shower and Zoe was still sitting on her bed.

"You going to class today?" Kristin asked as she put on her makeup.

Zoe didn't respond. Didn't look at her. She sat curled up in her bed, her head down, staring at her fingernails, picking off the chipped polish.

Kristin turned to her. "Zoe?"

Zoe burst into tears, covering her face with her hands.

"What's wrong?" Kristin asked.

"I have something to tell you. And you're going to hate me."

Cold enveloped Kristin's body. "What did you do?"

"You know how someone stole my laptop?"

"Yeah."

"Well, I, uh…"

"Just say it."

"I…recorded us—you and me—having sex. The video was on the laptop."

Kristin's heart spiraled into her stomach and she tasted bile in her mouth. "Are you kidding me? You recorded us? Why?"

"Just for me. So I could watch and remember." Tears rolled down her cheeks.

"And now it's in the hands of some stranger, who

could put it on the internet? Dammit! How could you?"

"I'm sorry. I never thought—"

"You never think things through before you do them, that's the problem."

Chapter Thirteen

His heart a cold, clay lump at the bottom of his stomach, Sean hit replay for the third time. The shock wasn't as great this time as when the image of Kristin—his sweet Kristin—first appeared on the video having sex with Zoe.

Her long, sexy legs were splayed wide, knees bent up by her ears, opening herself to Zoe's mouth and tongue and fingers. Her voice moaning out instructions that would bring her to pleasure faster. Her face in full-blown rapture when satisfaction gripped her. Her calling out his name in joy.

It was a scenario he had witnessed a dozen times but with one exception: it had been his face in her pussy, his mouth drinking her sweet honey. It had been his tender loving that put the look of perfect bliss on her face and made her call out his name.

His stomach turned as he watched the woman he thought was his pleasure her lover. She rolled over and dove into her roommate's cunt like she was a woman starved for the taste, her hand reaching for her own insatiable clit. Her ass rose up in the air and she rocked forward and back, the way she did when riding his cock. Zoe screamed out her pleasure, followed by Kristin's low moans.

There the video stopped. He started to watch it again, but knew there was no need. The images were burned into his retinas, his brain, his heart, like a hot brand that had labeled him a fool.

She had fooled him good and made him think she loved him. That he was the only one for her.

"Oh, fuck me." He cursed aloud, then louder, then roared it at the top of his lungs, a long, drawn-out moan that bounced off the walls of his room and down the hall.

****

Kristin read Sean's text again, looking for clues between the letters as to what happened to make him end their relationship.

"Kristin, we're over" didn't give her much to go on, not the first time she'd read it and not now. If she could just talk to him, hear his voice, get him to open up, she could clear up whatever misunderstanding must be playing out.

She dialed his number again. Her call went to voice mail after a couple of rings. He was refusing her calls.

"Sean, I don't know what's wrong, why you're mad at me...if you're mad. Oh, God, I don't know what you're feeling, but I—" Her voice broke; she swallowed back tears and tried speaking again. "Please, call me."

The words of Sean's jilted lover, the one Randy sent to her, flooded her mind. "He'll fuck you then dump you...End it now before he breaks your heart." Never in a million years had she believed he'd do the same to her. But he had. He had fooled her good, made her think he loved her. She never saw it coming. She dropped her phone in her jacket pocket, covered her face with her hands, and cried.

"Kris?"

Kristin felt a hand on her shoulder and looked up into Mason's worried face.

"Are you okay?"

"Yeah," she said, and quickly wiped the tears from her face with her fingers. But there were too many, and they kept coming. "No."

"Aw, babe. C'mere." He hugged her to his chest and let her cry.

After a moment, she pulled back. "I'm sorry. I can't seem to stop crying."

He pulled a couple of paper napkins from the fast food bag in his hand. "Here, take these."

She took them and dabbed her eyes, but the flimsy paper couldn't tackle that much moisture.

"I've never seen you cry, except when your grandpa died—Oh, man, did somebody die?"

She shook her head, but her mind was screaming *Me! The second I read Sean's message.* "Sean and I, uh, we broke up. Actually, he broke up with me. I'm not taking it well, obviously."

He squeezed her arm. "I'm sorry. What happened?"

"I don't know." She gave a hopeless little shrug. "He didn't tell me why he broke it off. If I understood why, I think I could deal with it better, you know?"

"Yeah, no one knows that better than me."

"What do you mean? Who dumped you?"

"Well, Zoe."

"What?"

An awkward little laugh gurgled in his throat. "You knew we broke up, right?"

"Yeah, but she said you broke up with her."

He shook his head.

"I'm confused."

It was his turn to shrug. "We went to my room after the movies that night, started, you know, making out like we always did. Afterward, she told me we were through and left. No explanation. Won't return my calls. Won't talk to me. She looks right through me now, like I'm not there."

Kristin put her hand on his arm. "I'm sorry. I had no idea."

"That girl is trouble with a capital T—wild, rude, and impossible to control—and that's exactly what I loved about her. I miss her. But I'm moving on. And you will, too."

She sighed, her breath shaky. "I don't think I can."

"I know it feels that way." He hugged her then eased back. "Hey, I hate to desert you, but I gotta get to class. Call me later and we'll grab some food, talk, get drunk, whatever."

She nodded. "Thanks."

He was a couple of steps away when she called out his name. "Would you take her back, even after what she did?"

He nodded. "In a heartbeat." He waved to her with his bag of food and headed across campus.

On her way back to her room, she thought about what Mason had told her. Zoe always had a motive for her actions. The question was, why break up with Mason and then lie about it that night? What was she up to? Kristin wondered whether she had succeeded in getting what she wanted from the action. Knowing Zoe, she had…and left behind a trail of dead or wounded souls.

Mason's comments also made her wonder whether

there was a connection between Sean breaking up with her and Zoe's admission that she had recorded the two of them having sex and that the laptop with the videos was now in the hands of a stranger. Had Sean seen the video? Was that why he wasn't talking to her?

If he broke up with her simply because she'd been with a woman, then maybe he wasn't the right man for her after all. No, he'd just come out and ask her about it. She was sure of it. He said he loved her, and when you love someone, you don't just toss them away.

But something had happened between their night of passion and this morning. But how could she fix it if she didn't know what it was? If he wouldn't even talk to her? If she had to track him down and ambush him to get him to talk, that's what she'd do. She wasn't going to let go of the love of her life that easily.

Chapter Fourteen

Sean sat at the bar staring into the tall pint—his fourth—between his hands. It had been sitting long enough for the foamy head to dissolve into the dark amber liquid. Part of him worried that if he started drinking to forget Kristin, he wouldn't stop, and he didn't have his mates here to keep him calm and safe like he did back home.

Ah, home. He missed it. For the first time since arriving in America, he wished he'd never come. He could've gotten his heart broken at home and gone to his local pub in Dublin with Ian and Jack and Shane and his other friends who would help him see that he was better without the bitch who wronged him. But no one here had his back. Not the acquaintances he'd made. Certainly not the woman who'd betrayed him.

"Something wrong with the beer?"

He didn't have to lift his eyes to see who had spoken. He knew the voice belonged to Raena Ortiz, the bartender who had been trying to engage him in a conversation and other things since that first night a week ago when he'd sat at her bar.

He shook his head. "The beer's fine."

"Then I'm guessing the problem's with you."

This time he did look up. The corners of her berry-hued lips curled into a smile meant to be seductive. And it was. But he wasn't interested in seduction.

"Good guess."

"Wanna tell me about it?" The light shining in her coal-black eyes told him she'd be a good…listener.

He dug some bills out of his pocket. "If I bore ya to tears, lass, you'd stop with the pretty smiles. And right now, that's the best part of my day."

Forcing a smile he didn't feel, he dropped the money on the bar, grabbed his drink, and stood. Feeling his world tilt to the left, he grabbed the bar with one hand, steadied himself, then picked his way to the back of the darkened room. He slid into a two-person booth, choosing the seat that put his back to the raucous crowd beginning to form.

Two guys stumbled past him on the way to the jukebox. A quick glance told him it was Mason and Randy. He scowled, wondering whether Randy would move in on Kristin now that he was out of the picture. Just the thought of Randy's slimy hand touching her made him want to break it in a dozen places.

Anger bubbled up in him as he recalled the day Randy had brought his world crashing down around him. He was still torn between thanking him and pulverizing him for telling him about that video of Kristin. He shifted in his seat and fisted his hands on the table, trying to stem the desire to visit vengeance on the guy's face.

The two left the jukebox, Mason in the lead. He glanced at Sean then away. Then, as if suddenly recognizing him, he stopped.

"Hey, dude. I didn't see you." He slid into the facing seat.

Sean nodded a greeting.

"Hey," Randy mumbled, his head down, and stood

as far away from Sean as possible while still being part of the group.

Sean gritted his name between his teeth.

"Hey, man, sorry things didn't work out with you and Kristin." Mason continued. "You guys seemed really solid."

"Yeah, well, you know how it goes."

"How did she take it?" Randy asked, a slight quiver to his voice.

Sean shot him a look and was pleased when the little snot looked ready to bolt. "You stay away from her." He pointed his finger at him.

"Oh, I'm seeing someone," Randy mumbled, shuffling from foot to foot, like he was nervous at the topic. His gaze cut to Mason. "I'm going to order our drinks." He rushed off.

Silence enveloped the dark table and shrouded the two sitting there.

"I talked to her the other day," Mason broke through in a low voice when Randy was far enough away to not overhear. "She's not taking it well."

Sean's head lifted and his eyes bore into Mason's, as if looking there would allow him to see Kristin as he'd seen her. Disappointed, he dropped his head again. "She'll get over it."

"I've known Kris since high school and, in all that time, I've only seen her cry once—when she lost her grandfather. The other day, man—she cried the whole time I was talking to her. Like she couldn't stop. She's hurting, bad."

The words hacked off another slice of Sean's heart, and he felt himself bleed out, taking with it his last reserves of strength.

"Well, that fucking makes two of us!" he said and pounded the table, making beer slosh out of the glass and puddle on the table. As if seeing the beer for the first time, he grabbed it and gulped down half of it before taking a break to breathe.

"What the fuck happened between you two?" Mason asked.

"Ask her," Sean said as he swiped his mouth with the back of his hand. Talking about Kristin made him feel like his skin was being scraped off to the nerves.

"I did. She has no clue why you dumped her."

Sean didn't respond.

"At least tell her why. It'll help her move on. Zoe didn't give me a reason for dumping me, and I..." He shook his head. "I'm still fucking stuck on her."

The warm tingly effects of the beer flowed through Sean's blood and heated his slogged brain, but he heard Mason's comment clearly, and something about it bothered him. "Zoe said you broke up with her."

"Dude, the girl's hot and wild, she wants to fuck all the time, she sucks better than a vacuum, and she was into me. Why in hell would I want to give that up?"

"Because she's fucking crazy."

Mason's lips thinned and he shook his head and leaned forward. "Just talk to Kristin."

"It won't change anything."

"Maybe not for you. But it will for her. If you ever did care about her, you owe it to her to tell her why you don't anymore. Look, Randy's signaling that my beer's up, so I'll leave you to scowl into yours." He started to scoot out but Sean stopped him.

"How did she look? When you talked to her."

Sean thought he saw a spark of anger flash in

Mason's eyes as he pulled up the image, as if he wanted to punch Sean in the face, and his words confirmed it.

"She looked like she'd been fucked over. I've never seen her in that kind of pain, even when Nick pulled his shit on her."

And you caused it. Mason didn't say the words, but Sean felt them. Like knives to his core. He nodded twice and dropped his head in his hands.

"Don't be a pussy, man. Talk to her. You owe her that much." Mason walked away.

Moments later, Raena slid another beer in front of Sean. He looked up, his eyes saying he didn't order it.

"On the house." Rae rubbed his back and let her hand slide up into his hair, caressing his head. "You look like you need it."

He stared up at the blatant offer in her dark eyes and she took it as an invitation. She dropped a knee onto the seat beside him and leaned toward him, showing him her ample cleavage and pressing her large breasts against his arm. Then her mouth was on his, her tongue in his mouth. She tasted warm and spicy, like whiskey. He drank deeply, the taste numbing his broken heart for an instant.

She squeezed his leg, high on his thigh, her long fingernails brushing his dick, which twitched at the touch. She released his mouth, but held on to him with a look in her eyes that said how much she wanted him.

"I get off in a couple of hours," she whispered, rose from the seat, and moved back to the bar with a smile on her face.

She was already gone when Sean remembered to nod. Maybe a fast, no strings fuck was just what he needed to start getting over Kristin.

****

"It ain't even two yet, *bruja*!" the second-to-last customer complained as Raena escorted him out.

"How would you know, Diablo," she said, "you're too drunk to see the clock."

"I see good enough."

"Good. Then you can see to tell the Tavern Taxi driver how to get to your house."

She watched at the door to make sure Diablo got into the safe-ride-home car before locking up tight. Then she turned her gaze back to where Sean stood, waiting for her.

She sauntered over to him, unbuttoning her shirt as she did. She untucked it from her tight black jeans, pulled it off, and threw it at him. He caught it one-handed and tossed it onto the bench where he'd waited for her to come to him.

Her black bra showcased her big titties to their best, but at this moment, the lingerie was nothing but a hindrance. As if reading his mind, she reached around her back and unhooked it. Her breasts, free from their restraints, plumped as his eyes fondled them, and her tight, dusty pink nipples peaked.

The hunger in her eyes made him squirm—and not in a good way. He fought to ignore the fist slamming into his stomach when she tossed her bra aside. When she raked her fingers through his hair and pulled his face down to hers. When she ground her lips against his and undid his belt. When her quick fingers unbuttoned his jeans and moved to his zipper.

Suddenly, the blood in his veins turned heavy and cold, and his body froze. He broke the kiss and caught her hand, removing it from his boxers.

She tried to pull him back into the kiss, but he moved his head.

"Raena."

"What's wrong?" He heard the frustration in her gravely voice, the raw need.

He stepped back from her and quickly fastened his jeans and belt.

"Something I said?" she asked, covering her breasts with her arms.

He felt like an asshole of the first order, knowing she probably felt ridiculous standing there, exposed, literally and figuratively. And it was his fault.

"Raena, you're a desirable woman."

"Ah, *mierda*." She released the breath she had been holding. "But?"

"My heart belongs to someone else."

"No problem, honey," she said. "That's not the part of you I want."

He smiled his apology.

"Let me guess—that woman you've been in here trying to drink off your mind?"

He retrieved her shirt and held it out for her.

She slipped her arms into her shirt and fastened the button over her breasts. "This woman of yours must be pretty damn special."

Even though Kristin broke his heart, he had to agree with Raena. Kristin was special. He'd never met anyone like her. It would take him a long time to get over her. He knew that, but he couldn't make himself answer Raena's question.

She nodded as if she knew the answer. "She cheat on you?"

His continued silence answered Raena's question.

She scoffed a gentle rebuff. "Yet you're still faithful to her." She shook her head and narrowed her eyes at him. "She doesn't deserve you, and you don't deserve me."

What he deserved was a kick in the arse for what he'd been about to do. He still loved Kristin, no matter what she had done. He didn't want another woman. He didn't want to be the kind of guy who hurt a woman just to get over the one who had hurt him.

He needed to get out of there.

He needed Kristin.

****

Sean found one of the few payphones in town at a sketch gas station on Central and dropped in two quarters. Yeah, he could use his phone, but he didn't want her to know it was him calling in case he couldn't find his voice. He punched in her number and held his breath.

It rang three times before she picked up. Her voice, sexy and sleepy, blew through his soul like a cool breeze on a sizzling summer day, bringing with it every memory they'd made together. The feel of her skin, the taste of her mouth, the rush of being inside her body. He felt like half a man without her by his side.

"Hello?" she repeated. "Who is this?"

His mouth moved, but no sound came out. He couldn't force himself to say the words he had called to say. *Meet me, Kristin. Let's talk. Let's work this out so we can get back to each other, where we belong.*

"Sean? Is that you?" He heard hope in her words, and they stung like icy shards.

"Kristin," he whispered her name.

"Sean." Her voice rose, tears breaking her words

into pieces. "Please, come over. Let's talk about what went wrong. Whatever it is, I want to fix it."

He opened his mouth to beg her not to cry when images of her and Zoe superimposed themselves over her lies of love, making him swallow the tender words he'd wanted to say. Feeling his heart tighten, he squeezed his eyes shut and hung up.

He shouted her name and a curse into the cold, velvet night, wishing that he had the courage to go to her now and say the words that would turn things around for them. In the end, he only turned toward home, sadness filling him.

****

"It's three in the morning! Where the fuck do you get off ordering me here, Randy?" Zoe spat the words, her hands in fists. "Our business is done."

"The way I look at it, it's just started."

Zoe grabbed his balls through his shorts, squeezed, and twisted them. "That's where you got it wrong."

She released him, and he fell to his knees, his hands cupping the injured dangles. Considering her job done, she turned to leave. "Don't call me again," she said over her shoulder.

"Do you think Kristin and Sean would be interested in knowing you're the one who posted the video to the internet just to break them up?"

Randy's words pulled her back like she was tied to a rope he yanked in his hands.

So...The little dipwad was threatening to tell Kristin who broke up her perfect relationship. He had to know that as soon as he did, she would rat on him and Kristin would hate him. But still...She wasn't willing to risk losing Kristin.

"What do you want?"

He took in a deep breath, released it, and struggled to a standing position. "I want you at my beck-and-call for a month."

Zoe slapped him. "You son-of-a-bitch! You think you can screw with me? We had a deal, and I lived up to my part of it. You don't get to come back later and renegotiate."

"New deal. You give me what I want, and I don't tell Kristin what you did."

She moved closer. "You sure you want to fuck with me? You're the one who told Sean about the video, not me."

"You sure you want to risk losing Kristin?" he countered. "She forgave you for recording her, but I don't think she'd forgive you for intentionally using it to destroy her relationship with Sean."

"Do you want to risk that I might twist your balls off during one of your beloved blowjobs, or bite the head off your cock and let you bleed to death?" She leaned forward and bit his neck, not hard enough to draw blood, but enough to make him wince at the demonstration of what her teeth and her ire could do.

He jerked back, but wouldn't look her in the eye.

She smiled. "I didn't think so." She laughed, turning her back on him, and sauntered away, hoping he was too afraid of her to persist in his blackmail attempt.

"I'll tell her, Zoe. I mean it," Randy called out.

She screamed a string of obscenities as she stormed away. But in that string was the word okay.

Chapter Fifteen

Kristin sat on the bench, her eyes scanning the direction she knew Sean would come from. Unless he had changed his routine, he'd be walking her way in another five minutes or so. The electrified nest of snakes in her stomach strangled her confidence, and she took a few deep breaths to untangle it.

How many times had she practiced in the mirror what she would say to him when she saw him? It felt like a thousand at least. She had a plan for what to say and do if he took her in his arms, kissed her, and begged for her forgiveness for being such an ass. Another one if he agreed to talk, but immediately began accusing her of something she didn't do. And yet another one if he ignored her and walked away. She was hoping for the first one, but figured it would be the second or third.

She was tired of waiting for him to come to his senses. If she could get him to talk, she knew she could fix whatever was wrong between them. So she was taking matters into her hands. Her heart slammed into her ribs on its way to her throat when she spied him walking down the path that would take him into the archaeology building and his first class.

He'd grown a scruffy beard and mustache since she'd last seen him a week ago. And his hair looked like it did after crawling out of bed from making love all night with her. Overall, the look gave him a rougher, tougher, even sexier presence and accentuated the sweet mouth she missed kissing.

****

Last night's beer pounded in Sean's skull like a tidal wave as he headed to class, making his mouth feel like he'd eaten sand all night and his stomach feel like a fucking boxing match was going on inside it. The pain was strong, but not enough to kill the pain in his heart. It also wasn't strong enough to ease the shame of what he'd almost done with Raena. He'd let his dick do his thinking again and had almost entangled himself in another mess that he'd regret.

As he neared the building where his class was, he saw Kristin sitting on the bench. He felt like *shite* and wasn't up to talking to her about why he broke up with her. And he knew that's what she wanted.

She looked pale and thinner, and dark smudges had appeared under her eyes since he'd last seen her that morning he'd walked her home. She looked lost, shattered, beautiful. A twinge of empathy pierced his heart and, in that moment, the thought of taking her in his arms and kissing her back to happiness appealed to him. But the moment was fleeting, leaving behind it the bitter taste of anger when he thought about his own pain.

He hadn't had much of an appetite lately, either, and sleep was hard to catch—even harder to hold on to. The woman had demolished their sweet, budding affair. He would not feel sorry for her, and he would not allow her to lie her way back into his heart and crush it again.

Fighting the urge to vomit, he set his eyes on the path before him and steeled himself to pass her by.

****

Fighting the urge to throw up, Kristin wiped her hands on her jeans and stood, her shaky legs feeling like fifty pound weights were attached to them. They didn't want to move. But if she didn't move, Sean would pass by as if she were a ghost. She took a stumbling step toward him.

"Sean."

At first he ignored her, but when she called his name again, louder, he stopped in the middle of the path and glared at her, his face darkening like the late winter sky hanging thick and gray overhead. His mouth and eyes were narrowed and unyielding, mirroring his mind, she guessed.

He adjusted his backpack, stuck his hands into his front pockets, and kept walking, hunkered slightly, chin down, as if he were walking in a stinging storm.

She rushed after him. "Sean." She caught his arm and stopped him, pulling him toward her. "Talk to me."

His lips curled as if to spew harsh words, but he snapped them closed and shook his head.

Her goal was to push him, get him to spew, because it was better than being ignored. She pulled on the balloons of anger bursting inside her. "You owe me an explanation, O'Neill, and since you're too much of a *shitehawk* to return my calls, I'm here to collect in person."

"I owe you nothing." He turned away.

Well aware that she was taking advantage of the fact that he'd never harm her, she pulled him back around, put her hands on his chest, and grabbed handfuls of his shirt. She had to make an impression on him or he'd blow her off.

"Did you love me, Sean, or were all those pretty words just a trick to get into my panties?"

His blue eyes glared into her like ice, and his lips twisted into a sharp grin. "I didn't need tricks, darlin'. You were always more than willing to drop them."

The slur and derogatory use of his pet name for her broke off another chunk of her fragile heart, and she fought to ignore the pain. "But did you love me?" She hated the lacy whimper thinning her voice, hated that she was groveling.

His jaw worked as if he were chewing on the response to her question.

She pounded his chest with her fists. "Answer me, dammit!"

"When I said I loved you, I meant it." He roared the confession as if it angered him to speak it.

"Do you still love me?"

He shook his head, but did not speak. They stood in a bubble of silence for several long, painful seconds.

"You killed it." Gone from his voice was the explosive anger; in its place was tired misery, trimmed in quiet disgust.

"If I did something to hurt you, give me a chance to apologize, to fix it. Don't just break up with me and ignore me like we never meant anything to each other."

"There's nothing to fix. It's over." He pulled her hands from their death grip on his shirt, and then he turned away and moved toward the building.

"Give us a chance!" She screamed out her pain and dropped to her knees, not caring who heard or what they thought about her pitiful act of desperation.

He spun around and glared at her. "For God's sake, Kristin, you're embarrassing yourself."

She didn't get up, and he glared at her like he was torn between helping her and just walking away and was pissed she was making him choose. Three angry strides and he was back at her side, dropping his pack to the ground near her feet. Grabbing her upper arms with his powerful hands, he lifted her and stared into her teary eyes.

"You broke my fucking heart," he cried out and shook her. "There's nothing left in me to give you another chance." He released her. "I'm not..." he shook his head, jamming his hands in his hair. His clenching teeth made his jaw firm, his eyes shiny.

"I love you, Sean."

His eyes opened wide then narrowed again. It was the first time she'd actually said, "I love you." But would it be too late to matter?

Unable to speak another word, she buried her face in his chest and cried, great wracking sobs that flooded his shirt and bathed his skin with heat. She felt his body tense at her touch, at her emotion.

"Fuck!" He growled the obscenity into her hair then roughly yanked her trembling body tight against him. Wrapping one arm around her waist, one hand at her back, he held her close, his body like an inferno against hers.

She curled into the circle of his angry embrace, her hands and head tucked against his beating heart, and pressed into him with all her might. She wanted to dissolve into him, wanted him to absorb her body into his, make her his again. But when her tears had dried and all that was left were a few sniffles, there had been no joining. He hadn't let her in.

Sean picked her up and carried her to the bench. He

sat beside her, not touching, but she could feel his heat. He wouldn't look at her, but she saw the mist of pain emanating from him. He wouldn't talk, but she heard his fear of saying the words that needed to be said. Silence settled down on them like a heavy glass dome.

"Why wasn't I enough for you?" he said tiredly, making the first crack in the dome.

"You are! You're everything I ever wanted."

"Then why did you cheat on me?"

The accusation pushed her back. Her body went cold, her eyes wide, and her backbone stabbed against her belly. "I never cheated on you!"

"I saw you, Kristin. With my own eyes."

She saw the pain in his eyes, heard it in his voice. His emotions were real, even though his eyewitness proof wasn't. "What did you see?"

"You fucking another person."

He had seen the video. "Who?"

"Zoe."

He said the name like it made him want to vomit. It sliced through her like a blade, revealing the images burned in her mind of Zoe pleasuring her, her pleasuring Zoe. The images momentarily drained her courage to defend herself against the accusing eyes boring into her, and she closed her eyes, trying to shut them out.

"Your eyes never could hide the truth in your heart. So just admit it. Confession is good for the soul."

His harsh words stiffened her spine, and she opened her eyes, steadying her gaze at him. "Yes, Zoe and I had sex, but how was it that you saw us?"

"The video you two created was good quality. I saw and heard everything like I was right in the room."

Kristin's face flamed. "Who gave it to you?"

"I tell you there's a video of you out there having sex with a woman—the very video that destroyed our relationship—and you ask how I got it? Does it fucking matter?"

"No. What does matter to me is that you give us a chance to talk about this, get the truth out, and get past it."

Her words seemed to deflate him. His eyes dulled like the fire inside them had died. "The minute I saw you on that video, somebody else pleasuring the body that was supposed to be only mine to pleasure, we became broken and unfixable. Talk won't help that."

"Look. I know it must have been a shock for you to see that video, and I'm sorry it hurt you, but it happened before you and I got together. I didn't cheat on you. You and I both still carry the scars from cheating relationships. I'd never do that to you."

"You called out *my* name when Zoe made you come, which means we were together at the time you were fucking her, which means you did cheat."

Frustration spiked through her body at his unwillingness to even consider that she might be innocent. Since she had only had sex with Zoe once since the night Sean had walked her home, the video he'd seen had to be of that time. In her mind, it was before she and Sean were actually "together."

"First of all, at that moment, we weren't together. And second, did I miss the conversation where we decided we were going to be exclusive?"

He reared back like she'd slapped him. "We've been exclusive since we first met, and you know it."

"Why would I assume that?"

"Are you kidding me, Kristin? The night we made love, you told me you felt an immediate connection with me. Unless that was a lie, it sure sounds like you thought we were together from the very beginning."

"I knew I wanted a relationship with you that lasted beyond our agreement. But that's how *I* felt. I didn't know how *you* felt."

"I told you how I felt. I told you I loved you."

"Yes, but you told me after we'd made love. Before that, I had no idea how you felt. You offered me a week's worth of dates, a cup of condoms, and sex. Where in that plan was I supposed to read 'love and commitment?' Was I supposed to read your mind?"

"Okay. Forget the instant attraction we both felt. Forget that we fell in love at first sight. Answer this. If I'd been having sex with other women while we were going out on our dates, and you found out about it, like I found out about you and Zoe, how would *you* feel?"

She swallowed the bitterness that rose from her stomach at the thought of him with another woman. "I didn't have sex with Zoe after we started our dates, and—"

"Just answer the question, Kristin."

"I would hate it, but I wouldn't fault you because we never talked about exclusivity."

"Bullshit. Do you remember our first date? I walked you to your dorm after breakfast and when you thought I had another date that day, you were so pissed you wouldn't hold my hand."

"I remember. Even then, the thought of you being with another woman..." *ripped my heart out* "...upset me, but—"

"No buts. I wanted only you from the night I saw

you, so I stayed away from all women but you. It's clear now that you didn't feel the same way about me."

"I did! Even before our first date, I only wanted you."

"No. You also wanted Zoe."

"No!"

"Did she force you to eat her pussy? Force your legs apart so she could eat yours? Force you to come in her mouth?"

Her tongue felt thick, her face burned. "I told you—that happened before we had our first date."

"I don't believe you."

"I called out your name because, from the second I saw you, I wanted you. I...I wanted..." Her thoughts went ragged and trailed off as if they were too trivial and painful to finish.

"You wanted me but when I didn't give you what you wanted, you went to Zoe for relief, like she was some kind of god-dammed human vibrator." A scoffing sound barked from his curled lip. "You Americans really are a spoiled bunch."

The disgust and sarcasm dripping from his words acted like acid to melt her words of explanation as soon as they formed. Her emotions shredded by the pain and anger in his eyes, she turned her gaze to the noisy birds fighting over bread scraps along the banks of the pond.

"Just to make sure I understand," he continued, "you're saying that you can't control your urges. So if I'm not around to satisfy you, you'll find someone who can. Is that about right?"

"No, that's not what I'm saying." Her whispered voice showed she'd been wrung of strength.

"Then what are you saying?"

She faced him. "I…" She sighed. "I'm saying I love you. I'm saying I'm sorry that video hurt you. I'm saying…I'm begging you to move past this so we can get back to loving each other."

When he shook his head, she put her hand on his chest. "Look in your heart. You know the truth of how I feel about you. How you feel about me. And how we feel here is all that matters. You told me so."

"It's dead in there now. Everything I thought I knew about you is a pile of ash. I don't trust you, Kristin, and I…" he turned his face away from her, "…I don't love you anymore."

Her hands went cold and she dropped them from his chest. "No," she whispered and tried to swallow the pain coming up her throat as she felt her love take its last breaths.

"So," he said after the thick silence had widened the chasm between them, "I've told you why I broke up with you. Does knowing make you feel better? Does it make the pain go away?"

She shook her head and watched the birds scatter to the sky, wishing her pain would fly away as easily.

Without another word, Sean stood. He took his time to retrieve his backpack from where he'd dropped it. He walked away from her then, taking his heart and leaving her to absorb the fact that he didn't love her anymore. She had lost the man of her dreams, and there was nothing she could do about it.

Whoever said the truth hurts wasn't telling tales. Her heart lay in a cold lump at the bottom of her stomach, making her ache all over. Her eyes burned from a ring of fire lodged just under her eyelids caused not by tears, but by all the tears she couldn't shed. Her throat was raw from trying to swallow the bitter taste of truth and grief in his words. *I don't love you anymore.*

A long while after he'd entered the building, Kristin stood on shaky legs and, when they didn't buckle, she walked away from the bench where she'd had her heart shattered.

Distracted by her thoughts, and not paying attention to where she walked, she felt a jolt to her shoulder as she ran into a solid body. Regaining her balance with the help of the person's hand at her arm, she reached out to apologize.

"Sorry, I…" Lights popped before her eyes and she slumped into a veil of dark bubbles popping over her head.

"Kristin, are you okay?"

She swallowed, blinked a few times, and looked up into Randy's face. She nodded once, and moved out of his arms.

"Sorry about you and Sean," he said.

"You know?"

He nodded. "Word travels fast. Is there anything I can do for you?"

Staring at him through watery eyes, her lips trembling, she whispered, "I love him more than my next breath, and now he's gone. And there's nothing anyone can do about it."

Randy reached out and touched her arm. "I don't give a shit about Sean, but I do care about you. I see how miserable you are without him, how much it's hurting you. I love you, and I don't want to be part of the reason you're in this kind of pain. I'll tell you what I know, but it may not fix anything."

****

Kristin stormed up to the room she shared with Zoe, her brain on fire, Randy's words sizzling like hot oil in her body.

Zoe sat in bed, painting her toenails.

Kristin slammed the door and dropped her backpack on the floor.

Zoe looked up at Kristin then back at her toes. "You look pissed. Did you finally talk to Sean?"

"Oh, yeah. I talked to him."

"And? Did he tell you why he dumped you?"

"Uh, yeah. He said I cheated on him."

"Pffft!" Zoe muttered. "What a liar. You never cheated on him."

"That's what I said. But he had proof."

"Proof? Like what?"

"A video of me fucking somebody."

"Ouch! That's rough. So, who did you fuck? That PhD student who kept asking you out? No, wait...Jacob." She grinned. "The little tree-hugger charm you back into his bed?"

Kristin scoffed. "Who did I fuck? *You*, bitch."

Chapter Sixteen

Zoe stared at Kristin with a face showing no emotion. "Why am I to blame because you like having sex with me?"

"You recorded us having sex—"

"I already admitted that."

"You then posted the video to the internet and made sure Sean saw it." Kristin's stomach pitched at the toxic anger and grief swirling through her body. "Oh, God! How could you do that to me? You know how much I love him."

Zoe's voice stayed calm, but her eyes flashed defensively. "The person who stole my laptop must have—"

Kristin leveled a steely stare at Zoe. "I know about your deal with Randy, so don't even bother denying it."

Zoe opened her mouth as if to deny it further, then changed her mind and closed her mouth. She got up from the bed and walked over to Kristin.

"Yes, I posted the video and had Randy tell Sean about it, but I deleted it after—"

Before she could stop herself, Kristin sliced out with her hand and slapped Zoe across the face. The sickening smack of skin against skin ricocheted off the white walls. A ruby imprint of her hand materialized on Zoe's pale cheek, the physical blow knocking her backward a few steps.

Zoe's eyes widened in shock, and then quickly narrowed, drawing in her eyebrows and pulling her mouth into a tight pout. "Now you know how it feels to be betrayed by someone you love." Her voice spiraled higher with each word, showing she was on the verge of tears.

Rigid with rage, Kristin fought hard to keep from striking Zoe again. "I never did anything like this to you."

"Bullshit! Ever since you met Sean, all your time went to him. I asked you to sit with me at the movies, and you wouldn't because you're sitting with *him*. I asked you to have lunch with me, and you couldn't because you're meeting *him*. I asked you to double date with me and you said no because you want to be alone with *him*. I want to have sex with you and you said no, you only want sex with *him*. We were happy, you and me, before he came along."

"You and I were friends, roommates. I'm in *love* with Sean. I wanted a relationship with him, was building one with him, until you destroyed it."

"If he broke up with you just because you had sex with a woman, that relationship wasn't going to last anyway."

"It's not because you're a woman, it's because I slept with someone while he believed we were in an exclusive relationship. He thought I cheated on him. And you know that. It was all part of your plan."

Zoe reached out to Kristin, grabbing her hand. "I did it so you and I could be together again. I even broke up with Mason so it could be just us."

Kristin scowled at her and jerked her hand away like she'd touched something foul. "There *is* no *us*. You intentionally hurt me, Sean, Mason, and Randy—all for your selfishness. I don't want to be around someone like that."

"But all those times we made love, you said—"

"It was just sex. I was never in love with you. I was never going to be with you that way. We were roommates. Friends. Occasional sex partners. And now…"

"And now, what?"

"Now, we're nothing." Kristin pulled her suitcase out from under her bed and laid it open on the comforter. She dug into her closet, pulled out clothes, and piled them into the suitcase.

"What are you doing?" Zoe rushed over and grabbed her arm.

"I can't live here after what you did. I can't even look at you without wanting to hurt you." She shrugged Zoe's hand off and moved back to the closet for her shoes, but Zoe wrapped her arms around her, not letting her move.

"You can't go!" Tears streamed from Zoe's panic-stricken eyes. "I love you. Don't leave me. Please!"

Kristin broke her grip and pushed her aside.

Zoe collapsed onto her bed and curled up in a ball, crying, begging her, over and over, not to go.

Kristin packed enough to last until she could come back for the rest of her things when Zoe wasn't there. She zipped her suitcase, lifted it onto the floor, grabbed her backpack, and headed for the door.

"Oh, God, Kristin, don't go!" Zoe jumped off the bed and wrapped her arms around her waist. "Please!"

Kristin stared down at her. "How do you feel right now, knowing that I'm leaving and there's nothing you can do to stop it?"

"I feel like I'm dying inside."

"That's how I feel, too, because Sean broke up with me. It's how I feel because there's nothing I can do or say to convince him to take me back. What makes it even worse is that it was my best friend who helped bring this pain down on me."

"I'm so sorry! I'll fix it. If I can fix it with Sean, will you stay?"

Kristin shook her head. "It can't be fixed. He said so."

"I can't live without you."

"You'll have to learn because we're done."

Kristin stepped out of Zoe's grip, opened the door, and walked out, closing the door behind her. She heard Zoe's wild cries all the way down the hall. Only with the closing of the elevator door did they stop.

****

Sean jolted up in bed at the pounding on his door and grabbed his phone. Bleary eyes scanned the time, barely four in the morning. He cursed the early visitor.

"I'm not leaving, so you might as well open the fucking door."

The shouted words were slurred, but he recognized Zoe's voice. She'd wake the whole damned dorm if he didn't answer. He flipped on the lamp before crawling out of bed, storming to the door, and flinging it open.

"What the fuck do you want?"

"Get out of my fucking way and I'll tell you." Zoe pushed the door open and stumbled past him into the room.

She smelled like she'd showered with tequila and looked like she'd been tossed by a couple of wind storms. Her normally styled hair was in wild disarray, a big hole in the knee of her leggings showed smears of blood, and her unbuttoned sweater hung off her bare shoulders, giving her no protection from the biting cold weather.

She tripped over her own drunken feet and fell to the floor on hands and knees. She was laughing so hard she could barely move but managed to roll over and sit up.

Sean picked her up and set her down on his desk chair, then pulled the throw off his bed and wrapped it around her shoulders. Her skin felt like ice, and her lips held a blue tinge. He shook his head as he stepped away from her. Arms crossed over his chest, he glared at her.

She glared back, her eyes traveling up and down his nearly naked body. "You know, I hate your guts, but Kristin was right...you're totally hot, and I can see why she was horny for you twenty-four/seven."

The sounds of a crowd forming outside his door made him turn around. Mason, Randy, and several other guys from the floor had gathered in his doorway.

"Mason, Randy, get in here. Rest of you, go back to your rooms." He thought it would be a good idea to have witnesses, seeing that he had a drunken woman in his room at four-fucking-o-three in the morning.

Mason and Randy, shivering in their boxer shorts, T-shirts, and bare feet, shuffled inside blinking their sleepy eyes at the light. Sean shut the door.

"Mason." A smiling Zoe started to rise from the chair, but the movement seemed to make her dizzy because she plopped back into the seat. "I miss you. I never shoulda broke up with you. Come kiss me." She listed to the right and almost fell out of the chair, but Randy, who was closer, rushed to her and caught her.

She looked at the hand on her arm and followed it up to the worried face above her. "You dick. You broke our deal."

Randy jerked his hand away and moved back to stand by Mason, crossing his arms over his chest.

"What's she talking about?" Sean glared at Randy. "What deal?"

Randy shrugged like he didn't know, but his wide eyes told another story. "She's fucking drunk, man. She's doesn't know what she's saying."

Mason stepped forward and knelt in front of Zoe, taking her hand in his. "Zoe, what—"

"Oh, Mason. Mason. I love you soooo much." She leaned in to kiss him, but he dodged her sloppy alcohol-soaked mouth.

"What are you doing at Sean's at four in the morning?" he asked.

"Sean? Oh…the fucker." She stood, but her legs weren't cooperating. She swayed, falling into Mason. Her hand moved to her head. "I don't feel so good. I think I'm going to…" Her hand moved to her mouth.

Sean grabbed the trash can and handed it to Mason, who sat Zoe back down and put the can between her knees.

"God, I feel like shit," she said after the moment passed.

"How much have you had to drink?" Sean asked, eyeing the pallor of her face.

Zoe's bleary eyes found Sean across the room, and she took in his angry stare. "Not enough," she responded. "I can still…feel."

Drinking to kill the pain. That was something he knew about since losing Kristin. Sean shifted on his cold feet, staring at them instead at the eyes that were burning a hole in him. "Why are you here?"

"I did it."

"Did what?"

"I broke up you and Kristin."

His face tightened, and his arms dropped to his side and into balled fists. "Did she send you here? Well, it's not going to work. I'm not taking her back, no matter what you confess to." He opened the door and motioned for her to leave. "Go back to her and tell her—"

"Kristin didn't send me here. She..." Zoe hiccupped once, her face scrunched up, and tears flooded out of her eyes. "She's gone," she moaned.

Panic sliced through Sean and forced the question from his mouth in spite of his efforts to hold it back. He shut the door. "Gone where?"

"I don't know," she said, wiping her tears and her runny nose on her sleeve. "I don't know," she said again, the words filled with panic, right before she leaned into the trash can and threw up.

Mason held her hair back for her, then pulled off his shirt and gently wiped her mouth and tear-streaked face when she was done expelling the alcohol her body hadn't absorbed.

"Why are you telling me this?"

Mason turned angry eyes to Sean. "Leave her alone. She's not in any condition to answer a bunch of questions. I'm taking her to my room." He held her around the shoulders and helped her to her feet.

"She came to my fucking door!" Sean bellowed. "She's not going anywhere until I know why."

Mason sat her back down, but kept one arm around her in a protective stance Sean half admired, considering she'd dumped him and, hell, cheated on him with Kristin.

"She found out about my plan and she packed her things and left. She hates me! Says she can't even look at me."

"Your plan?" Sean asked.

Her gaze zagged to Randy, who looked away and shifted his weight from foot to foot.

"Zoe, what plan?" Sean repeated.

She looked back to Sean when he barked at her and answered him sharply. "Kristin was mine before you came along. We studied together, partied together, ate together, worked out together, had the hottest sex together. We were happy until you ruined everything!"

Mason was the only one in the room stunned by Zoe's confession. He dropped his arm from her shoulders and rounded on her. "You and Kris were lovers?" He turned away, putting his hands on his stomach as if *he* were going to be sick. He turned back to her. "You're a lesbian?"

"No, I'm not a lesbian. I just…I like sex. I love you…and I love Kristin. And she used to love me until *Sean* came along." She said his name like a curse.

Mason stumbled away from her and slid down the wall onto the floor, his head in his hands, trying to absorb this biting new reality.

"Okay, so you don't like me much," Sean said, prompting her to continue and not get sidetracked. "I get that. What did you do about it?"

"I thought of a way to break you guys up so I could have her to myself again. And it would have worked if *somebody* hadn't sold me out." Her eyes shot venomous darts at Randy, who wilted under her assault.

"What was your part in this?" Sean stared down at the slighter and shorter man who looked like he wanted to disappear into the wall.

"She said you were the only thing in the way of me having Kristin to myself. So I agreed to help her break you guys up. Plus she offered me sex." His eyes darted to Mason, who looked like he wanted to beat the shit out of him. "Sorry. She's really persuasive. And scary."

"We know what she did for you. What did you do for her?" Sean asked.

"Told you about that video of her and Kristin."

"So it came from her?" His chin pointed to Zoe.

Randy nodded.

"Did you tell anyone else about it? Show it to anyone?"

Randy looked like he'd been insulted. "No. I would never do that to Kristin."

Sean turned back to Zoe, who was all but falling asleep in the chair. "Zoe!"

Her eyes popped open and found his.

"Why are you telling me all this?"

"I have to stop the pain." She clawed at her chest and stomach and started crying again. "When Kristin left, I told her I felt like I was dying. She said that's how she felt when you left her. How could you do that to her, you bastard! She loves you so much. She thought you loved her, too. She said you were the one."

Sean knew the ache of betrayal, the feeling of wanting to die because it would stop the pain. "If she loved me so fucking much, she wouldn't have cheated on me," he shouted.

"You're an ass!" she yelled back then laughed. "That video was from the day after you walked her home from Randy's. Can you believe it? She'd known you a few hours—hadn't even gone on a date with you yet—and she wanted you. She was already fantasizing about making love with you. She was already…"

Zoe's breath caught in her lungs at the words she had to say. "She was already falling in love with you. It was my hands, my mouth, that made her come, and she called out *your* name! You wouldn't take care of her, but I did." She poked a finger against her chest. "I did. And she still wanted you more."

"Did she have sex with you after that?"

She covered her mouth with her hand as if she were going to be sick again. "I tried to…after your breakfast, after your stupid walk in the rain, after the night of the movie…" She shook her head as if trying to fling away the memory.

The night of the movie—the first time he'd touched and tasted her delicious breasts.

"She told me no. Said she was with you and wouldn't cheat on the man she loved."

Sean felt a tingling in his body and a weight lifting as the numbness began to melt slowly away. His heart raced at the glimmer of hope that Zoe spoke the truth. "Why should I believe you? This is probably another lie you two cooked up to make me look like an arse."

"You hurt her, bad, and you are an ass for it—but I know you did it because of what I did. I know exactly how she's feeling, and how you're feeling, because I feel that way too. And it sucks. I want to fix it so none of us feels this way anymore."

"If by 'fix it' you mean getting Kristin and me back together, it's not going to happen."

"Fuck, Sean!" Randy exploded from the corner.

"Quit being so damned stubborn. If Kristin loved me the way she loves you, I'd do anything—forgive anything—to keep her in my life. Do you want your pride or do you want an awesome woman who's beautiful and kind and hot and loves you more than...Do you know what she told me? She was crying her head off and she said she *loved you more than her next breath*. Shit, *I* almost fuckin' cried. Sometimes you can't have absolute proof about things, you just have to trust. If you can't see how much she loves you and how lucky you are, then you don't deserve her."

"They're right," added Mason from his spot on the floor. "Kris is the most caring and honest person I know. She'd never betray or intentionally hurt anyone, especially someone she loves. She loves you and you broke her heart for it. If you ask me, she's better off without you." He stood and pointed to Zoe. "Can I take her home now, or did you want to torture her a little more?"

"She cheated on you, dumped you for no reason, and treated you like shit. How can you just forgive her like nothing happened?"

"It's what you do when you love someone." He picked Zoe up, cradled her in his arms, and carried her to the door.

Randy opened it for him and followed him out. He paused just outside the doorway and turned back.

"You'll never forgive yourself if you don't fix things with Kristin," he said.

"Don't think I've forgotten the part you played in this." Sean added.

"No, I didn't think you had."

Randy shuffled next door to his room, giving Sean time to absorb everything he'd heard.

A different intensity of pain sliced through his body. Guilt. Remorse. Regret. Shame. That he was so quick to toss Kristin aside after all they'd meant to each other. That he didn't trust in the love they shared. That he wasn't even *willing* to consider her point of view.

He shut and locked his door and climbed back into bed. He was no fool. He realized that Zoe could be lying, even though her slurred, emotion-filled words rang of truth. Kristin had showed him her love in so many ways, in and out of bed. Maybe he *had* taken that love for granted. Hearing Mason and Randy and Zoe describe her love for him certainly shined a whole new light on it.

She loved him. Hadn't cheated on him. He believed it. He felt it. And his heart swelled at the truth confronting him.

As the sun rose over the Sandia mountains, so too did the solution that would rid him of his pain. He would win her back. He could live without his pride, but he couldn't live without Kristin.

Chapter Seventeen

Kristin moved into a one-bedroom apartment in the University-run housing complex for married and grad students. It felt odd not having a roommate, but being alone would give her the time she needed to work on her thesis and to work on mending her broken and battered heart. It would never be as whole as it was before Sean, Zoe, and Randy had their way with it, but it could be better than it was now, which was full of cracks and eaten away by the acid of grief.

There were days when all she did was go to class, come home, and cry. Sean was the last thing she thought about before going to sleep and the first thing she thought of when she woke. He filled her dreams almost every night.

She planned out every word she would say if he called and asked her to forgive him and take him back. When the break up was new, her response was a desperate and immediate yes. As she got used to being alone, her response was an angrier, "how can *I* trust *you* again." After almost a week had passed since she confronted him, with no word from him, she no longer thought about what she would say because she was sure the call would never come.

They were truly over, and it was time she took his advice and began the painful first steps of moving on.

****

Sean's finger hovered over Kristin's name in his phone list. *Call her, you coward,* he taunted. *Apologize. Beg her to forgive you and take you back.* He pulled in a shaky breath, released it, and hit send. It rang and went straight to voice mail.

Even though he had rehearsed what he would say when he talked to her, had a response for just about every argument she might come up with to not see him, when the tone to leave a message sounded, he suddenly couldn't remember one word of it.

"Kri…" His voice died on her name, his throat so dry he couldn't swallow. He covered the phone and cleared his throat, trying again. "Kristin, it's Sean. We should talk—I mean, I'd like to talk to you about…us. Meet me tomorrow after your class at that coffee shop in the library…you know, the one we went to after our walk."

****

Kristin's heart beat so fast it propelled her feet forward faster than her brain could command her to turn and run away. Her stomach spun as her eyes searched frantically for Sean's face in the crowd of coffee addicts occupying the dozen or so tables in the small shop. She heard her name and looked toward the area in the back, where several couches and coffee tables offered space for more leisurely sipping and conversation.

When her eyes found his, the breath left her lungs in one whoosh. The welcoming look in his gaze brought it back and lifted the corners of her mouth into a tentative half-smile, though she didn't quite have the confidence to make it a real one. She dug her thumbnail into the flesh of her finger, the pain ensuring her this was no dream. Her pulse buzzed in her ears and in her head, rejoicing but scared shitless in the moment.

Sean moved toward her, and she toward him. They met in the middle of the room and stopped, facing each other, trying to read the emotions hidden behind eyes locked tight.

"Hi," he said.

He looked happy to see her. "Hi," she responded, cautious but happy.

"How are you, darlin'?"

He called her darlin'! But could she trust him? "Fine. You?"

"Better now that you're here."

His hand cupped her face. Joy rushed through her at his touch and sped up her heart. She breathed in sharply and whispered his name.

As if that were the signal, they rushed into each other's arms, their mouths fitting and mating, pouring out the love—the hunger—they had stored up since being apart.

When someone bumped them and muttered, "Get a room," they parted. Smiling, his eyes shining, he took her hand and led her back to the spot he'd claimed on the couch for them. They settled down onto the worn cushions next to each other and kissed again.

Realizing they had an audience, they pulled back, but he kept his arm around her shoulders, keeping her close, and she held onto his other hand.

"I didn't think you'd come," he said, his voice soft.

"I almost didn't. I was afraid it was just some kind of a cruel joke."

He brushed a strand of hair from her face and cupped her jaw. "I'm glad you did."

"Me, too." She put her hand on top of his and kissed his palm.

"Kristin, I was an arse. I hurt you, and I'm sorry for that and for not trusting you."

She caressed his face, stared into his eyes. "I didn't understand how you could say you loved me, but then so easily throw away what we had."

"For the rest of my life, I'll be sorry for causing you that pain. But now that I know the truth, we can get back to where we belong—together."

She felt a cold fog slip between them and wrap around her neck in a choking grip. "Now that you know the truth?"

"Yeah, darlin'. I know what happened."

"What do you mean?"

"Zoe confessed everything—her plan to break us up, her making and posting the video and having Randy tell me about it, her admission that you stopped sleeping with her even before our first date. Everything."

Kristin's stomach clenched, and her heart tumbled to her knees. The euphoric haze she had stepped into when she'd arrived burned away, leaving her more disheartened than ever. Her smile faded and she pulled back from him, her hands gripping the strap of her purse.

Sean must have noticed something in her reaction because his smile faded and his face froze into a mask of confusion. "Are you okay?"

She swallowed hard, struggling to pull the words from her battered heart. "You believed *her*. Not me."

He shook his head, confusion in his eyes and not understanding her point. "What?"

"You loved *me*, but you didn't trust me enough to believe that I'd never hurt you like that. You hate Zoe, but you believed her. Explain that to me."

"I was hurt and pissed off. I wasn't thinking straight."

She kept talking as if he hadn't spoken. "Until someone else gave you proof that what I said was the truth, you couldn't—wouldn't—believe me."

"Dammit, I love you. I was wrong not to believe you. I'm sorry, and I'll never make that mistake again."

"Neither will I." She grabbed her purse, her knuckles almost white from the tight grip she had not only on her purse but on her emotions.

"What does that mean?"

"It means I accept your apology, but I can't be with someone who has so little faith in me or our love that he'll believe everyone *but* me." She turned away from him and ran out of the coffee shop. And he didn't try to stop her.

****

Stunned by Kristin's reaction, Sean sat glued to the couch after she ran out. He thought they'd be celebrating their reunion by now, maybe headed to his room or hers, but instead he was left trying to figure out *what the hell happened.* Feeling curious eyes on him, he left the coffee shop and started home, going over everything they'd said, trying to pinpoint where it all went wrong and why she was so mad, so disappointed, with him.

He stewed for days over Kristin's words, finally coming to the decision that he was better off without her. He went to the bar with some of the guys from the archaeology department several nights a week, trying to drink her out of his mind. But even the stoutest drinks couldn't erase the memory of her face, her voice, her touch.

"Fuck her, man," slurred his officemate, Mark, and patted his back. "You gave her your heart, and what did she do? She kicked it to the curb and stomped on it. You're better off without her."

Kurt, who rounded out their trio, nodded, grunting his agreement.

But Sean knew he'd never believe that. He took out his phone. "No, I can make it right again."

A chorus of unasked-for advice roared from the table.

"She won't even talk to you, man."

"Don't do it. Never a good idea to drunk-dial your ex."

"No, really. She'll listen this time." Sean stood, staggered a bit, then righted himself. "She loves me."

The guys tried to get him to sit down, but he refused and made his way to the door. He stepped out into the cool, March night. The chill in the air acted like a slap in the face to rouse his senses. He thought of home.

The St. Patrick's Festival would have started today. Were he home, he'd be in the local pub with his best mate, Ian, and others from the dig team, playing trad and dancing and drinking real beer. He for damn sure wouldn't be in this lifeless bar drinking piss for beer with guys who didn't understand the depth of love in an Irishman's soul.

But if he were home, he'd be even farther away from Kristin. And he was already as far away from her as he could handle.

He scrolled through his phone, stopping on the picture he'd taken of them together the night they'd made love. They were in his bed, wrapped around each other so tight they were a part of each other, their faces glowing and glistening, smiling and facing each other instead of the eye of the phone's camera he held above them.

"You love me. You can't stop loving that fast."

He stared at the picture until it swam before his eyes, then he dialed her number. She answered on the second ring, and not with the warm hello he'd hoped to hear.

"I asked you not to call me anymore."

"Hello, darlin'. It's me, the man you love more than your next breath."

"Don't use my words against me, especially when you're drunk."

"I'm Irish. I'm incapable of getting drunk."

"Goodbye."

"Kristin, wait."

Silence.

"Kristin?"

Silence.

"Kristin!"

"What?"

The panic slid away when he heard her voice.

"Ah, Kristin," he exhaled her name on a sigh. He leaned back against the wall of the bar and stared into the blanket of stars overhead. "Darlin', I need to see your eyes...touch your face...smell your skin...taste your mouth. Let me come over. We'll talk all night, shout at each other, cry on each other, wrap our bodies together in a knot so tight nothing can break us again.

We'll watch the sun come up in each other's arms and, in the morning light, you'll see the proof of how right our love is, no matter what idiotic things we've done to each other. Say yes. Let me take you back to our Honahlee."

He paused, waiting for her answer, for the yes he needed to hear. He only got her whispered voice saying his name. He heard the tears in the spaces between her breaths. Heard the dead silence that told him she had hung up. Felt the knife in his heart that told him her answer was no.

He shoved the phone into his pocket and held up the wall until the cold froze the alcohol warming him and seeped into his bones. Then he started the walk home, his foggy brain sloshing ideas around for getting her back.

Spring break, which was a few short days away, would give him time to get her to come to her senses like he'd come to his.

****

Kristin dropped the bag of cherries into her cart, not taking time to check her list. With spring break in full force, and nothing to distract her from thoughts of Sean, she lived on automatic. She had once bought cherries from this store, so she was buying them today.

Sean's latest words replayed in her mind constantly. She had never heard such passionate, genuine-sounding words from any man who claimed to love her. Everything about him screamed his love for her. So why couldn't she take that small step and open her heart to him again?

It came down to fear. She was afraid to care that deeply again. Afraid that if he hurt her again, she wouldn't survive it. The flipside of knowing such great love was the possibility of knowing great pain.

"Excuse me, darlin', can I reach around you to get some of those cherries?"

Kristin shook herself out of her daze and looked up at the man standing beside her who had spoken in a lovely Irish lilt. Her heart flipped onto its side when her eyes tangled with his dark blue ones and saw a quirky grin on the sweetest mouth she had ever tasted.

Her eyebrows came together in a scowl. "What are you doing here?"

His eyebrows lifted, giving his face the look of innocence he was probably going for. "Buying cherries."

"Cherries? Really? That's your story?"

"I like...cherries," he said, his eyes settling on her mouth before drifting back to her eyes, his grin growing wider and more dazzling the more her face flushed.

"They're all yours." She turned her cart to move around him, but he stepped in front of it.

"I've seen you around, darlin', but I don't think we've met. I'm Sean."

She knew what he was doing—trying to start over—but she had already face-planted on the bottom of that muddy pool once. But seeing his hand outstretched toward her, hearing his voice float through her like the melody of her favorite song, rooted her in place, making her unable to move away from the spell he was casting over her.

His eyes and smile compelled her to respond and, before she knew what her body was doing, her arm had extended and her hand had made the easy glide to his. His touch was as warm and comforting as she remembered, and it made her insides tremble. She forced herself to remember to breathe. She forced herself to remember her name.

"Kristin."

"I see you like sushi." He nodded to the package in her cart.

She glanced at the package then back to his face.

"I've never tried it meself," he said, "but I'd like to. Any tips for a first-timer?"

Noticing he still held her hand in his grip, she pulled away and gripped the shopping cart handle with both hands.

"Don't buy it from the grocery store."

"Why are you buying it here then?"

"It's easier than eating alone in a restaurant."

The look of pity on his face pissed her off. "That better not be pity on your face, Sean O'Neill, because if it is—"

His eyes flew wide in mock surprise. "Pity? Naw. That was my 'thinking' face."

At her silence, he continued. "Ask me what I was thinking."

She shook her head, not wanting to play this game. But after a moment she asked, "What were you thinking?"

"So glad you asked. I was thinking we should go have sushi together. At your favorite restaurant. I could use a lesson in all things raw."

The flow of energy filling her body during their casual conversation turned ice cold at his suggestion. "No." She tried to steer the cart around him and escape, but he stood in her way, holding onto the cart.

"No expectations, no demands, just sharing a meal.

We won't discuss anything you don't want to discuss. Hell, we don't even have to talk if you don't want."

Paralyzed from her feet to her vocal chords, she could only stare at him, remembering how much he'd loved her and how much he'd hurt her. "No."

"You don't want me to poison myself by eating bad sushi, do you? Do you really want that on your conscience?"

She didn't want him to be charming and cute. She didn't want to respond to charming and cute. One hand rose to her mouth and she plucked at her lips to cover a little grin.

He picked up the cello-wrapped sushi from her cart. "Does that little smile you're trying to hide mean I can put this back?"

She dropped her hand, letting her gaze dart to his before quickly settling on the plate of nastiness. "I can't believe I was going to buy that."

He laughed, and she almost joined him but swallowed the mirth at the last second. He convinced her to put back the few items in her cart so they could go to dinner that night.

"My bike's over here," he said and started walking toward it. "We can come back for your car."

She didn't walk with him. "No, I'll meet you there. I need to go home and change."

His gaze took in her flip flops, shorts, long-sleeved T-shirt, and ponytail. "Why? You look...perfect."

Seeing the longing in his eyes, she turned away from it. "I'll meet you there," she said, wrapping her words in a tone that barred further argument. She told him the name of the place and he captured the location and directions on his phone.

****

As the hour of their dinner approached, doubts filled her thoughts.

I should have walked away when I first saw him in the store.

Why should I run away from someone I want so badly?

I should call him and cancel.

It'll be great to be with him again…it's been so long and he looked so damn good.

She sat on her bed in her bra and panties for a full fifteen minutes, arguing with herself and weighing her conflicting desires. When she finally left her apartment late, she still wasn't sure she was doing the right thing. She just hoped she wouldn't regret it too much.

Chapter Eighteen

Sean was already seated at a table when Kristin arrived at the restaurant nearly fifteen minutes late. He walked up front to meet her as she came in, a warm smile on his face.

"I thought you'd bailed on me."

"I almost did."

He put his hand on her lower back and escorted her to the table. "Glad you didn't." He held out her chair for her before taking his seat next to her. A waiter came to their table and handed her a single yellow daffodil.

"Sean asked us to bring this out when you arrived. Please take your time with the menu. I'll be back in a moment to take your order."

She turned to Sean. His eyes were shining so bright she had to look away.

She looked at the flower, then at him. "Why?"

"Renewal."

Her mother's early teachings floated back, reminding her that today—the spring equinox, Ostara—was seen as a prime time to get back things once lost. Is that what he had in mind? She dipped her nose into the cup of the flower and inhaled its spring-time fragrance. No flower better represented renewal than the daffodil, so he got that right. She wondered whether he had called his friend Ian's mother, who was something of a witch, for advice.

"Are you hoping we'll experience a renewal?"

He smiled. "I thought we agreed not to talk about us?"

She shook her head and grabbed the menu. She felt his eyes on her, but refused to look up and risk losing all control. First a smile, then she'd be romping in the backseat of her car with him.

"Do you know what you'd like to try?" she asked.

He held his arms wide, his hands toward her. "I'm completely at your mercy."

"That's a risky place to be."

"I trust you, darlin'. Completely."

Their flirty sparring and the bees buzzing in her stomach told her that she was the one in a risky place, not him.

Thankfully, the waiter showed up then. She ordered items that she liked and that she thought Sean might like. When the food arrived, he stared at the plate with a look that said he wasn't sure he could take a bite out of the colorful and artfully arranged raw chunks. To his credit, he smiled.

"How do we…do…this?"

She picked up the long slender envelope at her plate and opened it, taking out the wooden chopsticks. He did the same. She placed the chopsticks, one then the other, in her hand, demonstrating how to hold them. She reached into the plate of food, picked up a piece of yellowtail, dipped it in the wasabi, and placed it on her plate. He tried to follow her lead, but the sticks wouldn't cooperate.

"This is the hardest thing I've ever tried to do," he admitted good naturedly as one stick clattered to his plate for the third time.

Chuckling, she got up and moved to stand behind him, placing the chopsticks in his hands. Standing this close to him, touching him and not kissing him, was the hardest thing *she'd* ever done. He smelled so good. His skin was so warm. When he turned his head toward her and stared at her lips, her knees went weak.

"Pay attention," she teased. "There are no forks here, so if you want to eat, you gotta learn the sticks."

"If you can use a fork to eat ice cream, surely I can use my fingers to eat this?"

"Sure you can...you and the two-year-old over there in the booth."

Sean turned in time to see rice and bits of food spill from the toddler's mouth onto her T-shirt. His hearty laugh warmed her pink parts.

Mr. Overachiever soon got the hang of the sticks and was able to pick up the food from the serving dish, move it to his plate, then back to the service dish without dropping it all over the table and into his lap.

"All this work has made me hungry. When do we get to eat?"

She explained what everything was.

"Which one do you like best?" he asked.

"The yellowtail."

He inspected the plate again. "I don't see any with tails."

She pointed to the piece on her plate.

"Okay." He picked up one like it from the serving plate, dipped it in a little wasabi like she'd showed him, and brought it to his mouth, pausing. "If you have to rush me to hospital, tell them I'm allergic to penicillin and oxycodone."

She laughed and watched him intently as he put the

whole piece in his mouth. Chewed tentatively, then with more enthusiasm. Swallowed.

"Well?" she asked, surprised at how eager she was for him to like it—to like something she liked.

"I like it. I didn't expect to, but I do. What else?"

He tried the eel and squid next, which he liked. The tuna, not so much. The vegetable rolls and the fried tofu pouches were also winners, as was the tempura shrimp and California rolls she'd ordered in case he couldn't stomach raw.

She was impressed at how eagerly he tried everything and did so with gusto. That was his way, she realized. Everything with gusto. It was one of the many things that had made her fall in love with him. A warm rush tingled across her skin at the knowledge.

After they finished everything on the platter, he suggested they order some sake or another pot of tea. She could tell he wanted to stay awhile, to talk, to subtly remind her how well they fit together. But she knew it was a mistake to get any closer to him, so she refused, saying she had a lot of work to do the following day. They split the bill—at her insistence.

"Don't laugh, but I like sushi more than green chile cheeseburgers," he said as he walked her to her car.

She blinked her eyes and opened her mouth in shock. "I never thought I'd hear you say that."

They laughed.

"This was fun. Aren't you glad you didn't bail?"

"Yeah, I am." And she meant it. "I haven't had good sushi in a long time."

"So it was just the sushi you enjoyed? Not the company?" His voice was low and she felt it drum in her heart.

"It wasn't just the sushi."

"Maybe we can do it again sometime." His gaze caught hers and held, making her feel like she was standing on the crumbling edge of a deep abyss. A dervish of emotion spiraled in her heart, warning her to break the connection before she fell in.

"It's late. I should go." She turned, hand on her car door, but he caught her hand.

"It's not even nine. Let's go get some ice cream. Chocolate…" he tempted.

"Thank you, but no." She tugged her hand, but he wouldn't let go.

"Coffee?"

"No." She pulled her hand away.

"Kristin," he said. "Don't go."

She felt herself getting lost in his eyes and his voice again, captured by the feelings his one touch set loose in her, and she couldn't force herself to break free.

His hand moved to her face, caressing her cheek. "Stay with me. Just a little longer. I miss you."

Because she didn't move away, because she didn't resist and tell him no, he dipped his head and touched his lips to hers.

In that instant, the renewal he'd talked about burst into being inside her. Senses and feelings bloomed. Desire flooded her cells.

It felt so good with him, so right. But it was wrong. Without trust, it would always be wrong.

She shivered and pushed out of his arms, folding hers in front of her like a shield. "I can't do this, Sean. I don't have the courage to let you in again."

He took her hand and put it on his chest where his heart lived.

"Do you feel that? It started beating again the moment I saw you in the store today and you spoke to me. I've felt dead inside since we've been apart."

A spark of anger forced her to jerk her hand away. "When you threw me out of your life, you not only broke my heart, you broke all of me. I can't give you what you want. I'm not whole."

"Neither one of us is whole because we're apart from each other. I love you, Kristin, and I know you love me. Take me back, and we'll both begin to heal."

Shaking her head, she moved away from him. "I don't want to love you anymore. It hurts too much."

He stopped her. "You don't mean that."

She closed her eyes. "Yes, I do."

"Look, maybe we moved too fast the first time. But we can start over. Take it slow. Give you time to learn to trust me again."

Her skin tingled when he slid his hand up her arm, and she noticed a slight jolt to her heart as if it were trying to beat again. She backed away from him, from his talented hands, his pleading eyes, and his enticing voice.

"Your heart may be beating again, Sean," she pulled open her door, "but mine's still scarred and bleeding. Fast or slow, it won't survive another round with you."

"Promise me you'll think about it."

She shook her head knowing that it was all she would be able to think about now. "No promises." She got in and closed the door. It broke her heart to see him in the rearview mirror, standing where she'd left him, watching her drive away.

****

The following night, as she climbed into bed, she received a text from Sean. "Thanks for not bailing on dinner last night. I enjoyed it."

She didn't respond, and he didn't follow up.

The night after that, she received another text. "Sweet dreams."

Another night, another text. "Craving wasabi and that yellowfin thing. Have to make a run to the grocery store."

She chuckled, and her fingers ached to text back, "It's yellow*tail*, and DO NOT GO TO THE GROCERY STORE!" but she resisted. Then she sent it anyway. And couldn't go to sleep, a ball of anxiety tumbling in her stomach, until he texted back, "Whew! I resisted. Thanks, darlin'."

The following night was a quote: "Feeling fear doesn't always mean you should stop doing something. Push on. The best surprises are often waiting for you just on the other side."

"Another old Irish saying?" she texted.

"Something my da always said. Night, darlin'."

He texted her every night for a nearly a week. But at the end of that week, there was no text.

She tossed and turned all night, contemplating what this meant. The thought gnawing on her brain when she rose with the sun the following morning was that she had been wrong to see him again. She would not make that mistake again. Would not listen to his pleas or his promises again. She would truly get on with her life without him.

After an hour of mind-clearing, Qi balancing, yoga, she showered, ate breakfast, dressed, and prepared her backpack for a long day of research at the library. The drama this semester had put her behind, and she had precious little time left to complete the first draft of her master's thesis. She slung the pack over her shoulder and opened the door.

There on the welcome mat was a single daffodil, its stem wrapped in a wet paper towel and foil, and a DVD that had "Play Me" written on it in Sean's bold script.

She took the flower and DVD into her bedroom, sat on the bed, loaded the DVD into her laptop, and hesitantly hit play.

Sean sat on his bed in a T-shirt and sweats, looking into the camera.

"Hey, darlin'." He grinned and scratched his hand through squirrely golden locks, which stood on end. "Since I haven't had any luck getting you back using my charm and good looks, I thought I'd try something else—" He leaned over and picked up a guitar and held it in position to play, putting his hands in place. "—like making a complete arse of myself."

He plays the guitar? Kristin thought. *I didn't know that. Why didn't I know that?* In her musings, she realized she'd missed something he said, so she rewound it.

"This song is called *To Make You Feel My Love*. The song pretty much says what's in my heart. So…" He took a breath and released it. "…here goes."

His fingers strummed the strings, and soft, soulful chords strummed inside her. He began to sing the words of his heart, sweet lyrics in a raspy, edgy voice. She listened to the song intently, as if the words themselves held the key to getting her life back.

The sincere expression on his face and in his voice brought tears to her eyes. She let them fall and wash away the anger for and mistrust of this man she loved.

His final words ended on a slight crack in his voice as he gently plucked the strings of the guitar, playing the final soulful notes. Then he opened his eyes and stared directly into the camera, into her eyes.

"Kristin, I messed up, darlin'…bad, and I hurt you. Give me a chance to make it up to you. I'll make you happy. I promise." He put down the guitar and picked up his phone.

The ice block enclosing her heart melted at his words, at his sincerity, at the amount of love that came through the screen from him to her. She felt the broken pieces of her heart fusing together.

Sean got up from the bed and turned off the camera. Her screen went black. She reached out to start it over, to watch it again, but then his face filled the screen again.

"Oh, in case you've deleted my number, it's…" He left his number and the screen again went black.

Kristin had never deleted his number. She scrolled through her list, found his entry, and was ready to hit the button that would connect her to him when his face again filled the screen. She chuckled and stopped to see what he was up to.

"Sorry to interrupt you from deciding whether to call me, but I forgot that there was something I wanted to show you." He walked backward and pulled off his T-shirt as he spoke, giving her a grand view of his chiseled chest and stomach. "Something that might help you decide."

He untied his sweats.

Her heart beat faster in her chest as his sweats dropped to the floor and he pointed to the only stitch of clothing he had on—boxers, the green ones with big red lips across Kiss The Legend.

"The ones I was wearing the night we met. The ones that made you fall in love with me. You couldn't take your eyes off of them."

Kristin smiled and ran a finger over the image. "I remember."

"If you come back to me, I'll wear them every day for you. I'll let you wear them if you want. Or I'll buy you a pair in your size and we'll spend all day and night wearing nothing but our matching boxers."

He stood there grinning at her, looking a bit like an overgrown leprechaun. Cute, full of mischief, and just barely hiding his pot of gold.

"One last thing I want to show you." His eyes grew heavy and he tucked his thumbs into the waistband of those boxers, tugging them lower.

Her breath caught in her throat when she saw a shadow of his dark thatch and what looked like the start of one fine erection that could be hers.

As he moved the boxers lower, he moved closer to the camera, hiding the image she craved. He held the boxers up to the camera before tossing them over his shoulder.

"You don't get to see unless you call me." The joking mask fell away, revealing a serious face on her screen. "I love you, darlin'."

He held up his phone and the image again faded to black. This time he did not come back to deliver another message meant to entice her. But then, maybe he knew it wouldn't be needed.

Chapter Nineteen

Her heart pounding against her ribs, adrenaline pumping through her veins, and love overflowing every cell of her body, Kristin shot out of her apartment and was at Sean's dorm parking lot in ten minutes. She stood at the locked front door to his dorm when she realized that, since it was still spring break, she might not be able to get in. That he might not be there. That she had raced over for nothing. Then she remembered the side door the guys usually left unlocked. It was unlocked, and she ran up the back stairs to his room.

Sean answered the door in nothing but a towel. Ah! Sometimes the biggest risks return the biggest rewards!

"Kristin? Hi!" he said, surprise filling his voice and lighting his eyes. "I thought you'd call."

She fought to keep her face expressionless, stoic even, but inside she was about to shimmy out of her skin. "I thought you deserved a face-to-face. But I can leave."

"No, no. Showing up is great. Perfect."

She dropped her eyes and bit her tongue to keep joy from bursting into laughter. "Can I come in?"

"Of course." He moved aside and closed the door after she'd walked through.

She looked around the tiny room, remembering the love they'd made here. It was like she was back in the Honahlee they'd created—she felt magically happy and at home. Her memories acted like gas sprinkled on the flame of desire sparking inside her. It didn't matter that they'd known each other so short a time. It didn't matter that he'd made a mistake. It didn't matter that she still nursed a healing heart. She loved him and wanted him in her life.

She felt him behind her, his hands on her shoulders, and she shivered. He turned her toward him, his eyes hopeful but anxious, with that little half grin of his parting his lips, his eyes brighter and bluer than she'd ever seen them.

They stood together silently, searching each other's eyes for answers.

"Nice DVD," she said.

His eyes dropped sheepishly, as if a little embarrassed by it. "I wasn't sure whether it would help me or hurt me, what with my terrible singing and plucking."

"No, it was beautiful. I liked it."

"Good. So…Is it good news you're bringing me?"

"I'm afraid not."

He dropped his hands from her arms and seemed to stumble back a hair's breadth. "Oh." The tiny word slipped from his mouth like a groan.

She moved forward. "Uh, yeah. You said something the other day about going slow this time. Well, I'm sorry…" She put her fingers on the little knot where he had tucked in the tail of the towel and yanked it free. "…that's completely unacceptable." She tossed the towel aside. "I've been without Mr. Blarney far too long to go slow."

"Ack, woman. Why do you insist on calling him such a wimpy name?" He grabbed his cock and lifted it toward her. "He deserves a name more fitting of his monolithic stature."

She laughed and took the monolith in her hands. "How about The Legend? Does that appropriately reflect his magnificence?" She stroked him as she spoke, thrilled with her power to make him grow long and hard.

On a sigh, his eyes closed. "Darlin', you can call him whatever you want."

"Sean, I miss you. And I don't just mean Mr. Blar—uh, The Legend. I want you in my life, in my heart, in my bed." She laughed and tossed a glance over her shoulder at his bed. "Any bed. Tell me you still want me."

"I still want you." He took her hands in his, kissed them. "I prayed you'd come back to me."

"Well, I'm here. So why haven't you kissed me?"

He grinned, put his hands low on her hips, and pulled her to him. "God blessed man with two heads, but cursed him with the inability to use both at once. I wasn't thinking straight."

"Another old Irish saying?"

"Actually, it is." He smiled at her. "Forgive me, Kristin."

"Forgiven."

Joy burst inside her as his lips took hers. The heat of his kiss made her feel like she could dissolve into a mist between his hands.

His fingers tugged the hem of her shirt up, and she lifted her arms so he could pull it off. While he unhooked her bra, she flipped open the button on her skirt, yanked down the zipper, and let the material drop to her feet. His hands cupped her breasts and feasted on them with his hungry mouth, licking and sucking the pink points.

Her hands moved to his hard dick, but he lifted her up in his strong arms and carried her to the bed, laying her, naked and desperate for him, on the rumpled sheets.

He kissed her as he lay beside her, the stabbing heat and pressure of his cock against her side. Her hungry mouth rose to meet his. Her pulse throbbed in her pussy, like it was calling to him, telling him she was ready for him...past ready.

"I want you inside me. So much." She growled more than spoke the words.

"For once, darlin', I won't make you wait...too long."

His eyes held her in place as his hand crawled up her thigh to the wet spot between her legs. She opened herself to him and released a long sigh when he slipped his finger into her wet pussy. She stroked his dick, circling her hips against his hand, begging for more.

He released a shaky breath. "I've missed you, darlin'. So much. The feel of you. The taste of you. The smell of you. It makes me feel alive."

"I missed you, too." His fingers were nestled at her heat, sending hot shivers up and down her spine. She felt the desire rolling off of him, off of her, and she wanted to take it all inside her, use it to drive them both into oblivion. She was arching against his hand, panting with the need to have him inside her. "Which is why you really need to get inside me now."

He chuckled and rose over her, letting his dick jab the entrance to her pussy. She guided him closer and rubbed herself against the head of his magnificence, letting it distribute their juice onto each other. She cried out when he pulled back, opening her eyes. "What are you doing to me?"

She saw him rolling a condom on the erection that would soon be all hers. "Shit! Tomorrow, we're getting tested so we can do away with these fucking condoms," she growled in frustration.

He laughed. "I'm clean, darlin', but I'll do whatever you want."

"What I want is—"

He plunged into her, sending a rush of breath sliding from her mouth. "Oh, God!" A contented smile appeared on her face. "Thank you." She was where she was meant to be.

The moment stilled for her, and she absorbed the feel of him inside her. His smell. The weight of him. The love in his eyes. The touch of his hands.

Then his mouth took her lips and time started again. Her nails clawed his ass to bring him even closer to her. His hips thrust against her, his cock moving in and out of her pussy in one long sensation of pleasure. Urgent for each other, they sped up, moving together, lifting each other higher.

Her legs clutched his waist, her arms his back, holding him tight, burying him inside her, creating their own world. She ignored the sweat beading on her forehead, on his, and for long moments forgot to breathe, and just kept up the sweet rhythm that would carry them to the end where they would live or die together.

She plunged off the peak into the abyss, her whole body releasing, convulsing with the force of her orgasm. "I'm coming, Sean! I'm coming."

He was still pumping into her, helping her ride out her wave, when she felt him go rigid, every muscle in him straining with his release. He groaned and pressed even deeper into her pussy as he came, the flare of pleasure bursting in his blue eyes.

He collapsed onto her, his flesh filling her and hers hugging him, their hearts pulsing blood throughout their joined bodies.

"I love you." His voice was rough and his breath was as erratic as hers. "So much. I'm glad you came back."

"I'm glad you wanted me back," she said as he kissed her mouth, again and again.

"I'll always want you. Always love you."

"I'll always love you."

He put his mouth against her chest and dropped kisses here and there on the flushed skin that covered her heart. "I know. I see it in your heart. I feel it in mine. And that's all the proof I'll ever need."

****

"Which drawers are mine, darlin'?" Sean asked as Kristin walked into their bedroom. He held a stack of T-shirts in one hand and a stack of boxers in the other.

They had semi-shared her apartment since getting back together in March. He couldn't move out of the dorm until the end of the semester because he had RA obligations. But now, here in mid-May, he was moving in with her completely. They had a couple of days to themselves before his archaeology field school started.

"The bottom three are yours; the top two are mine."

"No way two drawers are enough for all your clothes," he said, putting his things away.

She crawled on the bed to watch him unpack. "Well, I *am* taking the closet."

He smiled. "Of course."

"I have a lot of clothes and shoes."

"I noticed." He grabbed balls of socks from his suitcase and tossed them into the drawer with his boxers.

"You like me to look good, don't you?"

"Darlin', it's not the clothes that make you look good." He put jeans and sweats in the third drawer.

"You're just saying that because you prefer me naked all the time."

He looked back to her. She had stretched out on the bed and lay with one arm flung back beside her head on the pillow, the other low across her stomach. Her legs were spread slightly, knees bent with one up and the other out to the side. Her breasts thrust high in her tight T-shirt, showing her hard nipples, and her short shorts left little to the imagination.

The day they got back together, they went together to be tested for STDs. Both received a clean record, and she got back on birth control pills, so they had quickly dispensed with condoms. He was glad. There was nothing better than being flesh to flesh with her.

"I'd keep you naked day and night if you'd agree to it. I love your body so much."

"Show me."

He pushed the suitcase from the bed and it crashed to the floor. The mattress dipped under his weight when he joined her and lay on top of her. Taking a wrist in each hand, he brought her arms high above her head.

She ran her tongue across her lips, tempting him, and her eyes went heavy. He dipped his mouth closer to hers for a kiss, and she rose up to meet him, but he pulled back, teasing her. He dipped in again and, when she didn't move toward him, he brushed his mouth over hers, giving her a taste of what was to come.

"You like to torture me, don't you?" she whispered and licked his lips before he could pull away.

"Torture?" he said and gave her a little grin. "Darlin', this is called pleasuring." She opened her mouth to protest and he pressed his mouth to hers, taking her breath, giving her what she wanted.

Small moans rolling in her throat had him pulling back from her again and moving down to kiss along her jaw, lower to her neck, across her chest and between her breasts. Without giving her time to prepare for what was coming next, his mouth came down on her nipple and sucked her through her shirt.

She moaned and arched up into him, wanting more. "The other one, too," she begged. His mouth left her breasts and shifted down to the bare skin of her stomach. His tongue dipped into her navel and grazed the sensitive skin just under the band of her low-rise shorts.

"Lower," she said, and he released her wrists so he could unfasten her shorts. But she beat him to it, unfastening them and pushing them down so he could go lower. Her hands yanked off her shirt, baring her breasts to his eyes, hands, and mouth.

It filled him with love to know she desired him that much. "I think you're glad I'm here," he said and let his tongue lave the flesh she had bared. It turned him on that she watched him taste her and made him want to give her even more, to give her everything she wanted.

"I am. So glad." Gasping as he nibbled down her

stomach to her mound, she thrust her pelvis at him, urging him on. "No one has ever made me feel the way you do."

"And no one ever will. I'm your last lover, Kristin."

He gripped the sides of her shorts and pulled them off, panties included. Burying his face in her pussy, he drew the eternity symbol on her clit with his tongue, over and over, before plunging deep into her pussy. Her hips thrust against his mouth. She wanted him inside her. He wanted inside her.

"Get naked with me." The words crawled from her mouth, low and urgent, and he knew she wanted him as much as he wanted her.

He sat up on his knees and she followed, pulling off his T-shirt and his boxers until he was as naked as she was. She trailed her fingers down his chest, his stomach, and into the nest of black curls at his crotch.

One touch of her hands to his hard rod sent a bolt of desire through him, hardening him even more. Then she took him in her mouth and his entire body sizzled. He caressed her head as she licked him, sucked him, teased his rigid flesh, letting her know how much she pleased him. Her movements drew rumbled moans of pleasure from his mouth that he barely recognized as his, and he had to have her now.

He eased her up onto her knees and lifted her until she sat on his lap. Anchoring her legs around his hips, she guided him to her hot spot, and he slid in. The overwhelming feeling of being sheathed so fully in her love hit him as it always did, and he felt himself giving everything over to her. She wanted all of him, and he wanted to give her all of him.

His ever-present concern over not hurting her in

place, he started slowly, plunging himself into her an inch at a time until she was slick and hot enough to take all of him and was grinding against him. She grabbed his back and pulled him closer to her.

"Don't be easy with me. I want all of you inside me."

Taking her word, he grabbed her ass with his hands, his fingers digging into her flesh, and held her still while he pounded in to her, hard and deep. His eyes were hard on hers, drunk with the smell and sounds of their fucking. He hit the tip of her cervix, then pulled out again, thrusting, withdrawing, plunging, withdrawing, fast, hard, again and again, until he felt like he was losing his mind from the heat and pleasure and desire washing over him.

She let her head fall back, as if she were luxuriating in the feeling of him so deep inside her. She needed him. She needed his cock. Hard and fast.

"Oh, God, Sean! Fuck me!"

"Fuck you like this?" His voice was rough, seething as he rammed into her.

Her hips lifted against his assault. "Yes! Yes!"

Their bodies rocked hard into each other, "You want my cock in your sweet pussy all the time."

"Yessss! All the time."

His voice, her voice, his words, her words, his movements, hers, their love fused into one giant incendiary device that was set to explode.

"Ohhh, fuck, Sean, Ahhhh! Yes!" she moaned, thrashing against him, quivering from the heat and force, and biting his lip until he tasted his blood. It was as if the explosion sent her into the air in a million fragments, all filled with hot pleasure.

He forced himself harder into her, now, throat growling, hips grinding, cock jamming, grunting with every breath. So fast, so fast. So fucking good.

"Come inside me, Sean. I want your cum."

Her words, her voice, the feel of her got him to the top and he jumped. His arms held her so tight she couldn't breathe, and his cock impaled her to the hilt.

"Arhhhh, Fuck me, Kristin, Fuck. My Kristin!"

He felt his cum, hot and pulsing, hit the top of her pussy, again and again as he found his release in her body.

They collapsed onto the bed, still holding each other, panting, groaning at the strength of their release, feeling ripped apart by it.

When she'd found a breath, she used it to whisper sweet words that left no doubt that what they had was real and precious, even though they both knew it had a time/date stamp on it that could expire come August.

"You're my world, Sean."

He sighed against her and nodded in agreement. "And you're mine, darlin'."

****

The summer flew by on eagle's wings. Kristin and Sean grasped every moment they had together, held them tightly in their hands. Time stood still for a few precious moments when they made love, but it wasn't enough to stop time completely. July was already half over. She refused to dwell on it, to ruin the present by dreading the future. But the future was galloping toward them.

She slid the veggies, cheese slices, and chopped green chile into the fridge. By the time Sean got home, he could fire up the grill for the burgers. She laughed at herself and the surge of domesticity that had taken them both over. She got up in the morning with Sean and showered with him. He made their breakfast, and she sent him off with a packed lunch made with love. She had dinner going when he got home from the field school, and he cleaned up afterward.

He was her world, and she was his, and that was enough.

During the day, she plowed through her thesis. She wanted her evenings and nights free for him. Their time together was moving fast, and she didn't want to be tied to her computer or to the library when she could be tied, so to speak, to him.

She glanced up at the clock in the kitchen. He was due home any minute now. Excitement surged through her, making her stomach twitter and her heart patter. How was it possible that she loved him more today than she did yesterday? But she did.

Her heart sped up when she heard a knock on the door. Forget his key again? She rushed to the door, a smile on her face.

"Forget your key a—"

Her joy vanished with the rest of her sentence. Her heart jumped to her throat, and her head begin to throb behind her eyes.

"Hi, Kristin."

Chapter Twenty

The lump Kristin swallowed tasted bitter. "Zoe."

"At least you remember my name." Zoe chuckled, a thin sound that slipped from her mouth almost as an afterthought.

"What do you want?" Kristin asked.

Zoe shrugged one shoulder, giving that sorry little-girl look. "To talk. And apologize."

"I'm not interested in either." Kristin shut the door, but Zoe grabbed it before it closed.

"Please, Kristin. I'm seeing a therapist for my...issues. She said I wouldn't be able to forgive myself and move on until I asked for forgiveness from the people I hurt."

"What if those people aren't able to forgive you?"

"All I can do is ask. I can't control whether you accept it or not."

Though Kristin had doubts that Zoe could transform herself on the inside, there was no question she had transformed on the outside in the four or so months since she'd seen her. Her normally wild hair was tamed into a sleek ponytail. Her makeup was natural and toned-down. She wore jean capris and a T-shirt, instead of ass-bearing skirts and chest-revealing spaghetti-strap tops. Her tone was even different—softer, less abrasive, and less demanding.

"It'll just take a few minutes. Please?"

After a pause, Kristin stepped back and opened the door.

Zoe smiled sweetly and stepped inside, glancing around. "Nice place. I always wondered what these apartments looked like inside. One bedroom?"

"Have a seat." Kristin sat on the chair and pointed to the couch.

Zoe sat, perching on the edge of the cushion instead of climbing on and tucking her legs under her, like she used to do.

The two former friends/roommates/lovers stared at each other for a long moment. Kristin wondered whether Zoe was reliving memories of another time.

"Never thought of you as the 'apron' type. It's cute."

Kristen felt her cheeks heat, wishing she'd thought to take off the domestic goddess costume before answering the door. "I'm cooking dinner."

"Is that why your face is red?"

Kristin heard the teasing in Zoe's voice, but she wasn't moved to play along. "I don't want to chat. Say what you have to say, and then go." Kristin recognized the pout on Zoe's lips, but without the garish pink gloss she used to favor, the action looked more remorseful than huffy.

Zoe dropped her eyes to her hands in her lap. She swallowed then met Kristin's eyes.

"I'm sorry for the way I treated Sean, Mason, and Randy, and especially you. Your friendship was everything to me, and I treated it like it was nothing. I betrayed your trust, and I hurt you. I don't know if you can—and I wouldn't blame you if you can't—but I'm asking you to please forgive me."

Zoe's eyes were shiny with tears, and her voice trembled with the emotion behind the words. Kristin felt her heart thaw a degree or two for her former friend for at least having the courage to come here and face her with her wrong-doings.

"I forgive you." She tried to keep her voice neutral, but she heard the frost on the words. She had said the words, meant them, but there was still a lot of emotion tied up in what Zoe had done to her and Sean...and Randy and Mason, for that matter. She was forgiving her so she could forget her.

Zoe's body released a sigh. "Thank you. You don't know what this means to me."

"Let me tell you what it means and what it doesn't mean. Just so that we're on the same page."

Zoe nodded at Kristin's crispness, wiping tears from her eyes with her fingers. Gone were the long, painted talons.

"It means I forgive you for what you did because I don't want to give it any power to affect me or my life." Kristin felt thick bands squeezing her body as she talked about this with Zoe. A hot pressure throbbed at her temples and in her stomach. But she pushed forward, knowing it would help to bring closure to it. "It means I've moved past what happened and have no unfinished business with you. It doesn't mean we are friends or ever will be friends—or anything else. Are you clear on that?"

"Yes."

Kristin stood. "Good luck in your therapy. I hope it helps you find happiness."

Zoe stood, too, giving her a weak smile. "Do you really mean that?"

"Yes."

As if all this honesty was just too overwhelming for Zoe, her tears burst forth in a torrent, and she rushed toward Kristin, wrapping her arms around her just as the door opened. Kristin's arms raised to Zoe, not for a hug, but in a purely defensive move. She pushed against her.

"Hey, darlin', guess wh—" Sean took two steps into the room and stopped, all color draining from his face when he saw Zoe hugging Kristin.

Kristin moved away from Zoe, who turned toward Sean.

"Hi, Sean," Zoe said. There was a roughness in her voice that told Kristin she still had issues with Sean, no matter what she'd said about what she'd done.

Sean's face went from shocked white to angry red in a matter of seconds, and his eyes flashed with rage as he slammed the door and stepped toward his nemesis. "What the fuck are you doing here?"

Her eyes narrowed. "I came to see Kristin."

Sean's stare zipped to Kristin, and she could see the hurt and confusion in his eyes, knew in that instant that he thought the worst of her: that she and Zoe were at it again.

"I came to apologize to her, and to you, for what I did. For—"

"For damn near ruining our lives. We can't forgive you for that."

Zoe lifted her chin defiantly. "Kristin forgave me."

He stared at Kristin as if she'd stabbed a sword in his back.

"You should leave," Kristin said to Zoe, walking to the door and opening it.

Zoe brushed past Sean on the way to the door. At the door, she stopped and turned back to him. "I know you can't forgive me, but I truly am sorry."

"You're only sorry your plan didn't succeed."

The corners of her mouth lifted into a restrained smile as she held Sean's hate-filled gaze. Then she turned back to Kristin, her smile genuine. "It was really good seeing you. Thanks again." She stepped outside into the heat of the day, leaving Kristin and Sean to deal with the deep freeze she had created.

Kristin had barely closed the door when Sean exploded.

"I can't believe you let her in. What were you thinking?"

Kristin knew how mad he was by how thick his accent had become. "I didn't realize it was her. I opened the door because I thought you had forgotten your keys again." She sighed deeply before continuing, "She apologized for what she did and asked for forgiveness. I gave it to her."

"You gave it to her," he mumbled and shook his head. "Gave her what? Forgiveness...or something else?"

"What are you insinuating?"

"I come home to find you in the arms of your ex-lover. What do you think I'm insinuating?"

Kristin's eyes and mouth pinched into tight lines of anger and pain. "Go to hell!" She stormed out of the living room and into the bedroom, slamming the door with a force that shook the walls.

Seconds later, the door flung open. Kristin lay on the bed, face down and crying. She could feel him standing beside her quietly, as if he were swallowing every fighting word he'd come in to hammer her with. She felt his hand settle on her back, gently rub it.

"Darlin', I'm sorry. I didn't mean what I said."

She rolled away from his touch and faced him, tears filling her eyes. "You're never going to trust me, are you?"

Pain damped the flashing anger in his eyes and he looked beat down, like his spine had no strength, no energy to stand much less fight. "It's not that. Not really."

The urge to pull his body down to hers and mold herself around him was strong. But she resisted. He looked like he was on the verge of sharing some real truths with her, and she didn't want to stop that. Plus, she was pissed at his totally unfounded accusation and lack of trust.

"Then what is it?"

He stood beside her, shaking his head.

She pulled him onto the bed. "Talk to me, Sean."

He lay next to her and his eyes found her face. "I loved you from the first night I saw you at my door, even though you were nearly naked, wearing my next door neighbor's T-shirt—inside out, by the way—and asking for a cup of condoms so you could have marathon sex. I loved you even when I saw you having sex with Zoe. I loved you when you dumped my arse and made me fight to get you back."

"Is there a 'but' in there?"

He licked his lips. "You invited Zoe in to our Honahlee. You forgave her for almost destroying us. It made me wonder whether there's a part of you that wants to be with her...wants to break up with me. And that scares the shit out of me."

Tears caught in Kristin's throat at the deep emotion flowing from the man she loved. He was hurting, and so she hurt too. She scooted closer to him, curled into his chest, wrapped an arm and a leg around his body, and hugged him tight.

"I love you," she whispered against his mouth. "Only you. But as much as I love you, I won't put up with jealousy and mistrust, especially since I've done nothing to deserve it. If anyone breaks our relationship, it'll be you, because of your lack of trust."

He hugged her so tight it took her breath away. His eyes found hers. "I do trust you."

She smiled. "And I trust you."

He swallowed. Hard. Closed his eyes. "I need to tell you something."

The look on his face scared her—serious, remorseful, the need to confess something hurtful.

"When I thought we were over, I..."

...slept with another woman. He didn't say it, but she knew it was coming. Felt it burn inside her, eating up all the air in her lungs. She didn't want to hear it. Didn't want to hear how he'd shared his body with another woman. She put her fingers over his mouth.

"No." She shook her head. "I don't want to know. You're with me now. You love me. That's all that matters." The words tumbled out of her mouth like boulders to block his need to confess.

"I didn't do it, Kristin," he mumbled between her fingers. She let him move aside her hand and finish his statement. "I couldn't."

Kristin closed her eyes in relief. She'd meant what she said about it not mattering, but knowing that he hadn't gone through with it was everything to her.

"Forgive me?" he asked.

Seems like it was her day to forgive. "Forgiven." She kissed him softly but deeply.

"I'm a lucky man that you love me."

She smiled. "Yes, yes you are. Why don't you show me just how very lucky you feel?"

His hands tugged the strings of her apron.

****

Sushi from their favorite restaurant and Japanese beer filled the bag in the backseat, Kristin was flying high as she drove her way home to Sean. Their time had worn down to a few short days, and she was going to make the most of each one, filling every minute with pleasure.

She smiled as she thought of the night she'd planned. They'd share a sensuous meal then make love in the shower. Then they'd make love all night in their bed, trying out some new edible oils she'd picked up as well as new positions from the Kama Sutra book she'd bought.

Kristin was still smiling as she pulled into their parking lot. She might need him to take her up against the living room wall. Just to take the edge off.

Sean stood near his motorcycle, talking to a stranger.

She parked and got out of the car, grabbing the bags.

He took the bags from her hands when she approached and gave her a quick kiss on the mouth. "Kristin, this is Tyrone. Tyrone, Kristin."

Kristin smiled and was shaking the man's hand when it hit her. She spun back to face Sean. "You're selling your bike."

He stared into her eyes and nodded.

Sean's fellowship had ended the day before. His visa would expire in a few more days and he would be leaving America, leaving her, and going back to Ireland. Seeing him sell his bike was the first tangible sign that the end was upon them. Feeling tears burning her eyes, she looked away and blinked, fighting to hold on to her emotions.

She cleared her throat and managed a smile at Tyrone. "It's a great bike. You'll love it. We've had a lot of fun with it."

Sean set the bags down at his feet and slipped his arm around her shoulders, holding her tight against his side.

"I've wanted a bike like this for a long time," Tyrone said. "I'm glad to get it at such a great price. Speaking of that..." He fished his wallet from his pocket and counted out hundred dollar bills into Sean's hand. Sean handed over the key, and they shook. The deal was done.

"Here's the helmet." Sean picked it up from the pavement near his feet and started to hand it over when Kristin put her hands on it, stopping him.

"Tyrone, sorry, but do you mind if I keep this?"

He looked from her to Sean and back. "Uh, sure. No problem. I have one at home I'll be using anyway."

She smiled her thanks and tucked the helmet against her chest, holding it to her heart like a precious keepsake.

Sean and Kristin stepped aside, giving the new owner room to approach the bike, climb on, and start her up. They watched, arms around each other, as their bike rolled away out of the lot and down the street.

Tears rimmed her eyes, not for the bike, but for

what it represented. Soon she would have to watch Sean roll out of her life just like the bike.

Sean wiped away the moisture caught in her lashes with his thumb. "Why do you want this nasty old helmet?" His voice was soft, tender.

"It's yours," she said, her words filled with emotion. "I'll need it when you're gone."

"Are you going to paint my face on it and sleep with it?" he teased gently. "Kiss it goodnight? Shower with it?"

"Don't tease me, Sean. It's all I'll have of you when you're gone."

"Ahhh, darlin', no. That's not true. I'll be beside you always, with my heart and my love."

"I can't see those things, smell them, hold them in my hands." She held up the helmet and looked at it. "You wore this every day, your fingerprints are all over it, your smell is part of it. I look at it and can see you with it on, smiling. I remember how your hair would stick up when you took it off and how I'd try to smooth down the kinks and you'd laugh."

"If I'd known it meant that much to you, I never would have tried to sell it."

"Well, if you're tempted to sell anything else, give me first right of refusal."

"You got it." He kissed her and picked up the bags. "Let's go in, darlin'." With his arm around her shoulders, he led her to their apartment. "I'm starving."

"There's sushi and beer in one of those bags."

"Uh, not for food."

She smiled and curved herself tighter against him. "Oh. Then you'll want what's in the other bag."

****

Sean had waited as long as he could to join the security line so he could have as much time with Kristin as possible. But the time had come. He had to go now or risk missing his flight. Still they held each other tightly, both finding it almost impossible to separate.

"The offer's always open to come live with me and finish school in Dublin."

She was too grief-stricken to cry or to speak in more than a whisper. "I'm so close...I need to finish here. After that, if you still want me—" Pain choked off the rest of her sentence.

"I'll always want you."

She knew she'd love him for the rest of her life whether he did or not.

"When you have your degree in hand, I'll come back and ask you again."

She nodded, and they kissed, a desperate, crushing kiss meant to make a lasting physical and emotional impression on both of them. They shared that last moment of passion before he pulled away and picked up his backpack.

With a last longing look at her, he turned and walked toward the line that would take him to his plane.

"Sean!" she called out.

He stopped and turned around as she rushed into his arms.

"We'll be together again." He cupped her face between his hands, stared into her eyes. "I promise. I promise."

She nodded.

He kissed her and then left her arms again. This time she let him go, watching every step he took as he snaked his way through the line that took him farther away from her. He paused at the entrance to the secure area, looking for her. Smiled. Touched his fingers to his mouth and sent her his last kiss.

She forced herself to smile, not wanting his last image of her to be of a sad, tear-streaked face. She raised her hand in goodbye as he stepped into the secure area and headed down the terracotta-brick walkway to his plane.

She stared after him until she could no longer see his blond head towering above most of the people heading the same way. Only then did she force herself to turn around and take that first stumbling step into her new life…a life without him.

She made it to her car before collapsing in on herself. How would she ever get by without him? Through her pain, she heard a soft ding sound. A text. She considered ignoring it, but the thought that it could be from him pushed her to dig into her purse and pull out her phone.

It was from him. "If you wait for me, Kristin, I'll come back for you. I promise." Also included in his text was a link to a video. She followed it and saw him with his guitar in hand, sitting on their bed…in his wonderful, stupid boxers.

"Darlin', this is my promise to you," he said and began to play *The Promise*. In the words of the song, she heard his love, his sorrow, and his promise that he would come back for her if she'd wait for him.

When the song ended, her fingers flew over the buttons. "I'll wait for you, Sean. I promise."

Chapter Twenty-One

Kristin's rational mind knew that long distance relationships rarely worked out, but that didn't stop her emotional heart from holding out hope that hers would be the one that did.

When the frequency of Sean's calls, texts, and emails slowed, her mind argued that the chance had faded for them. Her heart countered that it was simply his job was keeping him busy. But when her graduation day arrived that blue-skied, sunshiny December morning with no word from him, her mind and heart formed the same conclusion: he'd moved on.

She went to her department's graduation ceremony at her mother's insistence, hiding behind the neon sunglasses her class had decided to wear, the fog of grief making her distracted and disjointed. The guy behind her in the lineup had to elbow her to walk across the stage to get her diploma when her name was called and then, later, to progress down the aisle at the ceremony's close.

As she and the other graduates moved down the aisle to applause and cheers, she glanced into the crowd of happy onlookers for the first time to find her parents. She had been too lost in her own misery throughout the ceremony to look for them, and it shocked her how suddenly and keenly she needed to see the faces of people who cared about her.

She saw her father first, a head taller than most in the crowd, with his perfectly styled, still-dark hair shining and his normally tight mouth slanted into a smile that seemed to suggest he was proud of her. Standing next to him, her mother smiled through a torrent of tears. That her mother was crying was no surprise. What was surprising was her hand holding onto the arm of the much younger man beside her. A tall man, with squirrely blond hair, shining dark blue eyes, and a heart-stoppingly familiar grin on a kissably full mouth.

Kristin stopped in her tracks, slid up her sunglasses, rocked back a step oblivious to the fact that she was blocking everyone behind her. She stared at the handsome, sexy man beaming with love and pride at her. The man moved toward her with his eyes locked on hers. She stepped out of line to let the others pass.

Was it really him? Could he really be here? In the same room? Standing in front of her?

"Congratulations, darlin'." Sean held out his arms and she needed no more proof, no more encouragement, and no more convincing that it was indeed him.

"Oh, my God! Sean?"

She threw herself into his arms, delirious at the feeling of having them so tightly around her. He kissed her and she drank in the comforting and exhilarating taste and feel of his mouth. Her body—and heart and mind—heaved a sigh of joy and relief. Everything was right, now.

"What are you doing here?" Tears of joy stung her eyes, and she couldn't stop smiling.

His eyes sparkled, and his smile mirrored hers. "I came to ask you something."

"You could have called."

"Something this important deserves a face-to-face. But I could leave if you'd rather I call."

She flushed at the memory of the last time those words were said. "Don't you dare!"

He took her left hand. "When I left in August, you said you had to finish your degree before we talked about our future. Well, darlin', that's a diploma there in your hand, so I'm back to ask whether you still want a future with me."

"Yes. More than anything."

He blew out a breath as if relieved by her answer. "Then I have one more thing to ask you." He kissed her hand and slowly dropped to one knee.

She dropped her diploma. Her right hand flew to her mouth and tears swam in her wide eyes, blurring her vision. "Sean?"

The room seemed to have gone silent, like they were the only two people there.

"Forever isn't long enough for me to show you how much I love you, Kristin, but marry me, and every day I'll be at your side showing you. I promise to be yours only—in body, mind, heart, and soul—forever. Say you'll be mine, too..." He reached into his pocket and pulled out a ring, perched it on the tip of his finger. "...by accepting my ring, the symbol that my love for you is precious, solid, and eternal."

Tears as fat and shiny as the diamond on the engagement ring rolled down her smiling cheeks. She nodded and managed to whisper yes as he leaned in to slide his ring on the finger of her shaking left hand.

He stood then and wrapped her up in his arms. She put her hands on his face and stared into his shiny eyes.

"I accept your love, your promises, and this...Wow! This damn-fine symbol."

He chuckled.

"I love you, Sean. I'd be honored to be your wife, your lover, your friend, your partner. Forever." She leaned forward then, her mouth at his ear. "As long as I get to kiss The Legend whenever I want."

He threw his head back and laughed. "You got it, darlin'," he whispered, then pulled her into a long, languid kiss that left no doubt in her mind that she'd made the right decision.

About the Author

Welcome to love, picante style.

I began writing and selling short romances in college to support my bad habits...er, my weekend entertainment. I graduated to novel-length erotic romances in 2009 with my first book, *Hot Summer Fling,* under the name Toni Zuma. My first book writing as Sophia Ryan, *In The Bad Boy's Bed,* soon followed and several more are in progress.

I write the kind of books I like to read: stories where sexual heat sizzles off the page and the characters fall into lust and love. When I'm not writing about passion, I'm indulging in it—yoga, hiking, laughing with friends over hot chile and cold beer, and watching the Sandia Mountains turn the color of ripe watermelon at sunset.

I live in the sunny southwest with the loves of my life.

Visit Sophia at
http://sophiaryan.webs.com

To chat with Sophia Ryan and other Wild Rose Press authors of erotic romance, join us at www.groups.yahoo.com/group/thewilderroses.

Also Available

One Hard Ride

by

M.M. Bordeaux

Amanda Sloane's passion has been solely focused on becoming a well-respected, NYC art appraiser. With that appetite sated, she can no longer ignore her body's carnal desires.

Tasked with authenticating an uncataloged Randell painting that could be worth millions, she meets a trio of Texas ranch hands who take her on an erotic ride imagined only in her deepest fantasy. Between ranch owners, Jake and Justin Morgan, and their ranch foreman, Luke, the cowboys ignite in Amanda a raging fire of uninhibited sexuality.

For years, the Morgan brothers have fought off their greedy cousin's attempts to take their ranch, including poison and sabotage. Now, Jake is counting on the elegant and sophisticated art appraiser to authenticate his grandaddy's painting to stave off foreclosure on the family ranch. Awakening the big city vixen's sexual hunger has his body ablaze with need and his heart yearning for love.

Can Amanda give up the intoxicating pleasure of her sexual awakening? Or is Jake's love unconditional enough to encourage her to continue her erotic odyssey?

Chapter One

Amanda groped for her ringing cell phone, knocking the alarm clock and her vibrator off the nightstand before she had the damn thing in her hand. She fully intended to hang up but made the mistake of checking the caller ID.

"'Lo Sarah," she said sleepily. "What's up?"

"Time to rise and shine sweet cheeks. It's eight fifteen on a beautiful sunny day in Manhattan, and you owe me breakfast. Get your pretty ass out of bed and get dressed. I'll see you at Beans in twenty minutes. I've got a big surprise for you."

The cheery voice was like a suddenly raised window shade, flooding the room with bright light. "Jeez." She held the phone away from her ear. "How do you know I'm not already dressed? Maybe I've just come in from a two mile run."

"Yeah, right. And I'm the Queen of Sheba. It's just past eight on a Sunday, so I know you're still in bed. The question is, where and with whom? You still seeing that blonde Viking? Are you at his place or yours? I would really love to see the mast on that man's longboat." Sarah giggled.

"Well, you would be very disappointed, just like I was," Amanda groused. "And I'm afraid that relationship is over."

"You're kidding! After just a month? You two

seemed like the perfect couple."

"I guess things aren't always what they seem, are they?" Amanda's question dripped with sarcasm, but failed to breach Sarah's optimism.

"I want to hear all about it over breakfast. See you in twenty." The phone finally fell silent.

"Make it thirty!" she yelled, but Sarah was gone.

Leaning over the side of the bed, Amanda picked up the alarm clock and her vibrator, sighing as she sat the vibrator on the nightstand. It was frustrating to think that a battery powered piece of plastic could offer more satisfaction than a flesh-and-blood man. Why couldn't she find a man who could unlock her libido and awaken the sensual being she'd always been afraid to reveal?

Wondering about Sarah's big surprise, she took the vibrator into the bathroom for a wash-up and then took a quick shower. Scrambling through a drawer of lingerie, she selected a tiny thong in fine mesh trimmed in lavender lace.

She was very conservative in the way she dressed, except for her lingerie. Her one fashion indulgence was very erotic lingerie from high-end shops. The sexy panties and bras she wore, like her vibrator and shaved pussy lips, were her secrets, something only a few men ever got to see.

She slipped into the lace thong and looked in the mirror. She liked the feel of the thong on her ass and she didn't have to worry about panty lines. She also enjoyed feeling the material of her skirts and pants on her bare skin.

She kept the small dark triangle of pubic hair just above her clit neatly trimmed and, as she adjusted the panties, she made a mental note to make a wax appointment.

The matching lavender bra clearly showed her nipples through the transparent cups. Her nipples were large, sometimes embarrassingly so. When she was aroused or cold, the tips grew even larger, tightening almost to the point of pain.

She slipped into a pair of indigo skinny jeans and a black T-shirt. A pair of sandals completed the outfit. With a quick dab of makeup, she was off to meet Sarah at Has Beans, their favorite coffee shop/breakfast bar, where the walls were decorated with photos of celebs the paparazzi had lost interest in.

Amanda made it to Beans by nine and immediately spotted Sarah at their favorite corner table. It wasn't difficult. The neon pink mohair sweater she was wearing, which matched the inch wide strip of pink in her raven black hair, stood out like a beacon in a room crowded with New Yorkers dressed in de-rigueur black.

Sarah was an administrative assistant to Richard Patterson, Amanda's boss at Peabody, Patterson & Cope. She was also Amanda's closest friend.

In addition to Sarah's day job, she was a modestly successful artist, specializing in male nudes. The paintings were very popular among gay collectors, including their boss.

In appearance and personality, Amanda and Sarah seemed like polar opposites. Sarah, with her full red lips, eyebrow stud, and streak of pink in her coal black page boy reminded Amanda of a new age pin-up. She even wore bomber bras, garters, and stockings under her outrageous fashions, unless she was painting. Then her retro underwear was all she wore.

Amanda envied Sarah's wild non-conformist

streak, which was coupled with a wickedly uninhibited libido. She was sure Sarah never let a man walk away without giving her an orgasm. Even if it meant she had to bring out the whips and handcuffs. Sarah's uninhibited sexual lifestyle made Amanda's lackluster sex life seem even more depressing by comparison. But she did enjoy hearing about some of the outrageous situations Sarah found herself in.

"Hey girl." Amanda slid into a chair across the table from Sarah. "Love the outfit." Beneath the mohair sweater, Sarah had on a cone shaped bra that lifted and pointed her breasts like a fifties-era starlet.

Sarah smiled. "So tell me all, sweetie. You and Sven are no longer an item?"

"His name is Arne. And yes, we are no longer dating. What's in the box?" She nodded at a large box on the chair next to Sarah.

"You'll see. I want to hear all about your breakup with Arne."

When their waitress appeared, Amanda ordered a biscotti and cappuccino and they both ordered eggs Benedict. As the waitress walked away, Sarah asked, "Was the sex that bad?"

Amanda looked at Sarah in surprise then quickly leaned across the table. "Shhh! Keep your voice down." She looked around to make sure Sarah's comment hadn't caught some patron's attention. "What makes you think the sex was bad? There might be a dozen reasons we decided not to see each other."

"Name two."

Amanda tried to think of something. "Well…it might be…"

Sarah grinned. "Look. The man is successful,

handsome, and has a killer bod. I only met him once, but he seemed nice enough. Maybe even charming. And he certainly wouldn't dump you. So it must be him and it must be the sex. Right?"

Amanda blushed and glanced around again. "You're right. The man has no idea how to please a woman. I haven't had that many lovers, but I deserve more than a five minute grope and poke, even if it is followed by a sincere 'thank you'."

Sarah made a face. "That bad, huh?"

"Worse. The man doesn't have a clue."

"Any chance you could train him? He is damn good looking."

"I don't know." Amanda dipped her biscotti in her coffee. "We tried three times and it was bad every time. For me at least."

"Honey, three times in one night isn't bad."

"I meant three times in a month."

"Oh. That's bad. Did you tell him what you wanted? I mean, what you wanted him to do to you?"

Amanda blushed again, the glow rising from her neck and shoulders to her cheeks. "Well, I didn't say exactly what I wanted. But I hinted around and even suggested that we try oral sex sometime."

"And?"

"And nothing. I think it's too messy for him. Doing me, I mean. The man is a total priss when it comes to keeping things neat. The second time, we were at his place and he put towels down so we wouldn't get wet spots on the sheets."

"What about you doing him?"

"He never even asked. He just wanted to bang, bang, bang, get it done. Come and go, so to speak."

Sarah grinned and leaned back in her chair. "So this whole past month, you haven't had an orgasm?" This was said just as the waitress delivered their breakfast. Amanda glanced up to see the young girl smiling. When the girl left, Amanda leaned across the table and whispered. "Will you keep your voice down? Everybody in New York doesn't need to know about the sad state of my sex life. Or lack thereof. Besides, I've had orgasms lately. Just not with a man." She paused and frowned. "In fact, I'm not sure I've ever had an orgasm with a man. At least not in the classic big O sense."

Sarah leaned forward and lowered her voice. "Honey, you just need a good fuck with a man who will unleash your inner wildcat. Maybe I should set you up with one of my models. Seriously. Just for a nice fuck. No strings attached. With a guy who will do whatever you want."

Amanda smiled. "That sounds like an offer I'd be foolish to refuse. But for right now, I think I will. Thanks anyway."

"Okay," Sarah sighed. "You've got my number if you change your mind." She grinned. "Or if you run out of batteries."

There was a moment of silence as the two friends finished breakfast and sipped their coffee. *Maybe I should take her up on a nice fuck from a handsome model,* Amanda thought. *What could it hurt? Even if it would only be a mercy fuck.*

Glancing up, she saw Sarah looking at her with a Cheshire cat grin. "What canary did you swallow? And what's in the box?"

Sarah waited for the server to clear the table, then

handed Amanda the carton. The box was big, half the size of the table, but not very heavy. Amanda looked at her friend with a lifted eyebrow, and then slid the lid off the box. Inside, to her total surprise, sat a brand new felt cowboy hat. The hat was pearl grey with a black braded leather band around the crown. The crown was creased and the brim pre-rolled into wearing shape.

Sarah was grinning and squirming happily on her chair, unable to sit still. "Put it on," she said excitedly. "See if it fits."

Amanda looked at the hat, then at Sarah. She glanced at nearby tables and saw several people looking at her and the hat. "I'm not putting this on. And why on earth are you giving it to me?"

Sarah's grin grew brighter as she answered Amanda in a slow drawl. "Cause yer gonna need it shugga. Down thar in Texas."

Amanda stared at Sarah as if she were daft. "Texas? What the hell are you talking about?" Just then her phone rang.

"That will be Richard," Sarah said. "Don't tell him I told you about Texas. Or that I gave you the hat."

"You haven't told me anything about Texas," Amanda lifted the phone to her ear. "Hi Richard. What's up?"

"Mandy, darling." Richard sounded somewhat breathless. "Have you read your e-mail?"

"I only look at blogs and tweets on Sunday. And my laptop is at home. I'm having breakfast with Sarah."

"I know, sweetie. Has she told you anything? I told her I wanted to tell you."

"She gave me a cowboy hat. Said I would need it in Texas."

"You will, sugar. Maybe some boots, too. Do you have any cowboy boots? Never mind. You can buy some."

"Richard, would you tell me what in the world you're talking about?"

"You're going to Texas, sweetie. Tomorrow. Sarah's made all the arrangements. Tickets, hotel, reservations for a car. You leave tomorrow morning."

"It's too early in the day to be joking, Richard. And I didn't get much sleep."

"Darling, you need your beauty rest! And I'm serious. You are going to Texas. Tomorrow."

Amanda paused, trying to wrap her head around what she had just been told. "You're really serious?"

"As a heart attack, sweetie. I need you in Texas tomorrow." Her boss practically purred.

"But Richard, I don't do Texas. I do Western art but not on location. I barely know where Texas is. I may have flown over it once or twice." She glanced at Sarah, who was grinning from ear to ear.

"You don't have to know Texas sweetheart. Just art. Western art. This is right up your alley."

"Who's the client Richard? What is this all about?"

"A pair of brothers—Jake and Justin Morgan. They've got an honest-to-God cattle ranch out in West Texas about three hours northwest of Austin. Jake Morgan called me and said he wants to sell a painting. From his tone, I suspect he needs to raise some cash. Maybe cattle ranching hasn't been a growth industry for the past few years."

"What kind of painting Richard? Who's the artist?"

Patterson couldn't seem to conceal the excitement in his voice when he replied. "You won't believe this sugar, but the man sent me a jpeg of a signed Charles Randell painting titled 'Cowboy on a Horse.' Typical Randell scene."

"That could bring in a nice commission," Amanda said.

"Oh, that's not all. I've studied everything I could find on Randell. As far as I can tell, this painting has never been cataloged."

"Do you think it's real?"

"It could be. Morgan said the artist gave it to his great granddaddy back in the late 1800s. It's been hanging on a ranch house wall for a hundred years. If it is an unknown Randell, it will be worth a small fortune."

Amanda felt a slight constriction in her chest and realized she had been holding her breath. "No. It could be worth a big fortune if it's the real deal." She was trying to remember all she knew about one of America's most famous Western artists. He had given away lots of paintings and drawings when he was first starting out. "Jesus, Richard. This sounds exciting!"

"Go home and open your email. But do it in the bathroom because you're liable to pee your panties."

Amanda's mind raced. Charles Randell had done four thousand paintings, drawings, illustrations, and sculptures. Who could say he hadn't done four thousand and one, or four thousand and two? It seemed every twenty years or so a new Randell painting or drawing surfaced somewhere.

"This could be a major find Richard, if it's real. Do you know what the last unknown Randell brought at auction?"

"I do know, sugar. It made a very cool twelve

million. That's why you need to get your cute butt down to Texas. We need to make sure it's authentic, at least as much as we can. And we need to get the Morgan brothers to sign with Peabody, Patterson & Cope as their exclusive brokerage firm.

"This could be huge for us Mandy. We'll have to put it through the ringer to verify authenticity, but just in case it might be the real deal, we need you in Texas, shaking hands with the Morgan boys."

"I'll pack tonight," Amanda said, already wondering what she should wear. "Do you really think I need cowboy boots?"

"Wouldn't hurt," Richard replied. "And wear the cowboy hat. Put on some tight jeans, too. We need to take advantage of your natural ass-ets!"

"You know I could sue your ass for sexual harassment, Richard. I only let you get by with all that 'sugar' crap because you're as gay as a maypole."

"I know, darling, I know." Richard giggled. "Have fun in Texas. I can't wait to hear what the Morgans have hanging on their wall. You should plan on spending the night at their ranch. They have a guest room and there are no hotels or motels within a hundred miles. Call me as soon as you know something. Anytime, day or night."

Amanda clicked off and looked at Sarah, who hadn't been able to wipe the grin from her face.

"Texas!" Amanda said.

"That's right partner. Where they drive around with cow horns on the front of their land yachts. I've made your reservations. You change planes in Dallas. There will be a car waiting for you in Austin."

Amanda smiled then slowly lifted the cowboy hat

and sat it on her head, not caring that several people nearby were staring at her. "Texas," she said again.

"And cowboys," Sarah added. "Rugged, handsome cowboys."

"Yeah, right. Those ranchers are probably fat and fifty. I'm interested in seeing the artwork." She paused a moment. "I'm thinking about buying some cowboy boots. Want to go shopping with me?"

Sarah grinned then stuck her leg out to one side of the table. "No need to," she said, pointing down at her foot. "You can borrow mine."

Amanda looked down, then shook her head and grinned. Sarah was wearing a pair of pink ostrich skin boots. A wild collage of colorful jewels formed a peacock pattern on each side. "Thanks, but no. I don't think a rhinestone cowgirl is who they will expect from a prestigious New York art brokerage firm."

Amanda thanked Sarah for the cowboy hat, gave her an air kiss, and hurried home to look at the photo of the painting Richard had sent her. She spent the rest of the morning at the computer researching Charles Marion Randell. She couldn't find any Randell works that matched the Morgan painting. And from what she could tell from the jpeg, the Morgan work had the same brushwork, color palette, and style as a genuine Randell.

The more she researched, the more excited she became. At five thirty she decided to take a break and, on a whim, searched the net for Manhattan stores that sold cowboy boots. She found a shop called Wayne's Wild Wild West just blocks from her apartment. The shop closed at six on Sundays so she took a taxi, stopping to pick up batteries for her vibrator on the way. Half an hour later, she was back with a beautiful pair of hand-stitched boots in chocolate brown leather. Unlike Sarah's bejeweled and dazzling pink pair, her new boots had a simple design of an eagle done in gold stitching on each side.

By nine, she was packed for an overnight trip. By ten she was in bed, hoping to get a few hours sleep before getting up at five to catch her flight. Sleep, however, fell victim to the excitement of possibly finding an uncataloged painting by one of America's best known Western artists, and to the trip to Texas itself. She'd never thought about going to Texas. There were lots of places higher on her must-visit list. But now that she was going, even if just for overnight, she was looking forward to some scenery much different than Manhattan's concrete canyons.

Thank you for purchasing
this Wild Rose Press, Inc. publication.
For other wonderful stories of erotic romance,
please visit our on-line bookstore at
www.thewilderroses.com.

For questions or more information
contact us at
info@thewildrosepress.com.

The Wild Rose Press, Inc.
www.thewilderroses.com